I0831345

MYSTERY FROM THE PAST

By Giovanni Scialpa

This is a work of fiction. All of the characters, incidents, and dialogue, except for incidental references to public figures, products or services, are imaginary and are not intended to refer to any living persons or to disparage any company's products or services.

First edition

ISBN: 978-1-60402-400-5

Second edition

ISBN 978-0-9846502-0-0

RocCitybookpublishing.com

480-560-4933

Printed in the United States of America

ACKNOWLEDGEMENTS

To my associate Michael Rivoli, who has helped me write this story and has spent numerous hours listening to me and putting my thoughts into something understandable. I also want to give Shirley Rea a special thank you for helping me put the book together. And a big thanks to James Niger at Professional Instant Press who has helped me in many ways.

I hope you enjoy reading this inspirational family story.

Sincerely,

Giovanni Scialpa

INTRODUCTION

Let me introduce myself. My name is Giovanni Scialpa.

I have always wanted to write a story but early in my life, I didn't take it seriously. I was born in Italy in the city of Piazza Armerina, Sicily, famous today for being the site of a restored villa romana found in the late 1950's. People come from all around the world to see it. I lived there until I was 13 and started learning the trade of being a barber by my cousin Carmelo.

In 1950, my family moved to Belgium because there was no work in Sicily. My father worked as a coal miner and sacrificed a lot to support us. I enjoyed living there and learned to speak French.

In 1956 when I was 19, I went to Toronto, Canada with big ideas and looking for new opportunities. I was a barber but I wanted to write. I also took singing lessons because I always dreamed of being a singer.

I left for Rochester, NY in 1961 where my future wife lived and where I live today. I enjoy this city very much. It gave me a good opportunity for work and it was a smaller city than Toronto, which I liked. Even if we have to pay New York State taxes! I think it is one of the best cities in the United States.

I have been here in my barbershop now for 38 years and have met many wonderful people. On occasion, about 5-6 years ago, a friend would come by once a week with his guitar and we would serenade the customers with our singing and playing while I cut their hair. Everyone enjoyed it. Sometimes people would joke that I should charge extra for my haircuts because I was providing entertainment. I said it was on the house and they would laugh. I also have another good customer who comes in and jokes, "If you don't play the Italian music, I won't pay you." But I don't care if he pays me or not because his father-in-law pays me for his haircuts a year at a time. I have good customers and many stories I could tell.

Just recently I made a trip back to Sicily after 54 years to my home town and got to meet my cousins again, especially my cousin

Carmelo, who taught me to be a barber and my cousin Antonio, who I went to grammar school with and who is now a Monsignor in the church. It was good to be home again. This was a special trip that I had been looking forward to for many years. Then I went to Venice for several days, which I enjoyed very much. I was very impressed with the city. The city is unique and I hope someday to go back again.

All these years barbering, I have wanted to write but the time was never right. I had a family to raise and responsibilities. Sometimes as a barber, I would feel like a priest, listening to confessions, helping to comfort people but then that's part of being a good barber.

So now, it seems this is the right time to write and I really enjoy the process. For me this story is very special and I hope everyone likes it.

There seemed to be an invisible force behind me that propelled me to write this story, which is both truth and fiction. Some of my customers tease me and say if the story goes to Hollywood that I won't be a barber anymore. I tell them no, I'll always be a barber but then I would be a famous one and remember--I used to cut your hair!

I feel like a millionaire now, although it isn't in dollars and cents. I have good health and wonderful friends and family and look forward to my next book. I hope you enjoy this book.

Thank you.

Chapter One - The Beginning

It was 1918 and the Great War was over. It was time to pick up the pieces.

Patrick McCarthy, a mason contractor by trade, returned to his home in Belfast. He had spent many years fighting and he felt lucky and blessed that he was able to return home to a wife and two beautiful teenaged daughters who filled his life with joy.

The war, however, had taken its toll on his country's economy and he decided he would have to look elsewhere to provide for his family.

Luckily, his brother Tom had moved to Philadelphia a few years back. Patrick wrote his brother a letter telling him that he wanted to move to America and would dearly love to see him.

His brother was overjoyed and told him he would find him a job. With this in mind, Patrick and Tom started all the legal paperwork necessary to move his family to America.

As the months passed, Patrick, his wife Joyce, and their two daughters spent hours thinking about how life would be so much better for them in America.

Finally, on March 20, 1919 the day arrived to board the huge ship that would take the McCarthy family on their journey. They were sad to leave their country, friends and family, but they were full of joy and great hope for a better future.

On the way to America, the ship had to make a stop in Naples, Italy to take on more passengers. People wore coats because of the cold spring, but when the ship reached the gulf of Naples, it was almost like summer.

The green ocean and the sky so blue and full of light put a smile on almost everyone's face. When they got closer to the port, they saw palm trees which most of them had never seen before.

The people onboard felt like they were in a different world. They enjoyed the view of Naples as they approached the port and were disappointed when they couldn't leave the boat while it was docked. The boat would leave at dusk with more passengers.

As they docked, they saw people on the ground saying goodbye to each other, hugging and kissing and crying.

Joyce, Patrick's wife, said, "It's funny, a lot of people have a guitar or mandolin."

"When I was there a year ago," Patrick said, "my friends and I would go into town and have some food and vino. The locals would sing and write songs. They also made a dish called pizza that I really liked. They're leaving their country like we are, because times are hard and they have to provide for their families. I understand. They leave the beautiful city of Naples because they dream of going to America and doing better for themselves. They take with them the music that they love and which will help them remember their country. "Just like we do."

Among these passengers was a man named Carlo Martino, born in Sorrento. His father, a mason, died when he was young so Carlo had to go to work to support his mother and brothers. One brother, Angelo, had already gone to America.

When he was 21, Carlo joined the Army and served his country in the war. He was lucky to come back—he'd been a POW in a German POW camp.

One of his friends, a fellow soldier named Franco, came back early and told everyone that Carlo was dead. Franco, it seemed, very much liked Carlo's girlfriend, Marina, and wanted to marry her. Marina was very upset when she heard the news about Carlo's death, but Franco convinced her that Carlo would have wanted them to be married. So within a couple of weeks they tied the knot and moved to Naples.

A couple of months later Carlo returned home. His mother was overjoyed to see him. She had heard that he was dead but she didn't really believe that. After talking to her for a while, he wanted to see his girlfriend, Marina. His mother had to tell him the news, that she had married his friend, Franco, a few months earlier. Carlo was very angry and upset. He couldn't believe his girlfriend would do that, but he was mostly angry with Franco. What kind of a friend does that, he asked himself. Friend or not, he wanted to hurry off to Naples and confront Franco. His mother convinced him that going to Naples was a bad idea, and that he needed to let it go.

"What happened, happened," she said. "It's over now."

He finally decided not to go, but she made him promise on the cross that he would not go after Franco.

A few weeks later Carlo decided to go to America and be with his brother. His mother was upset that he was leaving again, but relieved that he'd be away from the whole situation. But she was sad, too. One son was gone already and another wanted to go, leaving her with only one son to stay with her.

"Mother, don't cry," Carlo told his mother. "There's not much work here and when I *do* work, people can't pay me. I'm going to America to make some money and then I'll come back for you."

He really meant well, but reality sometimes had a way of changing things.

The night before he was to leave for Naples, Carlo dreamt he was on a big boat. He dreamt about a beautiful blonde girl who told him, "Carlo, Carlo, I can't believe we're going to America." When he woke up, he wondered who this she was because he didn't know any blonde girls, at least not like her. He wondered what that meant for his future and most of all, who she was.

When he left Sorrento the next morning, he left behind a lot of friends and family who all wished him well and wished that they were going, too.

"I'm sorry about what happened here, but I'm sure when you get to America you'll find a girl who will love you," his mother said. "This is the greatest thing a mother can wish for her child. Be sure to write to me to let me know how you're doing, otherwise I'll worry about you and your brother."

Carlo was sorry to have to leave his mother again, but he wanted to forget what had happened and look toward the future.

When he reached the port, he joined the line, boarded and went up on deck to enjoy the sunshine and to eat the large pizza his mother had made.

As only coincidence can provide, Patrick McCarthy saw Carlo.

"Come esta Signore?" he said.

Carlo looked up and said, "Tu parli Italiano?"

"Si, a little," Patrick said. "I was in Naples last year when the war ended, and I learned a little Italian."

"I was in the war, too. Sit down with me."

Patrick sat down and introduced himself.

"I know you Irish love your beer, but I only have wine here," Carlo said.

"I've enjoyed wine for a very long time, since I was in Naples."

Despite the language barrier, the two men persevered and before long, it was as if they'd known each other forever.

During their conversation, Patrick saw his wife walking by with their two daughters so he called them over and introduced them.

Carlo shook hands with Patrick's wife and then his daughters. But as he shook hands with Patrick's daughter, Lisa, he remembered his dream. He realized then that this was the girl. He became so overwhelmed that he dropped his pizza.

As she looked into his eyes, she too instantly fell in love with him. Patrick saw so much love in Lisa's face when she looked at Carlo that he said to him in Italian, "Lisa e Bella."

"This is so funny," Carlo said. "I dreamt of a beautiful blonde girl last night who said, 'we're going to America' and here she is. Please, sit down and have some pizza with me."

"This is delicious," Joyce said. "I've never seen this before. What is it and how's it made?"

"My mother made this for me last night. It's made with dough, onions, olive oil and cheese. Then it's baked. It's been made in Sorrento since the eighteen hundreds. We all enjoy it very much."

Joyce smiled and said, "Carlo, when you get to America, are you going to open a pizza shop?"

"No, Signora, I'm a mason like my father was, and like Patricio. My dream is to be a builder in America."

Patrick saw that he was a very ambitious man. A good candidate to marry his daughter, Lisa, some day.

They spent the rest of the afternoon walking and talking. Then, just before dusk, the boat blew its whistle. It was time to leave. So with the sun still shining brightly and with summer-like warmth in the air, the boat started its journey. A lot of people on deck, Carlo included, started playing the guitar and the mandolin. They sang all the beautiful songs from Naples: *O' Sole Mia, Come Back to Sorrento, O Marie and Santo Lucia*. Songs they had played in Italy and would take with them to their new homes in America. Some were crying because they were leaving their country and all that was familiar behind. They were taking their songs in their hearts to America.

The next morning Carlo saw the McCarthy family again. For Carlo it was one of the best times in his life because he had found the girl of his dreams. He had fallen deeply in love with her and her with him.

They saw each other every day. Sometimes they'd go on the top deck to be alone so they could kiss and be with each other. Even though they don't speak the same language, they communicated in the universal language of love—and that love grew stronger and stronger every day.

At the same time, Carlo felt like he had a new family. His father had died when he was quite young and Patrick filled that spot in his life, even though he had only known him for a short while.

After a long trip, filled with sickness, they finally reached New York City. Luckily, Carlo and the McCarthy's had avoided whatever had befallen the crew and many of the passengers.

As they drew near Ellis Island, everyone went up on deck to see the Statue of Liberty. Carlo felt a tear wiggle down his cheek at such an awe-inspiring sight. He would soon be in his new country and he was excited to begin his new life in America. And even in the numbing cold and the blowing snow, nothing could deter him and every other passenger from remaining on deck until it was time to disembark.

Before leaving, Carlo gave everyone a hug and kiss on the cheek. Everyone except Lisa. He kissed her tenderly on the mouth and as he looked into her eyes, he knew she shared what he felt

"Patricio, tell your daughter that I love her very much and I promise I will be back to see her again. Ti voglio bene," he said to Patrick in Italian. "I have to go to my brothers first, but I'll come to see you all again once I'm settled."

The family was happy to hear that and gave him their address so he could contact them as he had with them. They would always remember the good times they had on the boat coming over.

"Thank you for being so kind to me," Carlo said. "I'll keep you in my heart and mind until I see you all again."

And with that, they shook hands and went their separate ways.

The Ellis Island inspection took quite a long time but after it was over, everyone looked for loved ones.

Angelo, Carlo's brother, and his wife waited anxiously at the pier. They were glad that he had made it through the war. Angelo had found a good job for him.

After he had disembarked, they embraced and expressed their joy at being together again. They drove to Angelo's house where they enjoyed a fine meal.

"And how are your mother and brother?" Angelo asked.

"They're well, but mother misses you. She was upset that I left because she didn't know when she would see me again, or you either, Angelo."

The look on Angelo's face said he understood. It also said that even if he wished, he could nothing about it.

A week later, at a surprise party to welcome Carlo to America, Angelo introduced Carlo to an Italian girl from Italy that he felt would be right for him. She was nice and incredibly beautiful, but Lisa had already stolen Carlo's heart.

Carlo knew his brother meant well so mentioning Lisa was not something he wanted to do. But after a few weeks, he decided he had to tell him, otherwise his brother would just keep trying to find girls for him.

One day when they were alone in the house, Carlo said, "Angelo, I appreciate very much that you're looking out for me and that you don't want me to be lonely—"

"I do it because I love you, Carlo."

Carlo smiled and said, "And I love you, too, but Angelo." He paused a moment, then, "This is very hard, Angelo."

"I don't understand."

Carlo took a deep breath, let it out and said, "Angelo, I met a beautiful Irish girl on the ship. I want to go to Philadelphia to be with her."

The news of Carlo's leaving obviously saddened his brother, but Angelo had always been very understanding. "I know what you're feeling, Carlo, I do. You must do what's in your heart."

And so within a few days, Carlo left for Philadelphia. Mr. McCarthy was very happy to see him again and Carlo was very happy to see Lisa again. Her two sisters, Dorete and Lisa, ran up to him and hugged him, tears of joy rolling from their eyes. They had much to talk about.

After catching up on what was happening in their lives, Carlo realized that he needed to get a job. Mr. McCarthy was a big help and found him a job as a mason. Patrick introduced him to his boss, who hired him immediately. His specialty was stone cutting and he was good at it.

When the boss saw how good he was, he thanked Patrick for bringing him to the company. He paid Carlo very well because of his ability. Patrick was very pleased to hear that. They worked well together and Mr. McCarthy knew this good working relationship would affect his daughter as well.

Carlo also went to night school to learn English. He knew he had to work hard to make his dream come true.

With Lisa's help, Carlo's understanding of the English language advanced quickly. Their relationship blossomed and the love they had for each other only grew stronger.

About a year later, Carlo and Lisa started thinking about getting married. Carlo presented Lisa with a beautiful diamond ring that caught the eye of all her friends. She was so happy in her relationship with Carlo that she spread happiness to all who knew her.

Carlo wanted to get married with both the Irish and Italian traditions, with singing and dancing. Carlo asked Patrick if he knew some traditional Italian songs and dances like the Tarantella.

"Teach me some Irish songs," Carlo said, "and we can have a combination of both at the wedding."

A week before the wedding Carlo invited everyone who'd be dancing to Patrick's house to practice. He had his mandolin and Patrick sang the Irish songs. The dancers practiced dancing. Everybody enjoyed the music and felt that it would be a beautiful wedding. By the time the wedding day arrived, they were confident that they were ready for anything. They hoped the marriage would be good and that they'd be very happy together.

Lisa and Carlo were married on a crisp, sun-filled April day. It was a beautiful wedding that would be remembered by all that attended, especially Carlo's brother, Angelo, who came from New York City.

Because money was tight, the reception was held in the church basement. But they didn't care, they loved each other and it was perfect. They had the singing and dancing of the combined Italian and Irish and everyone had a wonderful time. Even Angelo and his wife danced. An older Italian lady got up and danced the Tarantella. Everyone was happy for Lisa and Carlo. It was the first time they had ever experienced this combination of new music in their life and they thoroughly enjoyed it.

Lisa and Carlo stayed with Angelo during their short New York City honeymoon. He surprised them with tickets to see Enrico Caruso at the Metropolitan Opera. The gift was especially touching because the renowned tenor was also from Naples.

During intermission, Carlo and a few others went backstage to see him. Carlo shook his hand and said to him, "Could you please sing, Torna a Sorrento."

"I sing that song all the time at the end of my show because I come from near Sorrento," Enrico said. "It reminds me of when I was young and went fishing there."

After the show, they went to an Italian restaurant to celebrate their honeymoon. Then they went back to Angelo's house. Angelo and Carlo talked about how worried they were about their mother back home in Italy and how they hoped someday to see her again.

The next day they got ready to leave for home. They thanked Angelo for his surprise gift. They'd always remember their time in New York City. "Angelo," Carlo said, as they hugged each other goodbye, "I hope you'll come to Philadelphia some day when you have time."

"I'll try," Angelo said. "I promise."

But Carlo never saw him again because Angelo died in an accident a little over a year later. Carlo was very upset because he loved his brother very much and would miss him tremendously. It was hard for Carlo to write to his mother to let her know what had happened. But as fate would have it, she had died a few weeks earlier. Although the news saddened him greatly, not having to tell her about Angelo tempered his grief. That only left his one brother in Italy.

After the honeymoon, Carlo started working with Patrick. He felt like he had known him forever, as if he were his real father. He listened to him and called him Dad. He liked Patrick very much and was glad that he had met him on the boat. He had never expected to meet such wonderful people who had made such a difference in his life.

One day several months later, when Carlo came home from work, Lisa told him she had a big surprise for him.

"Amore, what's so special today?" Carlo said.

"It's a very special surprise. I'm going to have a bambino!"

Carlo felt his heartbeat quicken. "Lisa, thank you for this special gift. It'll make our lives complete," he said as he held her close.

Such joy and happiness filled their hearts. They told their close friends, Pete and Sue Palmer, who lived next door. And as only coincidence could provide, Sue had just found out that she was pregnant, too. They were going to name the baby Tom, if it was a boy.

Not long after Tom was born, Lisa had her baby. They named him Giuseppe after Carlo's father. The two boys were baptized together and everyone who mattered to them attended the happy event.

Life, Carlo decided, couldn't be any better. His job had worked out great, and he had a wonderful child. And now, Patrick had asked him to go into business with him as a partner. He didn't want 1923 to end, unless he could be guaranteed that 1924 would be just as wonderful.

For the next five years, life treated them like royalty, but by the end of 1928, things started to change. Jobs were scarce and the economic climate had clouded over. They had saved some money, though, so if problems arose, they could deal with them.

One day, as they were driving outside the city looking for jobs, they saw a big farm with cows and goats and pigs.

"Let's stop," Carlo said to Patrick. "I want to buy some cheese."

"Sure," Patrick said as they pulled into the driveway.

The owner, a portly man with a doughy face and a shock of dark hair across his tanned forehead, greeted them seconds after Carlo knocked on the door.

"Howdy," he said, "what can I do for you?"

"We'd like to buy some cheese," Carlo said.

"I think I can oblige you. Come on in."

"My name's Jerry and this here's my wife, Andrea," he said as he led Carlo and Patrick into the kitchen.

Andrea, as tall as Jerry was short, smiled and tended to a pot of something steaming on the stove.

The small talk that followed included the fact that both Patrick and Carlo were masons.

"Really?" Jerry said. "I'm looking for a mason. I need to make the barn bigger and I want to build a house for my son next door."

"We can do that," Patrick said, the confidence in his tone unmistakable.

"That would be wonderful," Jerry said, "but I can't pay you. I have the money for the materials, though. But I'll make a deal with you. If you help me with this, I'll give you twenty acres of land."

Patrick and Carlo thought it over and because business was slow, they agreed. So on weekends for the next several months, they worked on building the barn.

Not long after they started, they saw a sign for farmland for sale down the road.

"Let's ask how much they want," Carlo said to Patrick. "We could use the wood from the trees for firewood."

They bought one hundred acres at a very reasonable price.

After the barn and house were finished, Jerry invited them and their families over for dinner.

The night before, Carlo decided to make some pizza's to take with them. Jerry and his family had never had pizza before and they liked it.

"We have this kind of pizza in Sorrento, Italy," Carlo said. "I used the cheese you gave me."

"It's very good," Jerry said. "I'll make you a deal. Every time you make a pizza, I'll give you the cheese."

Over time, they became very good friends with Jerry who lived up to his word and gave them the twenty acres of land.

Times changed, though. The great depression of 29' forced Patrick and Carlo to dissolve their company. But again, their frugal ways helped them survive. Still, Carlo was very disappointed. He didn't think that this could ever happen in America.

"Carlo," Patrick said to him, "don't feel bad or disappointed. I have faith in this country. This is just temporary and better days will come. And when they do, there'll be more work."

"I hope you're right," Carlo said, "but what will we do now?"

One night at dinner with the family, Carlo suddenly remembered what his mother-in-law had said to him on the boat. "Are you going to start a pizzeria in America?"

Given the financial climate, Carlo thought perhaps that would be a good idea, so he told his family about it.

"We can start a pizzeria here," he said.

They laughed at first, but the more they thought about it, the more the idea appealed to them. Eventually, everyone agreed to help. Carlo started looking for a store in the city, found one that wasn't too expensive and bought it. They could get wood for the oven from their land and Jerry would probably help them with the cheese and flour.

Not much happened in the beginning, but word of mouth, so to speak, was their dearest friend. Once people tasted their product, they couldn't help but like it. Word spread and they before long, they had more than enough customers.

Carlo, who knew what it was to be hungry, sold the pizza cheap because he knew people didn't have a lot of money to spend. He even gave it away from time to time. "Enjoy my pizza," he said, "and when you have the money, you can pay me."

It was a philosophy whose time had come. The business quickly prospered, so much so that Carlo had to hire more people. He decided to introduce macaroni to the menu. Sometimes people would come in for the special and started to call Patrick Mr. Macaroni because it sounded like McCarthy.

"That's not my name!" he'd always say.

"Don't worry," Carlo said, "they call me Mr. Pizza!"

Considering the plight of other businesses, they considered themselves lucky to be doing so well.

Since the business *was* doing so well, Carlo decided to expand. He bought the empty building next door and enlarged his space. It became one of the first pizzerias in Philly. But they needed more help.

One day a young man walked in and asked Carlo for ajob. Carlo thought he looked Italian. He asked him his name.

"Salvatore, from Naples," he said. "I used to help my uncle make pizza and I do a good job. I like to sing when I cook." Carlo started to laugh because he remembered when he used to go to Naples on the weekends.

"I made a big mistake," Salvatore said, "I was working on a large ship. When it came to Philadelphia, I jumped ship. I thought I'd make a better living here but I didn't realize that jobs were so scarce. I'm living with my uncle now and I haven't worked for over four months."

"Salvatore," Carlo said, "go to work for me and make pizza."

Salvatore was overjoyed and started immediately. Carlo saw that he was doing a very good job—Salvatore's pizza was even better than his.

The business got better and better once Salvatore started making the pizzas. He added things like pepperoni and mushrooms and onions. People seemed to like it. He sang while he worked, and he was pretty to look at. His looks and his singing brought in a lot of young women.

Patrick laughed and said, "We should have called this place Show Time Pizza instead of Sorrento Pizza."

"Maybe our next store should be called that," Carlo replied.

One day, while Salvatore was making pizza, Patrick's daughter Dorete came in.

"Dorete," Salvatore said, "I want to teach you how to make pizza so you can help out."

She learned very quickly. She liked what she was doing and she also liked being with Salvatore.

After they'd finished, Salvatore, whom everyone called Sam now, said, "Now that you're good at making pizza I can teach you how to kiss, too, and how to make love. I'm told I'm very good at both."

She smiled coyly. "Before you can do either of those things, you have to marry me. You know my father."

"Of course I'll marry you," Sam said. "I like you very much and I think we'll make a good couple."

"I've liked you since we first met," she said, "not because you sing or make good pizza, but because you're a good person, honest and funny."

"I'll ask your father for permission to marry you."

One day, while Sam was making the dough, Dorete distracted him—his toss landed on a lady customer, covering her with flour and dough.

"Young man," she said, "watch what you're doing and don't watch the girls!"

Sam apologized profusely. Carlo, who had seen the incident happen, offered the woman free pizza and free dry cleaning.

"And next time you come in we'll give you another free pizza!" he added.

The woman smiled. Sam expected Carlo to be angry with him, but he wasn't. He knew what it was like to watch the girls.

Eventually, the day came when Sam asked Patrick for Dorete's hand in marriage.

"Sam," Patrick said, "you're a fine young man and a hard worker. You're very honest like Carlo, and I happily give my permission for you to marry my daughter. Welcome to the family!"

That said, he game Sam a big hug and a kiss on the cheek. Sam and Dorete were, of course, very happy her father had given his permission. Their love had grown day-by-day and they couldn't wait to get married and start a life together.

Dorete and Sam's wedding was filled with music and dance, both Italian and Irish. Everyone had a grand time. Because they had work responsibilities, Dorete and Sam took only a short honeymoon.

A few months later, Carlo and Lisa had another baby, a daughter they named Josephine. Sam and Dorete wanted to baptize her, which they did.

And so for another four years, life continued sweet and prosperous.

***

Patrick and Carlo decided to open another pizzeria, which they called Show Time Pizzeria. Salvatore became the manager. It did well too, and soon Sam was able to buy the business for himself and Dorete.

The depression was over now so Patrick and Carlo decided to go back into construction. They left the pizzerias to Sam and Dorete and started another company. The business quickly flourished. They never forgot about the bad times though and always put enough money away should things take a turn.

Carlo's son Joe was now about twelve years old. He and Tom had become best friends. They shared their most intimate thoughts and cared for each other like blood brothers.

They did exceptionally well in both school and football. It seemed that they had a special talent for the sport. Carlo wanted Joe to give up football and play soccer, like him, but Joe's first love was football.

With every passing year, he got better and better and in their senior year, Tom and Joe won their high school championship. Their fathers were very proud.

During that time, Tom Palmer was dating a beautiful Italian girl named Lina Mare. Her father's name was John. Tom became good friends with Mr. Mare. He went to their house many times for dinner and not simply because he liked lasagna.

"You Irish people like to drink beer and we Italians like to drink wine," John joked with Tom. "You like corned beef and cabbage and we like spaghetti and meatballs."

"Mr. Mare," Tom said, "thank you for inviting me to dinner because I like lasagna much better than corned beef and cabbage. I love Italian food but-" he gazed longingly at Lina- "I love your daughter Lina even more. I would like to marry her someday."

"Tom," John said, "as long as you're a nice boy and you go to college, I'd love for you to be my future son-in-law."

Tom and Lina dated all through high school. They went to the movies and they walked in the park where Tom would kiss her passionately and sometimes inappropriately, much to Lina's distress.

"Tom, please stop," she said, "I don't believe in making love before marriage. It's the way I was taught and I believe in it."

Tom sighed. "I'll be patient until we get married, I promise," he said.

Meanwhile, Joe Martino played the field. He was handsome, well-liked, and very popular, but he hadn't found one girl he could be serious about.

More than once, Joe said to Tom, "You're lucky to have found Lina. I know you really love her and she loves you. But I haven't found the right girl yet. Someday I hope to, though, and when I do I hope I'm as happy as you are."

After Joe graduated from high school, his family had a little party for him. They wished him good luck at college and hoped that if he didn't get to play football professionally, he could take over the family business.

Patrick made a speech. "Joe, I'm going to tell you a little story about when I met your father on the boat to America. I saw him on the top deck eating a big piece of pizza. That pizza looked so good it made me hungry. I remembered my time in Naples during the war when I had pizza for the first time. I saw him smile as I approached him. So I talked to him in Italian to see if he would invite me to share his pizza. When I saw my wife and your mother approach, I invited them over. That way we could share the pizza."

"So," Carlo laughingly said, "you wanted to eat my pizza and thought by introducing us all that you could get some more. But I have to say, this turned out to be the best thing that ever happened to me. To have this wonderful family become a part of my life. Patrick became the father that I never had because my own father died when I was young. Now I don't have to make any more pizza because your mother learned to make it better than I could."

"Joe, your father is a great man," Patrick said. "It was a great thing for us to meet him. He only did one thing wrong. He still never calls me by my real name. He calls me Patricio like he did the first time I met him on the boat. But I still love him!" They all laughed.

"Patricio," Carlo said, "remember, his name is Martino. Even though he's tall and blond and looks Irish, he's an Italian boy."

"Carlo, remember I gave my beautiful daughter to you, be nice."

"And I love her very much, Dad."

Joe and Tom wanted to go to college not only to further their education, but also to fulfill their dreams of playing pro-football. Lina was going to college to be a secretary.

Tom and Joe decided to go to Penn State. Unfortunately, Penn State was too expensive for Tom. But Carlo was prepared to give Tom a hand. He had the money and he also wanted Joe and Tom to be together. They'd been best friends since childhood; it would be a shame to split them up now. Tom was happy for the opportunity and promised to pay him back when he was able.

They started college in the fall of 1940. Everything went well for them. They did well in school and on the playing field. Then they got the bad news. The Japanese had bombed Pearl Harbor. They both received draft notices.

Tom was desperate. He wanted to marry Lina before he left. He thought that if he left her alone she'd find someone else. He talked to his father about it.

"You're doing the right thing, Tom. She's a good woman and she'll always be there for you."

Tom went to her father and said, "I'd like to marry Lina before I leave. Do I have your permission?"

"My daughter loves you very much and you're going away to serve your country," John said. "Of course you have my blessing."

Although it was rushed, in a week's time they were ready for the ceremony. Joe was to be best man. Lina was beautiful and the ceremony went off without a hitch.

They had the reception in the Mare's backyard. Sean, Tom's father, made a toast. "I'm glad my son married your daughter, Lina," he said to Lina's father, John. "I hope that they'll have a long married life together. I pray that my son comes back safe and we can all be together again.

It's my sincerest wish that our families will always be close."

Joe told everyone at the wedding that he was leaving in a few days. He was going before Tom. After the reception, he said goodbye to everyone and especially to Tom and his family.

"Joe, we have had a lot of good times together. I hope we see each other after the war and go back to the way we are now, friends forever."

They hugged and said goodbye, their eyes shiny with tears.

The next morning Joe's family and friends came to the house to say goodbye to him. Everyone wished him good luck and hoped that he would be safe and come back home in one piece.

"Joe," his father said, "if you happen to get to Italy, try to find your Uncle Vincenzo in Naples. He'd be happy to see you. He hasn't seen any of his family in a long time."

"I promise I'll try," Joe said. "It'd be great to meet some of our family."

"I wish you good luck, Joe," Patrick said. "You know I was in Italy in World War One. It wasn't easy but sometimes in life, we have to serve our country and this is one of those times. I hope someday we'll see you back home again. You're the only boy in the family and I hope one day you'll take over the company."

With tears in his eyes, Patrick took off his St. Christopher medal and gave it to Joe. "This is what I wore and it brought me luck. My mother gave it to me. I give it to you to keep you safe."

Joe was very touched and promised to return it safely. Sending a son off to war is always sad, and this was no exception. They all hugged and kissed him goodbye and told him fervently that they hoped he'd come back okay.

Tom and Lina left for a short honeymoon before Tom left. Everyone came down to the train station to say goodbye. And like every other soldier sent off to war, people cried because they didn't know if he would ever come back.

Before Tom got on the train, Lina said, "I'll always think of you and I'll pray that you'll come back to me soon."

"I want to take back the cross I gave you so that I have a piece of you with me," Tom said. "I'll give it back to you when I return."

He took the necklace from around her neck and put it in his pocket. He had given Lina the necklace when they got engaged. It had belonged to his grandmother. Then he put his arms around her, kissed her goodbye and got on the train. Everyone waved goodbye.

Basic training lasted six weeks. Joe went into the Army while Tom went into the Navy. Joe was assigned to fight in Africa and Tom the Pacific.

Joe was in Africa for almost two years before the United States victory. Joe's unit went to Italy where Joe, because of his heroism, was promoted to Sergeant. After two weeks, his unit arrived in Sicily. There he fought in another major battle that pushed the Germans out of Sicily. Following that victory, his unit went to Anzio, near Rome.

Joe recalled what his father had told him about his uncle who lived in Naples. So with his two best friends, Brian and Hector, Joe got into a Jeep and tried to find him.

Naples was torn up from the war, but they saw a bar and decided to stop and maybe have a drink. In his broken Italian Joe asked the bartender if he knew the street. The bartender said it was nearby. Then Joe asked him if he could make a pizza for them and he said he could.

While they waited, they drank a bottle of wine while two men across from them played cards. Joe thought one of them looked a little like his father.

His friends told him to get up and go over, which Joe reluctantly did.

"Scusa, signore," he said, "what's your name?"

The man didn't answer. Maybe it's my uniform, Joe thought. Maybe he's afraid of me.

"Mio papa, Carlo Martino?" Joe said.

Suddenly the man jumped up and hugged him.

"Mio dios, you are Carlo's son, Giuseppe! This is my nephew from America," he said to the others.

"Come with me," he said to Joe, "I want to introduce you to my family. They'll be so happy to see you."

"Sophia, Sophia, I have a surprise for you!" he called as he opened the door and ushered Joe and his friends inside.

"Keep quiet," Sophia yelled from the other room. "You always have a surprise for me, but then you come home with nothing."

But she *was* surprised when she saw Vincenzo with three American soldiers.

"This is our nephew from America," Vincenzo said, "Carlo's son, Giuseppe, and his two friends."

She hugged him and said, "This is a big surprise. Your father has always been very good to us. I hope he's well."

The three cousins, all around Joe's age, came home then and were equally surprised to see Joe. Everyone sat down and Joe told them about Carlo. They hoped that someday they'd all be able to get together.

"My father is very anxious to see you all again when the war's over," Joe said.

Food was scarce so he gave Sophia a big bag of macaroni and some food. Sophia thanked him and cooked some of the macaroni for dinner.

Joe and his friends stayed for two more days and when it was time for them to leave, Joe hugged and kissed everyone goodbye and gave Vincenzo fifty dollars to help out. Sophia hugged him, gave him a big pizza for the trip, and wished him well.

A few days later, while they were driving through the Anzio countryside, Joe heard singing. As they got closer to the source, he saw a beautiful young Italian woman singing and playing a guitar for a group of soldiers. He stopped to listen--she had the voice of an angel.

Afterwards, he approached her and said in Italian, "What's the name of that beautiful song?"

"*'Good Morning My First Love'*."

"What a wonderful title. My name is Sgt. Joe Martino. And you are?"

"Maria Bellini."

"You have a beautiful voice, Maria Bellini. May I walk you home?"

She paused a second, then, "Of course, Sergeant."

For some reason Joe felt an instant attraction to this girl, as if he had known her forever. He fell in love with her the moment their eyes met.

She introduced him to her mother, Mama Connie, and her little brother, Anthony.

"It's a pleasure to meet you," Joe said. He twisted his hat nervously and added, "I'll be in Anzio for a while. My father was born in Sorrento."

"Maria's father is fighting against Russia in the Italian army," Mama Connie said. She took a liking to Joe almost instantly and invited him to dinner.

"I apologize for the lack of food," she said as she served him a delicious plate of macaroni.

"I think you have a wonderful daughter and she has a great voice," he said after dinner. "I'd, uh, I'd like to get to know her better."

"You're welcome anytime."

Joe spent the next week getting to know Maria and her family. And he knew in his heart that she was the girl of his dreams.

Unfortunately, their squad would probably be moving out soon and he wanted to spend as much time with Maria as possible. He came up with a plan.

He invited his two best friends to Maria's house that night for dinner. He knew they didn't have very much food so he asked the cook if he could spare some spaghetti.

"For you sergeant, anything," the cook said and gave him several pounds. Then all three men drove to Maria's house.

Maria answered the door, Mama Connie right behind.

"I brought two of my friends with me tonight," Joe said. "Brian and Hector."

"You're both welcome in my house," Mama Connie said. "Any friend of Joe's is a friend of mine. But I'm afraid I have nothing but soup for dinner tonight."

"No problem, Mama Connie," Joe said. "I brought you a present."

Mama Connie was overwhelmed and hugged him tenderly. "We'll have a feast tonight," she said. "I made some sauce today with the thought that perhaps I could find some pasta. I also have some fresh ricotta from the goat. So please, sit down!"

Brian and Hector laughed and said, "We haven't had a home cooked meal in months. We can't wait!"

Mama Connie boiled the spaghetti and they sat down to eat. Before dinner, they said a prayer and thanked God for the food before them and for good luck in the coming days.

They started to eat and everyone was appreciative of Mama Connie's cooking. They asked for seconds and she laughed. "My boys, I love you like my own sons. You can eat all you want."

She brought out more pasta and sauce while Maria brought out a bottle of wine. Afterwards the men started singing some American songs, including, *God Bless America.*

Maria asked Joe what that meant. She could only speak a little English and some of the words confused her. Joe told her it is 'Dio Benedice Lamerica' and Italy too.

Maria, a talented singer and guitar player, brought out her guitar. She tried to play along and learn the words. Her playing brought tears to their eyes and afterwards they hugged her and thanked her for playing so beautifully. It reminded them all of the homes they had left behind and the hope that they all would make it back.

When it was time to leave, they all thanked Mama Connie and Maria for dinner and told her what a wonderful meal it was.

"You're all welcome to come here as long as you stay in Anzio," Mama Connie said. "I wish you well from the bottom of my heart. May God be with you."

"I'll pray for your safety and I hope someday to see you all again," Maria said.

"Signora Concetta," Joe said. "You have a wonderful daughter. She not only sings beautifully, but she has a wonderful heart. I love her very much. When I come back from the war I want to take you all back with me to America."

Brian and Hector got into the Jeep and Joe walked outside with Maria. "It's funny about what's happened in my life," he said. "When I was in high school in America I knew a lot of girls and had fun, but I never fell in love. You're the first girl I have ever felt that way about. I promise you, I'll take you and your family to America with me after the war."

They kissed goodbye and Joe got into the Jeep with his friends and left.

His friends kidded him about Maria on the way back but Joe told them, "This is the first time I have ever fallen in love and it has to be during wartime. Do you think this is my destiny?"

"Joe," Brian said, "things happen that we don't expect, good or bad. Who can see into the future?"

Joe thought about it and said, "If we make it back alive after the war, I want you both to be best man at my wedding." They shook hands and said, "For you sergeant, anything."

The next morning, they found they only had another few days left in Anzio before they had to leave. Joe wanted to spend as much time as he could with Maria.

That night he went back to her house alone. When she answered the door, Mama Connie asked where his friends were.

"We're leaving in a few days," Joe said, "so they're making preparations. They'll be here tomorrow night to say goodbye."

"Good, then I'll have time to prepare a farewell dinner."

She had Joe sit down and served him some homemade soup and bread, but not before saying a prayer for their safety and for her husband far away. Joe told her what a wonderful cook she was.

After dinner, Joe and Maria went for a walk around Anzio. Joe was going to miss the small town and the happy memories.

"Maria," Joe said, "I'm glad I met you. You have made my time here in Anzio wonderful." He paused a moment, then, and as the sweat beaded on his forehead, he said, "I'm going to miss you and your family, too. But I want to tell you, Maria, that I love you. I have never felt this way about a woman before. I faithfully promise you that when the war is over, I'll come back and marry you and take you and your family back to America with me."

"I like you, Joe, even though I don't know you very well," Maria said. "My mother likes you, too. She thinks you're a gentleman with a big heart."

They continued walking until they were outside the city where they heard the ringing of a bell.

"What's that?" Joe said.

"We're near the convent. The nuns have converted it into a hospital for the war. They're trying to help as many people as they can."

They walked on until they saw a statue of the Virgin Mary. They decided to sit down and rest on the grass. Joe looked at Maria and she at him. They knew what the other was thinking and before long, they started kissing each other passionately and with abandon, like two people who might not see each other again.

Joe, feeling bold and really not able to control himself, put his hands where he shouldn't have.

"Joe," Maria said, "what are you doing? I'm only seventeen. I've never made love before."

But, Joe, not to be dissuaded, kept on kissing her.

"Maria, I love you very much," he said. "And that's the truth. I'm not saying it so you'll make love to me. I'll be leaving in a few days and I just want to be with you."

"You're sure you're telling the truth? How do I know that you don't have another girlfriend or even a wife?"

"Believe me, Maria. I swear to God and promise you in front of this statue of the Virgin Mary that I don't have a wife or a girlfriend and I don't love anyone else but you."

For what seemed an eternity, Joe waited for a response. But Maria didn't say a word—she didn't have to—her kisses said it all.

Later, Joe promised Mama Connie that he'd bring his friends back the next night for dinner.

"Joe, don't forget," Anthony said, "you'll take me to America too, right?"

Joe laughed. "Of course I will."

***

Mama Connie served a wonderful spaghetti dinner the next evening and she said a special prayer for them to be safe. "I'll pray for you boys to come back here after the war and see us again. Hopefully, by then, my dear husband will also be back from the war."

After dinner, Maria brought out
the last of the wine from her father's cellar. They started singing and Maria played her guitar. They sang songs that reminded them of home. Then Maria surprised them by playing *God Bless America*. She had a sweet voice and everyone got a tear in their eye. She made them feel homesick.

They got up and hugged her and Hector said, "Thank you, Maria, you have a beautiful voice. It makes us think of our homes and all the good things we left behind in America."

Joe walked with Maria a little ways before he left. "Remember, Maria, what I told you," he said. "I promise you I will love you forever. I'll think about you while I'm fighting. And when I come back, I'll marry you. I'll always have you in my heart and the song that you sang the first time I saw you, *Good Morning My First Love*. You are my dream come true. I know our love is meant to be and I promise that it will always be true. I'll always hear that song when I'm in the front lines fighting the enemy."

"Yes, Joe," Maria said, "I love you too, and I believe you. I'll miss you and I'll think of you every day. I'll pray for you to come back safe."

Their unit left for Monte Casino the next day. It would be a difficult mission—the fighting was heavy and casualties were heavy.

Before he left, though, Joe wrote to his mother about Maria, the wonderful Italian girl who sang and played the guitar that he had fallen in love with.

About three weeks later Maria started feeling poorly while she was doing chores. It continued for a few more days. She tried to hide it from her mother because she wasn't sure why she was sick. But one day her mother saw her and said, "If I didn't know better, I'd think you were going to have a baby. Sergeant Joe's baby?"

Maria was surprised but happy. Now, more than ever, she prayed for his safe return.

Six months later, during Maria's second trimester, the town was heavily bombed by the Germans, killing her mother and brother and leaving her wounded. Luckily, a neighbor brought her to the nearby convent, which had been converted into a hospital.

Maria saw the doctor and rested for a few days. Her worries about the unborn baby were for nothing—the baby would be fine.

While there, Maria became friends with a young nun named Sister Theresa. Maria told her that she played the guitar, but it had been destroyed in the attack.

Sister Theresa told her she had a guitar and that she could use it when she got better.

When Maria started feeling better, Sister Theresa did just that. Maria's lyrical voice and playing made everyone around them happy. The war was forgotten while she played, by her and by everyone.

Maria decided to stay at the convent until her baby was born. They needed the help and she had nowhere else to go.

The week she was to give birth, a young boy; age eleven, took the bed next to her. His name was Rino and he'd suffered a leg wound from a rocket attack.

One night Sister Theresa, sensing that Maria didn't feel well, said, "I know your family was killed in the war, but is there somebody else who'd like to know you're having a baby? Perhaps the baby's father?"

At first, Maria felt apprehensive about discussing this, after all, she had sinned, but perhaps Sister Theresa would understand.

"His name is Sergeant Giuseppe Martino, Sister. We're going to be married after the war." She paused and wrung her hands together, then. "I don't know how you'd find him. I very much want him to be here, but it's impossible."

Sister Theresa took Maria into her arms and comforted her.

The next day Maria went into labor. She had a difficult time, but eventually she gave birth to a boy; but not just one. "I think there's another baby in there!" the doctor said.

After another difficult labor, she delivered another boy. The babies were fine, but Maria wasn't doing as well as hoped. The doctor hoped that with a little rest she should be fine. Maria thanked God for the two beautiful babies He had given her and prayed that Joe was okay, that he'd make it back to see his sons.

A few days later Maria started feeling better so she asked Sister Theresa to bring the two babies to her.

"What are you going to name them?" Sister Theresa asked.

"One after my father, Giorgio, and the other after their father, Joe Martino."

Later that night Maria kissed them goodnight, and said to herself, "I'm lucky to have two beautiful babies."

Rino, who had helped her, thought they were beautiful, too.

Later, while she was saying her prayers, Maria said to Joe, "We have made two beautiful babies. They look just like you."

Then she started to sing *God Bless America* and bless Italy too. "Someday we'll all be free. Then your papa will come back here and take us all back to America."

The next day Rino's mother came to take him home. While Sister Theresa was telling her about Maria and her two beautiful babies, Maria came over and said goodbye to Rino.

"Bono fortuna to you, Signora Maria," he said. "I hope you meet your Sergeant Giuseppe again." Then he left with his mother.

A few days later things took a turn for Maria. She started to bleed again. The doctor tried to stop it but to no avail. He didn't have the medicine to help her and she'd die if she didn't get the help she needed.

He went to see Sister Theresa. "I'm afraid she doesn't have long to live, sister. Only God can help her now. We must pray for her."

Sister Theresa told the other members of the convent what had happened and asked them to pray for her. They came to see her and told her what a joy she had been to them in this troubling time. They were all enormously sad.

Another day went by and she got worse. Maria knew that things weren't going well and that she was facing death. She asked Sister Theresa to please take care of her two babies.

"I promise you, Maria, that your children will be well taken care of," Sister Theresa replied.

"And Sister, please promise me that I'll be laid to rest near the statue of the Virgin Mary. Joe proposed to me there."

"Of course, child, now rest."

Maria closed her eyes to rest but an old gypsy woman came over and said, "Maria, don't worry, your babies will be well taken care of. I see that someday they will both be famous."

Maria smiled, but it was her last. She died peacefully, knowing that her sons would be fine.

They buried her where she had asked, by the statue of the Virgin Mary. The local carpenter made a big wooden cross and wrote her name, date of birth and death on it.

Also written on it were the words, *We will never forget you for being such a wonderful person. Rest in peace.*

After the ceremony, everyone gathered around the grave to say goodbye. They left with sadness in their hearts for someone who had died so young, leaving behind two newborns.

When Sister Theresa went to the American base to find Joe, she found out that he had died in battle several months earlier. Deeply saddened by Maria's death and now learning of Joe's death, she was confused as to what to do next. She knew Maria had no other family, so she sought the advice of the Mother Superior who told her they would keep the twins in the convent.

When the war ended several months later, the Mother Superior decided to bring all the orphaned children to an orphanage in Rome. Sister Theresa went along with the children to help insure they arrived safely.

When they arrived, she gave the officials the names of all the children, but she didn't tell them there was a set of twins—with so many children, she simply forgot.

When she returned to the convent, she went to Maria's grave. "Maria," she said, "your children are safe. I pray that they'll find good homes and be happy."

She never forgot about Maria or her two children and often went there to pray.

About eight years later, Sister Theresa went to Rome with the Mother Superior on business. She had never forgotten about Maria and her children and wanted to see what had happened to them.

She went to the orphanage and inquired about the two boys Giuseppe and Giorgio she had brought from Anzio so long ago. She told the officials they were twins. They were surprised that they had been separated, but Sister Theresa said she had forgotten to tell them that at the time because things were so hectic.

She found out that one child was adopted by a family in Venice and the other by a family in the United States. She was relieved to hear that. They were being well taken care of, especially the one who went to America. Maria had often talked about going there someday.

The first thing Sister Theresa did after returning home was to go to Maria's grave. She brought some flowers for her and said, "Maria, as I have promised you your children are fine. They're being well taken care of." Then she said a little prayer and went back to the convent, content that she had done her best.

Chapter Two – Giorgio's story

In 1946, things had begun to settle down. Giorgio Fiorino, a barber in Venice, had a daughter, Angela, and a wife named Marisa who was unable to have any more children. He had always had his heart set on having a son and it depressed him to learn they would have no more children.

He wrote to a friend who worked in an orphanage in Rome and inquired about adopting a baby boy. He knew there were many children left without parents after the war and he wanted to give one of them a good home. His friend, Franco, wrote back and told him that yes; there were many children available for adoption. This made Giorgio happy and he and his wife made plans to go to see them. They took the train for Rome the next day and then to the orphanage.

Franco greeted them, then introduced them to the orphanage administrator, a tall, willowy woman with a hawkish nose and an air of officiousness.

"We had our hearts set on a boy," Giorgio said as he took his wife's hand.

"I see. Well, several boys between the ages of one and two years old are available. Come, I'll show you where they are."

They saw a handsome boy with wavy brown hair. "What's his name?" Giorgio asked.

"Well, it's Giorgio," was the reply.

Taken by surprise, Giorgio suddenly grabbed his wife's arm and said, "This is the boy I want. It's an omen, I tell you."

They were allowed to spend the rest of the day with little Giorgio.

"We'll do what we can to expedite the paperwork," the administrator said. "What with the overcrowding and all."

Giorgio and his wife returned to Venice and waited for news.

A few weeks later, they received a letter from Franco advising them that it was time to come to Rome and get their new son.

Before they left, Giorgio stopped at his barbershop, saw the mayor and told him the good news about going to pick up his new son.

"His name is Giorgio just like mine and he has blue eyes just like me. I'm sure it's fate."

"Good luck with your new son," the Mayor said, "and bring him in one day so we can all meet him. Are you going to raise him to be a barber like you?"

"Yes, I'd like to, but I'll let him decide what he wants to be."

The next day Giorgio and his wife went to the orphanage and met with the administrator again. She had all the legal papers ready. Afterwards, they went to the nursery to greet their new son. He was dressed in a little blue suit and had a hat on that said *Welcome to Venice, little star.*

When Giorgio saw that he asked Franco, "What does this mean?"

"He's a very smart little boy. When we take him to mass he listens to the music and brings his hands up like he's conducting and smiles."

Giorgio's wife picked him up and said, "Giorgio, he has blue eyes like you. What a coincidence. He looks enough like you to actually be our son!"

Again, they thanked Franco for all he had done and gave a donation to him for the orphanage.

"If I come to Venice one day," Franco said, "you must give me a haircut."

"Yes," Giorgio said, "but I'm taking you to dinner, too."

A big celebration awaited them in Venice. Everyone wanted to wish them the best of luck with their new son.

Giorgio wanted his new son to become a schoolteacher like his grandfather. He wanted to keep the tradition in the family. But he also hoped that when he was old enough he would find his own talent and pursue it.

Christine, Giorgio's new sister, was happy to have a brother and liked to take care of him. There was lots of joy in the family.

He was a happy and active little boy and fit right in. Sometimes his father would take him for a walk on the Piazza San Marco. He was five at that time. There was always music playing and lots of things to see. Little Giorgio always wanted to hear the music. Sometimes he'd raise his arms like a little maestro and his father would laugh, as would the musicians. He loved the music and always asked his father to take him there.

When Giorgio started school at age six, he had a music teacher named Mrs. Gina. She taught him how to sing his first song. She was impressed by how fast he learned and by how strong a voice he had.

She told his father how talented he was and said he should encourage him to sing.
Giorgio asked his teacher to do the same by having him join the school choir.

He improved every week. His father was so proud of him. No one else in the family had this kind of talent. Giorgio Sr. knew he had made a good choice when he had adopted him, but of course, he often wondered who his real parents were. They had to have been very talented themselves. He felt blessed that he was able to adopt him and give him a good home and encouragement.

Five years later, during the summer of his eleventh year, Giorgio went to his father's barbershop and listened to an elderly man play the guitar.

"Sir," Giorgio asked, "would you accompany me while I sing one of my favorite songs?"

"Certainly," the man said.

Everyone was impressed with his singing and he would frequently come back and sing. He was so popular many people came there just to hear him sing.

One day the Mayor of Venice came to the barbershop for a shave.

He saw a crowd out front as he approached.

He went inside and asked Giorgio, "Is your son coming to sing today?"

"Yes, before his school recital."

The Mayor sat down and Giorgio put the shaving cream on his face.

"Giorgio," the Mayor said, "your barbershop has become a famous place since your son has been coming in here to sing. They're starting to call you the barbiere, 'The Barber of Seville'."

Giorgio laughed. "Mayor, since I'm so famous I'm afraid I'm going to have to charge you more for your shave."

"I don't care. I love to come here and hear Giorgio sing. For that I'd pay any price."

Just then, Giorgio walked in with his friend, Enrico, the guitar player. He greeted his father and friends and then sat down and started singing. His father was so enthralled watching and listening to him, that he forgot what he was doing, leaving the Mayor in the chair unshaved.

Giorgio started another song, an old Venetian song, which coincidentally the Mayor's mother used to sing to him when he was little. The many memories brought tears to his eyes. He got up and hugged Giorgio, forgetting he still had shaving cream on his face. Everyone started laughing but the Mayor was puzzled. What was going on?

Then he realized what had happened. He laughed and said, "See, Giorgio, you were so involved in listening to your son you forgot to shave me! For that I'm not going to pay you. Instead I'm going to give Giorgio a big tip."

"That's okay, Mayor. Besides, he needs the money for his education."

Before he left, Giorgio went over to the Mayor and thanked him for the tip.

"Don't worry about my father. Next time he won't take so long to shave you," he said.

"Giorgio, I enjoy your singing very much and I hope that one day you'll be a great singer. I'll never forget today and what happened here. Especially the last song which brought back so many memories. It was a song my mother used to sing to me when I was little. You sang it with so much feeling. I hope someday when you're a star you'll come back here to Venice and sing for us again."

"Of course," Giorgio said.

***

Five years later, at the age of seventeen, Giorgio earned extra money singing in the gondolas on the canals. Enrico played the guitar. Having once been a professional singer, Enrico knew talent when he heard it. He offered to send Giorgio to a voice teacher since his father couldn't afford the extra expense. His father accepted the offer, which allowed Giorgio to take voice lessons for several years.

He did very well on the gondolas and the public enjoyed his singing very much, which gave him the confidence he needed to become a professional singer and to study at the conservatory. So he saved all his money and worked hard.

One day a group of American tourists approached the gondola where Giorgio was singing, *Come Back to Sorrento.*

Among them were an elderly gentleman and his wife who were so overtaken by his singing, they cried. They were on a trip back to Italy after having lived in America for many years. The husband was from Sorrento and he was taking his Irish wife there to see the place where he was born.

"Your singing reminds me of someone I loved many years ago," he said. "Please, accompany me to a café and enjoy a cup of cappuccino with my wife and me."

At the café, Giorgio told them about how he wanted to go the conservatory of music and take voice lessons and that he was working on the gondola to earn money to do so.

When it was time to go, Giorgio was surprised and shocked when the elderly man presented him with a check for $10,000. "But you must use it only for the conservatory," he said.

"I promise," Giorgio said.

"One day I hope to hear you sing in America. Remember my name, Carlo Martino from Philadelphia. I'm giving you this money in memory of my son and also because I believe that with training you'll become a great singer."

Before they parted ways, Giorgio once again thanked him for the money. He told him that if he ever had the honor of coming to America and singing, he would look him up and thank him for his generous donation.

"You'll always be in my heart for what you're doing for me. I can never repay you for this."

Giorgio gave Carlo and his wife a hug and then went back to work on the gondola.

As they watched him walk away, Mrs. Martino said to her husband, "You must be crazy to give away ten thousand dollars to a complete stranger."

"I think he'll become a famous singer and if I can help him achieve that, I'll be a better person. Besides, he reminds me of our son, Joe, who I miss very much."

Carlo spent another day in Venice with his wife. They really loved the city. Then they rented a car to see more of Italy. They stayed in Florence for a few days. They went to the museums and art galleries and loved their time there. Then they went on to Rome, the eternal city. They spent quite a lot of time there looking at the ruins, the Trevi fountain and of course enjoying the food. Lisa, Carlo's wife, loved the food the most.

Then it was time to go back to Naples, Carlo's home town. He hadn't been back for 41 years. His only living relative was his brother Vincenzo, who still lived there.

When they arrived, Carlo said "I'm home now," the emotion evident in his tone. They found the street where his brother lived and parked. As he was getting out, his brother saw him, ran to him, and hugged him. They were so happy to see each other after such a long time.

"Carlo, you are finally back home," Vincenzo said. "I never thought I' see you again."

"It's always been my dream to come back home and see you again," Carlo said.

Everybody was there to greet them when they went inside. They shook their hands and hugged them and welcomed them both.

Sofia, the sister-in-law, said, "Everything is ready to eat. I made lasagna just like your mother used to make."

Carlo hugged her and as he remembered his mother, it almost made him cry.

"You know Carlo," Sophia said, "when we met Giuseppe during the war, we enjoyed him very much. He was a wonderful boy. Just like you, with a wonderful heart. Too bad he died in the war."

"He was my only son and I miss him," Carlo said. "He will always live in my heart. But life goes on and I know one day I'll see him again."

After dinner his nephew Vito came out with his guitar and said, "Uncle Carlo, here's your mandolin, join me."

Carlo happily obliged him.

Everyone had a great time and welcomed Lisa like she was one of the family, which she really appreciated.

The next day Carlo told his brother, "We have to go to Sorrento where we were born to see our home and our parent's grave."

When they arrived, they saw that everything had changed for the better and Carlo was happy to see that. After being there for a few days, he met some of his old childhood friends, his fishing buddies. They were glad to see him again.

The next day they left to go back to Naples to spend a few more days there.

One day while they were taking a walk with Vincenzo, Sofia and Lisa, Carlo saw Marisa, the young woman he'd been in love with long ago before he left for America.

"See that woman?" Vincenzo said. "Remember her?"

At first Carlo didn't remember, but the more he looked at her, the more focused his memory became. Marisa instantly recognized him. He hadn't changed that much. She had never forgotten him. They greeted each other and hugged.

"I'm sorry for what happened a long time ago, Carlo," she said. "I'm glad you look so well. I wish you much happiness for the future."

"I forgot what happened," Carlo said. "It was never your fault anyway. I wish you and your husband the same."

"He died ten years ago in an accident."

"I'm sorry to hear that. He was my friend at one time." Then they hugged again, said goodbye, and went on their way.

Carlo and Lisa spent the rest of their vacation in Naples. Carlo had a good time being back home again with his old friends and family. He was sad when it was time to go.

The family went with them to the airport and hugged him goodbye.

"Thank you for all you've done for us over the years and your generosity, Carlo," Vincenzo said. "And thank your wife for being such a wonderful woman. We love her very much."

"Thank you for letting us stay with you and showing us a good time," Carlo said. "I'll always remember this when I go back home. I hope we see each other again someday."

"Carlo, why don't you come back and live here in Italy again. We had such a wonderful time together."

"Vincenzo, my brother, you have to understand something. I've built new roots in America. That's where my family is now. I remember always when I left Italy many years ago. At that time there was no work for me and I left my family and my mother behind, who I loved very much. I came to America with a big dream, to have better opportunities and to start a new life. I soon realized I made the right choice. I worked hard and I started to achieve my dream and I became a successful businessman with the help of God and a good friend. I made a good living and after forty-one years my dream came true and I was able to come back home to Sorrento and see my family again. I've been very happy to see you all again and you gave me and my wife a great welcome. I see how much everything has changed. Everything's better now and I'm glad to see that. Italy is a beautiful country. The sea, the sunshine, the food and the history. While I was driving around, I saw many people from around the world enjoying themselves. For me now, America is my home. But in my heart and mind, I'll always remember Italy. Let me give you this poem that I wrote about her and how I feel. It's the same as I just told you."

Ricordo sempre il mio passato
Il paese dove sono nato, l'Italia.
Non avevo lavoro e sono emigrato
E ho lasciato la mamma e portato
D'into o core il ricordo del suo amore,
E la nostalgia della patria mia.

E dopo tanto tempo sono ritornato e
Ho trovato tutto cambiato.
La gente é differente, vivono molto bene
E io sono molto grato di quello che ho trovato.

L'Italia è sempre bella c'è il mare e il sole
Che brilla è fa calore.
L'Italia, l'Italia fa vivere in ogni cuore
La vita e l'amore.

Quanto ritornerò ricorderò per sempre
La patria mia lontana.
Io sono Americano, ma d'into o core mio
Sono sempre italiano.

"I understand Carlo," Vincenzo said. "My only wish is that someday you'll come back again."

"With the will of God, I will."

***

Enrico was waiting for Giorgio when he returned. When he saw the big smile on Giorgio's face, he asked, "What happened? I've never seen you so happy."

Giorgio showed him the check. “Can you believe this? An American tourist liked my singing so much he invited me for cappuccino and then gave me a check for ten thousand American dollars! He said it was in memory of his son. He made me promise to use it to go to the conservatory.”

Enrico was amazed. “I’m very happy for you. This will do a lot to make your dream come true.”

“It’s funny but when I hugged him, I felt a connection.”

“Giorgio, I wouldn’t worry about it. It’s probably just one of those rich Americans who just likes good singing and good music.”

“Perhaps. But now that I have some money let’s take the rest of the day off and go celebrate!”

Enrico laughed. “Yes, now that you’re a rich man you can buy me the biggest plate of spaghetti in Venice!”

“Don’t worry about it. If I become a great singer, I’ll pay for many dinners!”

Giorgio had a big smile on his face when he got home that night. He couldn’t wait to tell his father what had happened that day.

When his father saw his face and the big grin, he said, “Did you get a big tip today?”

Giorgio smiled, “You won’t believe what I got! Today I met a man and his wife who were visiting from America. He used to live in Sorrento. He requested a song and when I was done, he was so impressed that he gave me a check for ten thousand dollars in American money to use for voice lessons. He said he gave me the money because he felt a connection with me. I reminded him of his son.”

His father’s eyes went big with excitement. At first, he thought that Giorgio was playing a trick on him, but when he showed him the check, he believed him.

He told Giorgio to thank God for sending Mr. Martino to him when they went to church on Sunday. That’s exactly what he did.

After church, he told the priest that he wasn’t going to be singing in the choir any more because he was going to Florence for schooling. Everyone wished him well and said they would miss him and his singing. They hoped that he would do well and go on to become famous.

The Mayor had heard that Giorgio was going off to school and he wanted to help him along. He asked the local businessmen for their help. They collected some money and came to the barbershop to give it to him and say goodbye. They said they hoped he would be a great success and become a famous singer.

He thanked them and the Mayor presented him with the envelope of money.

Giorgio was touched and said, "Thank you all very much. I promise you that when I'm a success that I'll come back home and sing for you all. But before I go I'll sing one last song for you."

They called after him, "Bono Fortuna," as he left.

Giorgio was very excited to have received this money and very honored that the townspeople thought so much of him. When he got home, he told his mother what they had done. His mother told him that she had received a letter that day that said the conservatory was closed for the summer and would reopen in September. They were, however, happy that he was going to attend.

Giorgio decided to stay in Venice with Enrico, who was like a father to him. He could earn some extra money for his schooling.

Everyone was glad he was staying a little longer, especially the girls. His father told him it was okay to date, but not to get serious before he left for school. He promised his father that he wouldn't.

One day while waiting for customers, a beautiful young woman with blonde hair came along and wanted a ride. "Quando a bella, questa signora." (What a beautiful woman), Enrico said to Giorgio.

She smiled because she understood what they were saying. As they started down the canal, Giorgio started singing. She was very impressed. When they came back to the dock, she complimented them and offered a cup of coffee.

"My name is Monique Reno," she said, "and I'm from Paris. I'm a singer, too. I'm here visiting because my grandfather used to come here many, many years ago to visit. He was a chef in Paris. I haven't been back myself for a long time. I'm here for a week's vacation. I was very impressed by your singing. Would you be interested in coming to Paris with me? I can arrange for you to sing in the clubs. The experience will be invaluable. I can show you around the city, too."

Giorgio was very flattered. "Thank you for your offer but I'm leaving for the conservatory in Florence in three months."

"That's wonderful. But if you'd like to come for a month or so that'd be fine, too. It would be a good learning experience for you and you can stay with my family."

Giorgio thought a moment. He could treat it like a vacation. He'd have to work very hard when he started school anyway.

"You could also learn some French which might come in handy."

"Why would you do this for me?" Giorgio said.

"I like to help new talent and I think you're very talented. Think about it. I'll meet you for dinner in two days and you can give me your answer then."

Giorgio agreed and they made arrangements for where to meet.

As they were walking back home, Giorgio asked Enrico for his advice. Should he go to Paris or not?

"She's very beautiful, Giorgio. I'd go in a shot if she asked me to go to Paris with her!"

"I'll have to talk to my father about this."

But Giorgio had a hard time telling his father about what had happened.

"How was your day?" his father said. "Was it busy?"

Giorgio let out a breath and said, "We met a woman from Paris. Her family's from here, but she lives in Paris. She's a singer, Dad. She asked me to come to Paris with her for a few months because, well, she likes my voice. She wants me to sing in some clubs there and get some experience."

His father leaned forward and said lowly, "I don't think you should go, Giorgio. You should be spending the summer getting ready for school".

"It's a good opportunity for me, Dad. To learn about a new country and maybe learn a little French before I have to settle down."

His father finally agreed, although reluctantly. "I'll trust you to be back before school starts."

"Of course. Before school."

A few days later Giorgio and Enrico met Monique for dinner. She was pleased to see them again. "Please be seated. Dinner is my treat," she said.

Giorgio thanked her and said, "I've decided to go with you for two months. But I have to be back before school starts in September."

"A wise choice, Giorgio. It'll be good for your career." She signaled to the waiter. "A bottle of your finest champagne," she said. "We're going to celebrate."

After their wonderful dinner, they thanked Monique. She told Giorgio to meet her at the ferry dock in two days.

Walking home, Enrico told Giorgio that maybe this was a good idea to take a break before school and get some experience, perhaps of both kinds. They laughed.

Giorgio told his father that he had decided to take Monique up on her offer and that he'd leave in two days. His father was still a little bit worried but he realized that at age nineteen, Giorgio had to start making his own way in the world.

"I want to go with you to the dock and meet this woman," he said.

So several days later, they arrived at the ferry dock where Giorgio introduced Monique to his father. She assured him that she would take good care of him and that this was a good experience. "I wasn't too happy at first, Mr. Fiorino said, "but after thinking about it, I think it'll be good for him. But it's important that he be back in time for school. I also think this is a nice thing you're doing for my son. I trust my son very much and I know he'll be back in time."

Then Giorgio said goodbye to his father and wished him well.

"Don't forget to write to us," his father said, "and let us know how you're doing."

"I promise you, Father, I will. Goodbye."

***

Monique took him to her family's house to stay. The next day she took him on a tour of Paris. Giorgio was impressed and thought he'd made the right decision. He was also impressed by how beautiful the women were.

The next night Monique took him with her to work and introduced him to her boss, the owner of the cabaret. She told him Giorgio was a singer and hoped that he would let Giorgio sing there some night. He said he'd work something out with him.

Giorgio bought a French language book and hoped to be able to practice enough to know what the locals were saying.

He walked around the city with Monique every day, and at night, he went with her to work. One night she had a surprise for him—she'd made arrangements for him to sing.

"Are you sure?" he said. "I don't want to make a fool—"

"Hardly, Giorgio. You've got a wonderful voice. You'll bring the house down."

Giorgio had never felt more alone than he did while he stood stage center, with the spotlight beating down on him. He could smell his own sweat. He wiped it away from his forehead and squinted—maybe there's no one out there, he thought. Then someone coughed and the smoke from a cigarette wafted sinuously through the spotlight. No, he certainly was not alone. He looked to his left, at Monique in the wings. She smiled and prompted him. He took in a breath, let it out and started to sing. The first note went flat—the crowd responded with a gasp. He started over. And this time, as if by magic, he made it not only past the first note, but the whole song, and toward the end, even he had to admit that what came out of his mouth was absolutely beautiful. The crowd loved it. They even called him back for an encore.

Giorgio really enjoyed his time in Paris, but that first night on stage was by far the highlight of his stay. He knew he had made the right decision. He was feeling more comfortable singing in front of crowds and it made him feel more confident.

But like all good things, this too came to an end. It was almost September, time to go home. For his last night, Monique took him out for a special show and dinner. She gave him a gift, a gold bracelet. "Please wear this in memory of our time together in Paris. And when you're a big star, I'll come hear you sing."

"Thank you," Giorgio said. "And thank you for inviting me to Paris for the summer." He took her by the hands. "I've enjoyed this and my time with you very much. It's such a beautiful city. And as for the future, perhaps we'll see each other again sometime."

The next day, a Sunday, he took the ferry back to Venice. Everyone was at Grandmother Lucia's for dinner, there to surprise them. He hadn't told them when he was arriving.

"Let's say a prayer for my grandson, Giorgio, that he'll be back home soon," his grandmother said. And just as she finished, the doorbell rang and there was Giorgio! They all welcomed him back and he told them all about his trip when they sat down for dinner.

The next day Giorgio went to see Enrico. He told him about his trip and Enrico asked him if he'd had an affair with Monique. He smiled and said, "Perhaps, but please don't tell my father!"

When it was time for Giorgio to leave for school, his parents had a goodbye dinner for him and wished him well. Enrico asked him to visit when he had a chance and he promised that he would.

The next day Giorgio packed his bags and left for Florence where he was greeted by the teacher and shown around. His room, although small, was well-appointed and clean.

He didn't have to start for a week so he spent that time learning his way around the conservatory and the city. He loved Florence and had always regretted that he didn't have a lot of time to see more of it. But now that he had a week on his own, he went everywhere.

He especially liked the work of Leonardo da Vinci and visited all the exhibits scattered around the city. He also spent time at the sidewalk cafes drinking cappuccino and talking to people.

His time went by quickly and soon it was time to start classes.

When his teacher heard his voice, he was overcome. "God gave you a gift to sing," he said. "Be patient and listen to my advice and in time you'll be a great singer, known throughout Italy and perhaps the world."

So for the next three years Giorgio worked hard on improving his voice. He even sang in small theaters occasionally, but he knew that someday he'd sing in a grand opera house, before thousands of people. It was a dream, certainly, but one that was well within his reach.

While at the conservatory, Giorgio met an aspiring pianist named Rosa whose compliments were sometimes a source of embarrassment. Occasionally they would get together for a drink or go for a walk and in time they started a relationship.

Eventually, Giorgio was asked to sing at the big theater; his family was thrilled, as was he. But on the way home to celebrate that weekend, he had a car accident. As he lay in the hospital bed, he tried to remember just what had happened, but like most accidents, it was too difficult to bring the incident into focus. He did, however, remember what the doctor had said just minutes earlier. How could he forget?

"The operation was a success, Giorgio, but I'm afraid you may never sing again."

The doctor was gone now, and Giorgio was alone with his thoughts and his blossoming depression. Never sing again—was that possible? What would he do if he couldn't sing? What could he do? Just then, the door opened and in stepped his father, followed by the rest of his family.

While his family surrounded his bed, his father took his hand and said, "Count your blessings, Giorgio. You're alive and you will heal. And as for what that doctor said, well, what do they know? Rest assured, son, that we'll be there to help you every step of the way."

But even a simple spoken response was difficult. Still, he tried. "Thank you, Father. Thank you," he said haltingly.

Over time, and while he underwent the healing process, Giorgio often visited the conservatory. He also took walks on the grounds to relax and gather his thoughts.

One day he saw Rosa at about the same time she saw him. She hurried over and sat down next to him.

"Oh, Giorgio, it's so good to see you," she said. "When are you coming back? I do miss you."

He smiled and said, "I do want to come back, Rosa, more than anything, but I had an accident."

"Giorgio, are you—"

"I'm fine, really. I just, well, I may never sing again. The doctors aren't optimistic."

"Giorgio, I'm so sorry, really I am." She moved a little closer. "But you must believe in the power of God, Giorgio, and that with His help, you'll someday sing again. Tell me you believe that."

Of course, Giorgio wanted to believe that, but he'd made such slow progress, it was difficult to believe anything. Still, he smiled and said, "Of course, Rosa, of course."

She took his hand. "Come back to Venice with me. Keep me company on the train," she said. "Please, Giorgio."

Giorgio didn't hesitate. "I'd like that," he said. "Very much."

She played the piano for his family while she was there and everyone was impressed with her talent. Before she left, she again reminded Giorgio to never give up hope on his desire to sing again.

Giorgio rested and worked on getting his voice back. He went back to school and with his teacher's guidance, made significant progress. The hope he'd been missing had finally revealed itself.

During that period, he also got closer to Rosa and over time, they fell in love. She was, without a doubt, the woman for him, but he had to achieve his dream and even his love for Rosa was secondary to that.

It was around noon on a Thursday when his teacher called him into his office and said, "Giorgio, I think you're ready."

At first, Giorgio had no idea what he was talking about, and then it dawned on him. "To sing again? To sing in public?" he asked.

His teacher smiled. "Not only in public, but at La Scala, Giorgio. What do you think of that?"

Giorgio's only response was a moment of abject fear. LaScala, where only the world's best singers performed. LaScala, the place of legend. How could he possibly perform there? "I'm humbled," he said. "And terribly frightened."

His teacher smiled and patted him on the back. "That's to be expected, but please understand, Giorgio, that you've made incredible progress. I have real faith in you. Everybody does. You'll be wonderful."

Giorgio, however, wasn't so sure. And his fears were, unfortunately, borne out. His first performance went poorly. He understood that as soon as it was over. The audience clapped, but only politely, and as he walked off stage, he vowed that he would never sing in public again.

"Father," he said a few days later, "I'm going to teach. I'd make a good teacher, don't you think?"

His father looked at his mother then back at Giorgio. "You're afraid, aren't you, son? You're afraid that what happened at LaScala will happen again."

Giorgio let out a breath and said, "Wouldn't you be? I was terrible. Father, I have nightmares about that evening."

"Son, when you were younger, you went swimming and almost drowned. Do you remember?"

How could he forget? Water seeping into his lungs. Gasping for breath that wouldn't come. "Of course I remember, Father."

"And for a very long time, you vowed that you would never even take a bath again, let alone go swimming. But eventually, you did, didn't you? You looked that fear straight in the eye and overcame it. You'll do the same this time, son, I know you will."

His father was right, of course, and as time passed, Giorgio looked this fear straight in the eye and confronted it. He practiced, he sang, then he practiced some more, then he sang for his family and eventually he was even invited to sing in a small theater. As fate would have it, an American promoter was in attendance that evening.

His name was John Edwards. "Such a voice," he said. Just marvelous. Do you have an agent yet?"

Giorgio was both stunned and flattered. "No, I, should I?" he stammered.

"An agent can do far more for you than you can do for yourself."

Giorgio appraised this short, squat man with a ruddy complexion and a bulbous nose standing before him—how he could impress anyone was beyond him, but it seemed that this was the break he'd been looking for. He had to trust this man—and he loved his singing. "All right, yes. What now?" he said.

"New York City is where you should be, young man. That's where the people are, that's where the critics are and most importantly, that's where the money is."

"New York City, I don't know, my parents—"

"Let me talk to your parents. I'm sure that once they see the possibilities, it won't be a problem."

His father, however, was thrilled that Giorgio's dream might finally come true. "It's gonna take lots of work, and lots of time, Giorgio, you understand that, don't you?" he said.

"Of course, he does," Mr. Edwards interjected. "But he'll have to be able to go on a moment's notice. He needs to get a passport, too, and most of all; he'll have to be able to speak English."

"I know a teacher," Giorgio's father said. "You'll learn. You're a fast learner." He turned to Mr. Edwards. "He's a very fast learner, you'll see."

"I'm sure he is," Mr. Edwards said with a grin.

It only took Giorgio a few months to learn the language, or at least enough to get by. The night before he was ready to go, his family had a celebration and wished him luck. Unfortunately, he also had to say goodbye to Rosa. He didn't know when he would see her again.

The priest blessed him and wished him good luck. "Someday," he said, "you'll be famous and everyone will know your name."

"Thank you, Father," Giorgio said. "I hope you're right.

Mr. Edwards sent him money for the crossing and when he arrived in New York City, he was there waiting for him. He took him to the apartment he had rented for him and showed him around. Then they went out for a nice Italian meal to celebrate Giorgio's first night in America.

"Giorgio," he said, "I know you're probably thinking about the Met, but it's still a little early. You've got a great voice, though and it will happen, you'll see. In the meantime, I've arranged for you to sing in a nightclub. It'll be good for recognition. You see, Giorgio, first you have to be noticed."

The next day Mr. Edwards took him to meet the owner of the nightclub, a tall waif of a man with a deep baritone speaking voice. His thick, dark hair waved about as he talked. And when he spoke to

Giorgio, he spoke in platitudes. "It'll be great having a true Italian tenor here," he said. "They're gonna love you, kid."

Giorgio took the few days before his debut to acquaint himself with the city. He got a crook in his neck from looking up—and the Statue of Liberty simply took his breath away. But it was the sheer size of this city that overwhelmed him. Certainly, Naples was a good size city, but it was but a hamlet in comparison.

His sightseeing served him well—it kept him from dwelling on opening night too much. Still, the butterflies started hours before his first performance.

Scantily clad showgirls went on before him and he stood in awe, totally amazed by it all.

After they left the stage, Dino fisted the microphone and said, "Ladies and Gentlemen. Tonight we have a special guest, a tenor all the way from Italy. I'm sure you'll love him. Someday I know he'll become a great singer. So give a big round of applause for Giorgio Fiorino!"

Giorgio took the microphone and said, "Grazie, thank you, Dino, for your kind introduction."

Giorgio chose *Oh, Marie*, for his first song and while he sang, he realized that even the waiters had stopped to listen. An hour later, when he finally took a bow, the nightclub erupted in applause. The owner, of course, was very happy and planned a huge promotion.

After the show, he met a showgirl named Marilyn who fell in love with his voice and his presence.

"You have such a beautiful voice. The sky's the limit. You've got quite a future ahead of you, Giorgio. Quite a future, indeed."

"Thanks," Giorgio said, flattered beyond words.

A month went by and during that time, Giorgio sang every night. The owner was very happy—Giorgio was great for business.

Marilyn tried to befriend him; she wanted to have drinks with him, dinner, etc. She even wanted him to come to her apartment for dinner.

Giorgio refused and refused, but one night, when he felt especially lonely, he gave in.

"Marilyn, please understand," he'd said many times, "I'm engaged to a wonderful girl, a truly wonderful girl."

Her response was always the same. "And I wouldn't do anything to jeopardize that, believe me. I'd just like it if we could become friends, that's all."

But human nature being what it is, Marilyn and Giorgio did get together in a way that Rosa would most definitely have not approved of—they had dinner and then, after a few relaxing drinks, made love. And Giorgio, being a red-blooded male, discovered that making love to Marilyn was something he wanted to do; needed to do. He still loved Rosa, but a man had needs.

His career, however, was not moving as quickly as his relationship with Marilyn, and even she noticed his advancing depression.

"Don't be discouraged," she said. "Hang in there. It'll happen."

Giorgio appreciated the display of confidence, but he couldn't shake the thought of returning to Italy. And an incident a few days after their talk, only cemented his decision. While he was minding his own business, just walking down the street, a man just a few yards away got robbed and shot. All Giorgio could do was watch in horror—and before he could yell, "Police," the shooter had hightailed it down the dark, late night street.

The next day he decided to go back to Italy. He certainly didn't want to get killed. This was not the place for him.

He called Mr. Edwards and told him.

"Are you sure?" Mr. Edwards asked. "I mean, it was just an isolated incident. Please don't think that these things happen all the time."

"I'll come back when you get a call from the Metropolitan Opera," Giorgio said. "Thank you for everything, but my mind's made up."

He decided to leave without telling Marilyn. He knew that their affair couldn't continue. He knew it was cowardly to leave without saying goodbye, but he just couldn't confront her. She was in love with him, he knew that. It would be better this way. She'd get over him.

He went back to Italy feeling hugely disappointed and sad. And although he continued to sing in nightclubs and theaters, he still hoped to get that call from Mr. Edwards. He still hoped to hear that the Met wanted him.

***

A few months later, he was invited to sing La Traviata in Milan. He graciously accepted, but things didn't go well. He was too nervous and his performance reflected that.

But the next night, the phone rang. He picked up and for some reason, a thread of nervous energy traveled down his back before he said hello.

"Pack your bags, Giorgio," Mr. Edwards said, "the Met wants you."

Giorgio almost told him about his performance of the previous night, but he didn't. Instead, he said, "Thank you so much, Mr. Edwards. I'll be there as soon as I can."

He called his parents with the wonderful news, but before he hung up, he said, "Before I leave, I want to ask Rosa to marry me, Father. I love her very much and I want her to be with me as soon as possible. I don't want to be alone there. I'll find a place and then come back for her and we'll be married."

"Rosa is the right girl for you," his father said. "She comes from a good family. You're doing the right thing, son."

Giorgio decided to arrange a party before he left. He'd go see Rosa and be with her until then. Besides, someone might snatch her up if he waited too long.

Giorgio drove to Rosa's house in Florence and rang the bell. Her mother opened the door. "Giorgio, what a nice surprise. I'm glad to see you. Come in, come in!"

"Signora, I have good news," he said as he stepped into the living room. "I just got a call from Mr. Edwards. He's got a job for me at the Metropolitan Opera."

"Giorgio," she said as she hugged him, "I'm so happy for you."

"Where's Rosa, I have to share this news with her."

"She's in the backyard playing tennis with one of her friends."

Giorgio looked at Rosa's mother a moment and said, "Please don't say anything to her but before I leave I want to ask her to marry me."

"Oh, that's wonderful, Giorgio, just wonderful."

"I want to have a big party on Saturday at my friend Pino's restaurant. Will you and Mr. Rossi and Rosa come?"

"Of course, Giorgio. I'm so happy for both of you. You make a wonderful couple. Now go out back and surprise her."

Giorgio made his way out back and watched Rosa and her friend playing. She played well—he had even taken up the sport so they could spend time together.

Rosa ran over and gave him a hug and a kiss. "Giorgio, I didn't know you were here. I'm so glad to see you."

Rosa and Giorgio sat down after her friend said goodbye. He told her his news and asked if she'd come to the party, to which she readily agreed.

For the next couple of days Giorgio and Rosa spent all their time together. They didn't know when they would see each other again and they wanted to make the most of their time.

One afternoon, while they were walking in one of the beautiful Florence gardens, Giorgio said, "Rosa, I'm going to miss you very much. I feel so good when we're together, but I have to go to America for my career. You have been so good to me. You were close to me when I was sick and didn't think I could sing again. You give me so much encouragement and because of that, I owe my life to you. After I've settled down, I promise I'll return and marry you."

"I have never loved anyone else but you since the day I met you at the conservatory," Rosa responded. "The jewelry store owner's son, Gino, is crazy about me but I don't love him. He told me once you left you would never think about me again, but I didn't believe that. I knew you loved me and so I waited for you to come back."

"You were right not to listen to what anyone said. There has never been anyone else but you. Trust me and my love for you. I will love you forever. This is the promise that I make to you." And then they kissed, passionately and tenderly, that kiss a manifestation of their shared love.

Saturday night arrived, but in the mean time, Giorgio had gone to the jewelry store. The ring was far more than he could afford—but she was worth it.

Rosa was upstairs waiting for Giorgio to arrive with his parents. The doorbell rang—she thought it was Giorgio. It wasn't—it was a delivery boy with a beautiful display of roses for her.

"Rosa, I will love you forever. Love, Giorgio," the card said.

Not long after Giorgio arrived with his parents, and she thanked him for the flowers. He gave her a kiss and said, "You're as beautiful as they are." Then they got into the car with her parents and went to the restaurant.

"Welcome, welcome" Pino said. "I've got a special table just for you in the back room."

There was a surprise waiting there for them--Rosa's brother and wife and friends from the conservatory. She was very touched by what Giorgio had done and loved him even more.

"Champagne for everyone," Giorgio said after they saw down.

After the champagne was poured, Giorgio stood and said, "Salute. I will miss you all and I want to thank you for everything you have done for me. I hope someday when I'm famous that you'll come to New York City and visit me."

After the applause, Giorgio sat down and said to Rosa, "Stand up, turn around and close your eyes. I have a surprise for you."

Rosa did as asked and said, "Giorgio, what surprise do you have for me?"

He latched a gold necklace around her neck and then placed the diamond ring on her finger. The inscription said, 'I will love you forever.' "Open your eyes, Rosa," he said.

She was overwhelmed. "Giorgio, this is the most beautiful surprise I have ever had in my life. Yes, I will marry you," she said as she hugged him.

She turned to her family. "Bello, bello, what a beautiful ring. You're so blessed," they said almost in unison.

Mr. Rossi stood up and made a little speech. "Giorgio, I've known you ever since you came to the conservatory. I know you're not just a good singer but also a good man. I also know that one day I'll lose my beautiful Rosa to you and New York City. But I want you to know I'd be happy to have you for a son-in-law. I wish you good luck and success and don't forget to call us." Everyone applauded.

After everyone sat down again, Giorgio said, "This diamond ring is the symbol of my love. Before I left I wanted to show Rosa my love and devotion and for everyone to know what a beautiful woman she is."

He sat down and took Rosa's hand.

A man with a guitar walked over and asked if they had something special they wanted him to play.

"I want to sing a beautiful love song for my fiancée, Rosa," Giorgio said. "The song says that when I'm away from you I'd die for your love, but in my heart I'll love you forever."

It was a beautiful song and everyone sighed with envy at the happy couple.

Before dinner, the priest from the church where Giorgio was baptized blessed the food. Afterwards everyone congratulated Giorgio and Rosa again and then left, although reluctantly.

It was time for Giorgio and Rosa to part. They kissed, hugged, and promised to write and call. Rosa could only watch as Giorgio and his family walked out the door; she caught Giorgio's thrown kiss and held it close to her heart.

***

Mr. Edwards met him after he got off the flight from Venice. "It's time you met the conductor, my friend," he said.

Rehearsal times were arranged at the Met. The show was slated to start the next weekend, very little time for Giorgio to get his bearings. But the stress of a short week before the show served him well. He had little time to think about walking onto the stage and about the crowd of very learned people waiting to listen to him sing. It was only when he walked onto the stage that the butterflies began in earnest. He cleared his throat, smiled, and thought of something his teacher said. "Imagine they're all naked, Giorgio. How much of a threat can they be then?"

So that's what he did, and it worked. Even he was impressed by his performance and the audience echoed that sentiment. He received a standing ovation.

Afterwards, he thanked Mr. Edwards for his trust and faith in him.

"I always knew you were destined for great things," Mr. Edwards said." Hearing that, Giorgio began to feel that his dream might come true after all.

He called his family and Rosa and talked way too fast about what had happened. Even Rosa had to ask him to speak more slowly. "I understand, though, Giorgio, I really do. I'm so proud of you."

He called Rosa about every week. He told her all about what was happening with him and how much he missed her. Sometimes he'd surprise her by singing the song he had sung the day of their engagement.

***

The next six months raced by and during that short period of time, Giorgio became a star at the Metropolitan Opera. And just as importantly, New York City had become his second home.

Six months later, he went back home to see his family and Rosa. The first thing he did was to tell her how much he has missed her and she, of course, returned the sentiment.

One night his father took him for an espresso at the local café. "Giorgio, you've become a big success and you'll be spending a lot of time in America. I think it's time you and Rosa got married. It's not good for you to be alone. She'd be a great wife and it'd be good for your career."

"You're right, Father. I love her and I want to marry her. I have a month left before I go back to America. I think we should get married before then. It'll be a little rushed but you're right—she's the woman for me."

"First, there's something I want to discuss with you, Giorgio. Someone has made an offer to buy the barbershop. Business is great since you became a success. I don't do as much work now because I've got a barber working for me. Actually, Giorgio, I'm thinking of retiring."

"Retiring? Please, Papa, don't sell the barber shop. You don't know what it means to me. There are so many memories there. That's where I started singing. If you want to retire, that's fine. I make plenty of money now and I can help you out if you need it."

"No, Giorgio, I don't need your money, I'm doing okay. I didn't realize how much the barbershop meant to you." He looked at his son a moment, a tiny smile on his face, then, "So, it's settled. I won't sell it. Remember when we first named it The Barber of Seville? Now it's become famous."

"Papa, I've been thinking. I make a lot of money now and I'd like to send some of it to the orphanage in Rome. You know, where you adopted me from. I'm sure they could use the money. And I want to thank you, Papa, for adopting me. You've treated me like your own son. But I'd like to find out who I am and where I'm from. It's important to me to know my own identity. Like I told you before, sometimes I feel there's someone else in my life looking for me, like a brother or sister. I know you told me that as far as you know there's no one else, but I've always had this feeling that there's something more. Someday I hope to find out why."

"I understand, son. I do."

"Thanks, Papa. I was hoping you'd understand."

"Okay, Giorgio, don't forget about the banquet tomorrow night in your honor. The Mayor and ex-Mayor are giving it. They want to honor you for your accomplishments."

"I'll be there. I want to thank them for all they did for me."

They talked for a few minutes more and then Giorgio said, "Papa, let's take a walk. I'd like to stop in and see my old music teacher from grammar school. She still lives in the same place?"

"Yes, she does."

"But I have to wear a disguise. Too many people recognize me and I have such limited time here."

Giorgio put on a big hat but a few people still recognized him and said hello. He graciously accepted their compliments and even signed a few autographs.

When they reached Maestra Gina's house, Giorgio said, "Papa, don't knock, I want to surprise her."

He started to sing the first song she'd taught him long ago.

Her husband was sitting inside at the kitchen table having a glass of wine when he heard the singing.

"Some drunk is singing at our door," he said. "Go tell him to go away!"

"You are umbrioca (drunk) yourself," she said. "That's a very famous singer at our door," she said as she ran to answer the knock.

"O mio dio. (Oh my God)," she said to Giorgio, "I remember you like it was yesterday." And she hugged and kissed him. "Giorgio," she continued, "I'm surprised to see you and it's a great honor to have you here."

"Maestra, it's my pleasure. I never forgot the first song you taught me, about Venice, remember? And I remember when you said I'd be a famous singer some day. I told that to a lot of people in the conservatory. I never forgot what you told me. That's why I came to see you tonight. And I want to invite you to my wedding. You're one of the first people I respected in my life."

"Of course, Giorgio, I'd be honored to come to your wedding."

He gave her an autographed picture. On the bottom he had written, 'Signora Maestra, I'll always remember you in my heart for the beautiful song you taught me.'

Then he had a cup of coffee with her and her husband and he told them about life in New York City and how beautiful the city was.

"It's like a second home to me now, but Venice will always remain first in my heart because this is where my family is. And I have the best parents in the world."

***

Giorgio and his father were greeted by applause at the banquet the next night. Giorgio heard someone say, "Here's the Barber of Seville and his son!" and they all laughed.

Giorgio had never shaken so many hands–he wondered if he'd ever be able to sit down and have dinner. But eventually they did eat, and afterwards the new mayor gave a speech.

"Gentlemen, Signori, we have two special guests here tonight. The famous tenor, Giorgio Junior, and The Barber of Seville himself, Giorgio Senior.

"It's a great pleasure to have Giorgio and his famous son with us tonight and I know Giorgio will become even more famous. As you may or may not know, he's getting married before he returns to America and I want to thank him for inviting me to the wedding."

Then the ex-Mayor stood up and gave his speech. "Giorgio, welcome to Venice. Your voice is superb. I'll always remember when you came to the barbershop to sing. That was very special to me and I'll never forget it. I've always enjoyed your singing and I always gave you a tip, but never your father because he always took too long to shave me and sometimes he forgot all together because he liked to hear you sing too. That was okay because I too, liked to hear you sing. And it ensures that your father's barbershop will always be remembered. I want to give you a big tip now. The biggest ever. Giorgio, because you're very special to the people of Venice, I'd like to give you the key to the city. I hope someday that you'll come back to Venice and sing *La Traviata* for us. And I'd also like to thank you for inviting me to the wedding."

Giorgio was overwhelmed, he had never expected this. He went to the microphone and accepted the key from the ex-Mayor.

"I want to thank the people of Venice for being so kind to me. I'll always remember this in my heart. Even though I wasn't born in Venice, at least that I know of, I've always considered myself a Venetian. I grew up here, lived here, and consider it my home. I tell everyone that I'm a Venetian because I'm proud of that. But now I have a big tip for you both." He brought out two autographed pictures of himself to give to both Mayors. On one he had written, 'Always remember when I used to sing in the barbershop and you gave me a big tip. This is the biggest tip I can give you today.' He read it aloud and everyone laughed.

"At some other point in time I'll come back and give a concert here, but right now I want to sing the first song that I ever learned, which is so close to my heart. It's called *'Venezia La Gondola.'*"

The applause he received afterwards was as wonderful as any he'd ever received at the Met. And when he left, he silently vowed that he'd come back and do as the mayor asked.

***

That Sunday Giorgio and his family drove from Venice to Florence for dinner. Mr. Rossi and his wife welcomed them warmly.

"You're very welcome in our home," Mr. Rossi said. "We're very proud of your success and wish you even more to follow."

"Thank you for your kind wishes, Mr. Rossi," Giorgio said. "I hope they come true."

The comfort Giorgio felt here made dinner taste even better and when they were done, he stood up and said, "Mr. Rossi, Rosa and I have talked. I have a month before I have to be back and we'd like to get married before I go. I know it's sudden and really short notice to plan a wedding, but I want to take her with me when I get back. I hope I have your blessing."

Mr. Rossi jumped up and shook his hand, obviously overjoyed with the good news. "Giorgio, it's an honor to give my daughter's hand-in-marriage to you. I admit that I'm a little disappointed in one thing, though. I've always dreamed that when Rosa graduated from school that she'd accompany me on the piano while I played the violin in the symphony orchestra. She's my only daughter and it won't be very easy for my wife and I to let her go so far away. But because we know you and because Rosa loves you, your union has our blessing."

"Mr. Rossi, thank you again for your kindness and please don't worry about Rosa. I'll take good care of her. Besides, we'll be coming back to Italy on occasion so you'll see her often."

About then, Rosa's brother, Angelo, walked in and they told him the news. "I'd be honored if you'd be my best man," Giorgio said.

"I'm flattered, Giorgio. Of course I'll be your best man."

Almost a month passed—way too quickly as far as Giorgio was concerned—and the wedding was very close. Giorgio had asked the orchestra leader and the piano player to come to Italy for his wedding. They had agreed.

The wedding was a thing of beauty; flowers of all varieties graced the church and Rosa was the most exquisite bride Giorgio had ever seen. As he watched her walk down the aisle, he felt his legs begin to weaken. I can't believe this woman is about to be my wife, he thought. She's so radiant, so refined.

The reception was a whirlwind of activity; lots of kissing and toasting and smiling. Before Giorgio knew it, the time had come for them to leave.

They only had a little time in Florence before it was time to board the airplane for America and their honeymoon.

When they reached New York City, Giorgio showed Rosa around and she loved it. They decided to live in Giorgio's apartment for a while until they could find a house. They lived near the theatre, an area that offered lots of interesting things to see and do. Rosa missed Florence and all her friends and family, but she was married to Giorgio now and she loved him very much. Wherever he wanted to live would be fine with her.

Their house search started in the suburbs. After an exhaustive search, they finally found a house they liked. It had lots of space and lots of land so it would probably be quiet.

After all the moving and rearranging, Rosa found herself with a lot of time on her hands. She decided to go back to teaching the piano to children. She had always loved music and it would be perfect.

Life seemed ideal. Giorgio occasionally came home with flowers, which made Rosa happy, and they often went out with their friends, but the fact that Rosa was not getting pregnant tempered their happiness. A family would help make their lives complete.

Giorgio had been at the Met for about three years and his fame had grown. Eventually, he was offered *Othello*, a very difficult opera. But the maestro chose him because he felt Giorgio was up to the challenge. They had several months to prepare, but even with that amount of time, each practice lasted until the wee hours.

One day Giorgio was on stage when he suddenly had a terrible pain in his leg. He stopped singing and went back stage. He had to sit down it hurt so much. People asked him what was wrong, but he couldn't say why he had so much pain.

"All at once I just had this shooting pain down my leg," he said. He decided to quit for the day and go home.

By the next day, his leg still hurt, and it continued to hurt for two days after that.

He called the maestro and told him what had happened. "I'm sorry but I don't feel well. I've tried to practice at home but I can't."

"Take some time," the maestro said. "You'll feel better in a few days and then you can come back to work."

Rosa, of course, was worried. This was not like him. This was the biggest opera of his career and it would make him an even bigger success. A lot was riding on this. She begged him to go to a doctor.

A few days later, he finally decided to see someone. The night before he had a dream and in it, he heard a pain-filled voice, calling out. He had never had this experience before and he didn't know what it meant. Is it a premonition, he wondered.

He went to the doctor who examined him. The doctor shrugged and said, "Sorry, Giorgio, I can't find a thing wrong. Maybe this new show is causing stress. It could be what's causing the pain."

"I don't think that's it. I'm used to singing. I just feel sometimes in my mind that someone's calling out to me, as if they're trying to tell me something. It makes me feel a little depressed, actually."

"Forget about that. It's in your mind. Go back to the theater and I think you'll be okay."

Giorgio went home and told Rosa what the doctor had said. At the same time, his father called to see how everything was going with the new show. He told his father about his ailment and that he couldn't work.

"I know this is a big show for you," his father said. "Maybe you should see a psychiatrist."

But the maestro was concerned about Giorgio as well. If he couldn't do the show, he had to find a replacement for him. He didn't want to tell Giorgio yet because he didn't want to add to his depression. He decided to give him another week to see what might happen.

Giorgio decided to take his father's advice and called his doctor for a referral to a psychiatrist.

When Giorgio went to the office, he was pleasantly surprised. The psychiatrist had recognized his name. "It's a pleasure to meet you Mr. Fiorino. I'm a big fan."

They talked and Giorgio told him his problem. "Sometimes I feel as though someone is calling my name in my head with such emotion--like they're looking for me and can't find me."

"Do you have a twin?" the doctor asked.

Giorgio shook his head and said, "As far as I know, no. I was adopted. I don't know my family."

"That's the reason you feel like this. This person is calling you. They're having a problem in their life. I'll tell you a little story. I have a twin brother. Five years ago, he was in a car accident and I felt the whole thing. I stayed home for several days until he was feeling better because I could feel his pain. Giorgio, you must have a twin somewhere. You were in the womb together and bonded. Then you were born and separated. You've always felt this separation and always will until you're together again. Right now, something is going on in the person's life that's affecting you. Go on with your life, it'll pass. I know how you feel."

"That's the way I feel, like something is missing. I'm not sure if my wife or father understands. We don't know about this missing twin. I hope when I have the time that I'll be able to go to Italy to the orphanage and find out more about myself and this twin."

"Good luck. I'll look forward to your new show when it opens."

Giorgio thanked him and they shook hands. Finally, he felt better because someone believed what he was telling them about how he felt inside.

Giorgio told Rosa what had happened. She wasn't too sure if she believed him, but she decided to go along with it because she didn't want to add to his depression.

Later that day Giorgio's father called, he had been worried. He asked him how things were going.

"Papa," Giorgio said, "I saw a psychiatrist and you know what he said? He said he thinks I have a twin somewhere that I was separated from who's having a problem in their life, and that's what's affecting me."

"My son, according to what we knew when you were adopted, you had no family. This doctor must be pazzo (crazy) to tell you these things."

"Papa, you're the one who told me to see a psychiatrist! Who am I going to believe?"

"Son, you know how much I love you. I talked to Padre Mike and we're going to pray for you. You do the same thing with Rosa. Pray together. We did this when you had your accident and everything turned out okay."

For the next several days, they went to church and prayed and Giorgio took it easy. The maestro was more concerned now. He had one more day before he had to call Giorgio and tell him he was being replaced.

The next day Giorgio woke up feeling good, like he was back to his old self. Maybe the other person was getting well, he thought.

He called Rosa upstairs and kissed her. "Thank you for supporting me through this bad time," he said. "I love you so much." Then he got in the shower and started to sing. He felt just like he had before.

Rosa was glad he was back to his old self. He called the maestro and told him how good he felt and that he would be back to work that day. Then he called his father and told him he was back to normal. He was happy to hear that. He and the priest had been praying for him to get well. "God can work miracles when you pray with all your heart."

So the show got back on track and a month later, it was ready to open. Giorgio was worried about how good he would be, but once he started singing, he got back his confidence and started singing better than he ever had before.

The maestro was thrilled. He was confident that the show would be a big success. And if the standing ovation Giorgio received was any barometer, then it would be. Othello was technically difficult to sing and he'd done a great job. The Maestro, the musicians and anyone who could get close enough, congratulated him.

Mr. Edwards hugged him and said, "Giorgio, you were super. I knew the first time I heard you that you'd be great."

At that moment Giorgio felt a sense of accomplishment unlike any he'd ever felt.

Then Rosa came over, hugged, and kissed him. "Congratulations, Giorgio, you were brilliant. I love you so much. It's the best I've ever heard you sing. I knew since I first met you that this day would come and you'd be a famous singer."

The psychiatrist came back after the show and congratulated Giorgio. "Giorgio, this person, your twin, is well now and I hope someday you'll find him. That will be a very happy day for you and for him."

When Giorgio's father heard of his success, he called Padre Michael and asked him to join in the celebration.

In fact, Giorgio was now one of the best tenors in the world, a huge accomplishment for someone so young. And sure, the money was great, but the personal rewards were far greater. He has succeeded at something he wanted so much in his life. Now all he wanted was to be blessed with children. That would be the ultimate happiness.

But after a year of failure, Rosa decided to see a doctor about the problem. After a myriad of questions and tests, it was eventually concluded that a disease Rosa had contracted while in the conservatory had rendered her unable to conceive. It was the cruelest of times for her and for Giorgio. And every doctor offered the same opinion. She would never have a child.

But of course, human nature being what it is, Rosa and Giorgio still tried—a child of their own was not a dream they would dispose of as simply as one disposes of the morning trash. But seven years later, they realized that their dream would have to be altered, that although she could not conceive, they could adopt.

Giorgio knew a priest; Father Pedro in Peru. He wrote to him. Father Pedro replied quickly—yes, they had many children more than ready to be adopted.

Rosa and Giorgio met Father Pedro and he showed them around his orphanage. They found a little girl that Rosa liked, but they had to wait for the papers to finalize the adoption. For Giorgio and Rosa adopting a child was a new experience, but they also felt they'd love her just like they'd love their biological child.

They both realized there was a lot of paperwork, so they asked Father Pedro how quickly they could get the adoption processed.

"Two months, maybe sooner," he said.

No matter what, Giorgio and Rosa were determined to have little baby Lucia.

While waiting, they took a tour of Peru. They enjoyed its diverse landscape, its beautiful beaches and its towering, white-capped peaks. But even after they'd seen almost everything Peru had to offer, Father Pedro told them it would still be a few weeks before the adoption could be finalized.

So given the added fourteen days or so, Giorgio had a thought—he'd do something special for the children; a concert at the convent. The children and Father Pedro and his staff were immensely grateful—especially given the amount of money raised for the orphanage.

Not long afterwards, the paperwork was completed and they were ready to leave.

Father Pedro thanked Giorgio for the money he had raised for the children. "We'll say a special prayer for you and your family and we'll remember you in our prayers."

Giorgio hugged him and said, "What you do for the children will remain in my heart forever. Goodbye, Father. I hope I can return someday."

***

At the Metropolitan the next day, as Giorgio's friends offered congratulations on the new baby, he thought it would be a good idea to have a party, so he invited them all to see their new daughter.

The following Sunday all his friends gathered at his home. Rosa and Giorgio appreciated their generosity. They were so enthralled by the baby that they talked about adopting a baby boy who Rosa thought should be named Giorgio in his honor.

Lucia filled their lives with joy and happiness for the next few years. But they wanted to share this joy and happiness with their grandparents in Italy. So arrangements were made to fly to Venice.

The night before they left, Giorgio had a sore throat, but he didn't think much of it. If he really got sick, he'd see his family doctor in Italy.

They met his parents and grandparents in Rome the next day. From there, they drove to Venice. The parents were overjoyed to see them and the new baby. Great-grandmother's name was Lucia and she was happy they'd named the baby after her. She kissed her and said she already looked like she was part of the family. They got in the car and she held her in her arms. "Giorgio, mio bello," she said, "tomorrow night I want you to come to our house for dinner. We'll have chicken parmagian."

He laughed. "Yes, Mama Lucia! I've missed your chicken. No one can make it like you do."

The next day they went to Mama Lucia's for dinner. She had invited some other guests too, along with the mayor. They had a wonderful dinner and afterwards Giorgio told his father about how well things were going for him in his career. In fact, he had a concert in Miami the following week. "I'm happy for you," his father said. "Everyone is always commenting about how well you're doing."

Giorgio told his father about his throat, and that it was getting worse.

"Don't worry about it," his father said. "Tonight the priest and the doctor are coming over for a drink. Perhaps he can check it out for you or you can go to his office tomorrow."

Giorgio felt reassured, but still anxious. His throat was his career. If he was ill, his career could be over.

"I'm having a little sore throat that I think is getting worse," Giorgio told the doctor. "I can't let this get too bad and I was wondering if you would check it out for me. Can I come to your office tomorrow?"

"Come whenever you want," the doctor said.

Later, as they were having some wine and talking over old times, Giorgio started feeling even worse.

He was there bright and early the next morning. The doctor checked his throat and said, "This is more than a sore throat. There are some small growths there. I don't have to do this now, but when you get home, you should have your doctor check them out. I'm sure they're nothing but they should still be removed."

But the doctor's attempt at reassurance missed its mark. Giorgio had only heard, "Small nodules that have to come out."

"I'll give you something for the soreness," the doctor said. "Then go see a specialist."

When he got home, Giorgio told his father the news. His father hugged him and said, "Don't worry about it. Just do what the doctor said." He told the rest of the family and they all gave him encouragement.

"I have a concert to give in a few weeks," Giorgio said. "I'm concerned about my voice. Will I be able to sing?"

"Worry about your health now," his father said, "forget about the concert."

"I think I'll fly home next week," Giorgio said. "I know we were going to stay longer, but I'm very concerned about what this might mean for me. I've never felt this way before and I'm worried about having an operation and maybe never singing again."

"Don't worry about it," his grandmother said. "For now we're going to pray to Father Pio. We'll have faith in him that you'll be healed. No operation."

"I've heard the name, but I don't know much about him."

"I'll tell you a story about him. A few years ago before he died, your mother Christina and I went to see him. When we arrived, there were people from all over the world waiting to see him. When he came out for the mass, he made a speech. He said, 'My children, welcome. No matter your religion, we are all children of God. I'm not God. I believe I was sent here for a reason. I've done my best for Him and I've suffered with stigmata for Him. I am just a man. I don't make miracles. You have to believe with your heart, soul and mind that the power of God will heal you. I was chosen to bring the message and to read the Gospel of God to you and I believe God will heal you if you will believe in Him, whether you're well or not. Pray, hope and don't worry. Worry is useless. God is merciful and He will hear your prayer. You must speak to Jesus not only with your lips but with your heart.'

"The people were filled with joy when the mass was over. I was talking to a lady from New York there with her son. Her son had a tumor in his head and they had come there to pray that Father Pio would cure him and he was. So they had come back to thank him. I heard other stories like that from other people. So Giorgio, have faith in him and God and I have faith that you'll be well."

The next week Giorgio made plans to fly home. He was still worried, but he had prayed and felt a little bit better. He remembered what his grandmother said. "Just believe in yourself and Father Pio and all will be well. We'll pray for you too. Remember before when you were ill? We prayed then and you were healed."

But Giorgio felt there was more to it and that perhaps he did need an operation.

He went to see a throat specialist. He had some tests done and a biopsy sent out. "The growth seems to be getting bigger," the doctor said. "We're going to run some more tests over the next couple of weeks, but I think we'll have to operate, Giorgio. I'm sorry."

So for the next week or so Giorgio and his family prayed to Father Pio and to God. Every week his grandmother called him. "We're praying for you, Giorgio. Keep the faith."

Giorgio was very worried about not being able to sing again. He had told the conductor about his condition and everyone was worried about him and tried to be encouraging.

As time passed, however, Giorgio had begun to believe in God, and with that belief came the idea that he would be healed. He was trying to think positively. That night he had a dream that an old man with a beard appeared to him and said, "Son, you have nothing to worry about. God gave you a special gift to sing and you'll be singing for a long time to come. Sing, my son, sing *Ava Maria*. I always love to hear that song in church."

When Giorgio woke up, he felt like a new person. All his fear had disappeared. He woke Rosa and told her about his dream. "That must have been Father Pio," she said.

Giorgio had an appointment with the specialist the next day. He was told that he needed surgery before his condition worsened. But the doctor wanted to examine him again. What he discovered amazed him--everything was shrinking. He had never seen this happen before. He ran some more tests and told Giorgio to come back in a week. Giorgio told him about his dream and that he had prayed to Father Pio and to God.

"Keep on doing what you're doing," the doctor said. "It seems to be working. Sometimes God works in mysterious ways. Medically, we don't see this too often but spiritually you're doing the right thing. God is healing you. I'm glad for you because I want to see you up on that stage."

Giorgio went home with happiness in his heart. Rosa saw him looking so well and gave him a hug and kiss. He told her what had happened and she was ecstatic. With the will of God and his belief in himself, he was healing himself.

The next week he went back to the doctor, but he knew that he'd been cured. Again, the doctor was astounded--the tumor was almost gone. The doctor told him to come back one last time just to make sure. "I'm happy for you, Giorgio. It seems everything is going well."

Giorgio went home and told Rosa and then they called the family in Venice.

With tears in her voice, Mama Lucia said, "I told you that faith and belief in God and Father Pio would heal you."

"You were right, Mama Lucia. Thank you for telling me about Father Pio. I'll always thank you. I promise that next year we'll be back for a visit."

"God bless you, my son."

"Giorgio, keep on with your faith," his father said. "I'll tell all your friends that you're well. They'll be happy to hear the good news."

Giorgio called the conductor. "Tonight I'm taking the orchestra out for a special dinner to celebrate. Singing is my life and I'm very happy that I've been given the gift to go on singing."

So they went out to celebrate and everyone was glad that things were going to go back to normal. Giorgio was sorry that he had missed his concert in Miami, but he planned to make that up. He pledged to send a donation to Father Pio's friary in Pietrelcina and to different orphanages to help them care for the children in his name for as long as he lived in memory of Father Pio and God.

Giorgio went on with his career. The doctor came to see the next concert in New York. It was a mystery to him what had happened, but he knew that miracles did sometimes happen.

***

One night while they were eating dinner, they decided that now would be a good time to adopt a baby boy. Their daughter was two years old now and a two year age difference seemed appropriate. So they wrote to Father Pedro in Peru and made arrangements.

The night before they left, while Rosa was packing their suitcases, the phone rang. Rosa answered and heard a woman ask for Giorgio. Rosa asked who was calling and she replied, Marilyn.

Rosa called Giorgio into the room and handed him the phone.

"Hello," he said.

"Giorgio, this is Marilyn."

"Marilyn? I don't know anyone by that name."

"Please, Giorgio, hear me out."

Giorgio glanced at Rosa, still standing in the doorway, and then turned his back to her.

"I'm listening," he said.

"We met in New York, when you sang in a nightclub. Remember? I was a dancer."

Giorgio wondered if this was the same woman he had met years ago. He remembered that he had never said goodbye to her before he left for Italy. He had always felt bad about that because she had always encouraged him to become a great singer.

"Yes, I remember," he said. "And I remember that we were good friends."

She started to cry.

"Why are you crying?" he asked.

"Because I'm happy, that's why. It makes me happy that you remembered. But that's… Giorgio, I'm sick. I don't have long to live. I'm actually calling from the hospital. Please, listen closely. I want to die in peace so you have to know. Giorgio, I have an eleven-year old son. Your son. He has your name; Giorgio. Remember when we made love?"

Giorgio glanced again at Rosa then turned back and said, "Yes, yes I remember."

"He could find a home here, a lot of people want him, but he should be with his real father. You, Giorgio."

Giorgio was surprised and stunned but at the same time, he was glad to hear that he was the father of an eleven-year-old boy.

"I'm very sorry to hear about your illness, Marilyn. Very sorry. What hospital are you at?"

"Las Vegas General."

"I'll be in touch."

After he hung up, he turned to Rosa and said, "I met her a long time ago. A very long time ago."

Rosa crossed her arms on her chest. "What did she want?" she said icily.

Giorgio made a snap decision. "We were lovers, Rosa. Not for very long, just long enough to create a child. I don't know; it's a funny world. Maybe she's trying to blackmail me. She's dying. So she says."

"A child?"

"A boy. He's eleven now. She named him Giorgio."

"I see. Well then, why don't you go see this Marilyn and see if she's telling the truth? If she had called another day, we would have been on our way to Peru. Perhaps this is faith trying to help us make the right decision."

"Maybe you're right."

The next day Giorgio took a plane to Las Vegas and went directly to the hospital to see Marilyn.

"Thank you for coming, Giorgio, I didn't know if you would," Marilyn said when he walked into the room.

"Thank you for calling me. And I want to thank you for all the encouragement you gave me so many years ago."

"I knew one day you'd be a star. You have such a wonderful voice. And I want to thank you for being honest about not being in love with me, that you were in love with someone else. You know I was in love with you. I wanted a baby with you and I was very happy when I became pregnant. When he got older, he always asked me questions about when his daddy was coming home. I told him you were a good man and someday you'd come back to see him. And now you're here."

Just then, a young boy who looked like him walked into the room. Giorgio knew deep in his heart that this was his son.

The little boy walked over to Marilyn, kissed her, and said, "Mommy, I love you. I don't want you to die."

Marilyn caressed the side of his face and smiled, then turned to Giorgio. "See this man here?" she said. "He's your father."

The boy just looked at Giorgio for a moment as if studying a road sign. Giorgio smiled at him, not knowing what else to do. The boy walked over to him and said, "You're my father?"

Giorgio could only nod.

"We've been waiting for you for a long time. Why did it take so long? The kids in school ask me about when you're coming home. I never know what to tell them."

Giorgio could do nothing except hold out his arms. But again, the boy just looked at him, at least until Giorgio smiled and nodded, then it was like a dam burst. He rushed into Giorgio's arms and the two hugged. Giorgio, of course, was overcome.

"I promise you I will never leave you again," he said. "I'll take care of you when your mother is gone."

Giorgio looked at Marilyn and saw the tears. He hoped they were tears of joy, at least as much joy as she could muster, given the circumstances.

"Giorgio," she said, I appreciate your taking the time to see us. And to find out the truth."

Giorgio took his son's hand and together, they walked to the bed. Giorgio took Marilyn's hand.

"Giorgio, can you do me a favor," she said as she wiped away the tears.

"Anything," Giorgio said.

"I'd like to be buried next to my parents in New York City. Can you arrange that?"

Giorgio Junior turned away and started crying. Marilyn stroked the back of his head.

"Yes, of course," Giorgio said.

"Giorgio, I fell in love with you the first time I heard you sing. When you told me you had a fiancée back in Italy, I appreciated what you said, but it didn't matter. I wanted to be with you and have a baby with you, if God was willing, and that's what happened. That was eleven years ago. I never told anyone who his father was, not even my closest friends. I wanted to tell him who you were when he was older and better able to handle the news. He always asked about you but then I got sick. Remember our dinners where we talked about everything? You told me that you had started singing at age eleven in church and at the barbershop. Your son is doing that now. He sings in the church choir. The teacher tells me he's a good singer. When I heard that, I knew that he was following in his father's footsteps. I followed your career; you've done well for yourself. I know why you left for Italy without telling me. I know you didn't love me, but I had hoped that someday you would if I tried hard enough. I guess it was for the best. And we have a wonderful son. Did you ever marry that fiancée of yours back in Italy?"

"Yes, I did. Her name is Rosa and we've been married for ten years now. We tried for years but she couldn't have children. So a few years ago, we went to Peru and adopted a little girl from an orphanage. We were just about to leave for Peru again and adopt a little boy when I got your call. I flew here as fast as I could. I'm sorry that you're sick. I've thought of you often over the years. I was ashamed of myself for leaving so abruptly. But you were right. I knew you were in love with me and I wasn't with you. I didn't know how to say the words so I ran away. I've always wanted to say I was sorry. Will you accept my apology now?"

He picked up her hand and kissed it.

"Of course, it is forgiven."

"Knowing I have a son, flesh of my flesh, is the most amazing thing that has ever happened to me. To have a child, my own child. I promise I'll do my best to take care of him and to love him. I have a lot of years to make up for."

"Giorgio, I'm going to hold you to that promise. You've always been a kind and honest man. I know you'll take care of him and I know I'm leaving him in good hands."

Josie, Marilyn's friend, came into the room. Marilyn introduced them.

"Josie, this is Giorgio's father, Giorgio Fiorino."

Josie, a tall, attractive woman with red hair and small features, had obviously heard of him, who in New York hadn't, but the fact that he was Giorgio's father seemed hard for her to digest.

"Come to think of it, you do look like Giorgio. I think you should know that I was going to adopt Giorgio but now that you're here… I'm sure he'll be in good hands. Promise me you'll let me keep in contact with Giorgio. I've always loved him and I'd really like to see him from time to time."

"You may see him whenever you like. If you'll excuse me for a few minutes, I have to call my wife and tell her the news."

Rosa asked him if he was one hundred percent sure the boy was his.

"Honey, when you see the boy you'll know that he's my son. There's no denying it."

She laughed and said, "My God, this is a miracle. We wanted a son and now we have one. I'll love him with all my heart just the way I love you because he's a part of you."

After Giorgio hung up, he talked to Marilyn's doctor and asked him how long she had.

"Just a few more months at the most," he said.

The next day Giorgio took his son home to meet his family. Rosa opened the door and just stared at the boy—the resemblance was uncanny. She was overcome with joy. She hugged him and told him that she was so very happy to meet him.

Giorgio Jr. was happy to meet them, too, although he was also incredibly sad about his mother. He knew that they would make him feel welcomed and loved, just as his mother had.

Rosa had resented the fact that Giorgio had an affair, but she forgave him because Giorgio was such a wonderful gift to them. Things happen that we don't expect and sometimes it's for the better.

When Giorgio met Lucia, his new sister, he gave her a big hug and kiss. "I have a little sister," he said. "I've always wanted someone to play with. I'll love her and my new family."

Hearing that, Giorgio felt the pride swell within him. He had only Marilyn to thank for such a great son.

To celebrate his great joy, Giorgio invited his close friends to see his new son. Everyone was amazed at how much they resembled each other and how they had been reunited after eleven years.

Giorgio took his son with him everywhere; baseball games, shopping, sight-seeing and then finally to the Met. Giorgio was impressed and said he wanted to be just like him, a great singer which, of course caused yet another swell of pride in Giorgio.

A few days later, he and Giorgio Jr. boarded a plane for Las Vegas. It was time to see Marilyn for the last time.

Upon arrival, they went directly to Marilyn's room. Giorgio left them to return to New York City but promised to call daily to see how things were going.

After Giorgio left, Giorgio Jr. told his mother about all the wonderful places and things he had seen in New York City. He told her how loving everyone had been to him and that he felt he was going to be happy living there.

Giorgio called Marilyn and his son every day to see how things were going. His son was living with Josie.

After a few weeks, Giorgio received word that Marilyn was fading fast and had only a little longer to live. Giorgio was in the middle of a new show and told the director that an emergency had come up and he had to leave for Las Vegas. His son's mother was dying and he wanted to be there. The director told him to do what he had to do and they would do what they had to.

When he arrived at the hospital the next day, he went straight to Marilyn's room. It was easy to see that she didn't have much time left. With tears in her eyes, she gave him a big hug and said, "I'm going to die peacefully knowing that my son is with his father and will be well taken care of."

"And I promise you that he will be," Giorgio responded.

Seconds later, and with one last squeeze of his hand, Marilyn passed away.

Giorgio had Marilyn's body sent to New York City as she had requested. He went to his own priest and asked that he say a mass for her, even though she wasn't Catholic. The priest said he would. "I do this for you because no matter what she is, we all believe in one God."

She was brought into the church for the memorial service the following day. The priest had arranged for a young lady to sing *Ava Maria* at the services, but Giorgio Jr. begged his father to sing it. Giorgio said he'd be happy to.

After the church service, they brought her body to the cemetery where all of her friends gathered around and paid their last respects. They threw flowers on the casket.

Standing in front of her grave gazing down, Giorgio said, "I'll never forget the promise I made to you. I'll always take good care of our son."

Giorgio Jr. threw the last flower on the casket. "Mommy, I'm going to miss you," he said. "Thank you so much for taking care of me. I'll always remember when you held me in your arms and sang *Oh Marie* to me. I know you loved that song. And I know now it was because you loved my father so much and he loved that song. I promise you that every year on your birthday I'll come back here to sing *Oh Marie* to you in your honor."

Giorgio and Rosa put their arms around him.

"I know how much you loved your mother," Giorgio said. "Rosa and I will try to love you as much as she did and take care of you."

"Giorgio," Rosa said, "I can never take your mother's place, but I'll do my best to take care of you as she would have."

His sister came over and hugged him and he felt some of the depression drift away.

After the funeral, they all went out to lunch and everyone wished Giorgio the best of luck with his new son. Giorgio felt blessed that he had a good life. He had a wonderful wife and daughter and now he had the son he had always wanted. He felt truly blessed by God.

Rosa treated Giorgio Jr. like her own son. He was a wonderful boy, well-mannered and he got along well with everyone.

Later that evening Giorgio called his parents in Italy with the good news. He hadn't wanted to tell them until he was sure that Giorgio Jr. would be living with them.

"Mama, Papa, I have wonderful news. Rosa and I just adopted a boy. We're very happy. He's a wonderful child."

He didn't want to tell them that it was his child, that would involve too much of an explanation and his parents weren't up to that. His parents, of course, were happy to hear the news. Giorgio wanted them to come to New York to see their new grandson. They felt they should make the trip—they weren't getting any younger after all, and who knew how long it would be before they saw them again. This could be their last trip to the United States.

His parents left a week later. Giorgio was full of pride at his son meeting his grandparents for the first time. "Giorgio," his mother said, "It's amazing how much he looks like you. If I didn't know better, I'd think he was your own son."

"Yes, he does look a lot like me."

"It's incredible," his father said.

Giorgio smiled and said, "Mom, Dad, when we get home I have a story to tell you."

They drove back to Giorgio's home where they unpacked and had a fine dinner.

In the living room later, after the children were put to bed, Giorgio said, "Mama, Papa, I have a story to tell you. I didn't want to tell you on the phone. But Giorgio Junior is my real son."

His parents looked at each other then back at Giorgio; their expressions displayed their confusion. "Your son? How can that be?" his father said.

"I can hardly believe it myself. Do you remember when I first came to New York and sang in that nightclub? Before I left to come back to Italy? Well, I met one of the dancers at the nightclub. We were good friends and I was lonely and well, things happened. She fell in love with me, but I wasn't in love with her. And when I decided after the robbery to go back to Italy, I left without telling her. I'm ashamed about that. It seems that she was pregnant with my child and never told me. She contacted me a few months ago, and told me she was dying. She also told me about my son. I flew out to see her and met Giorgio Jr. We had a long talk and I told her I wanted to adopt him. I told her I would always take care of him and he would never want for anything. This wonderful woman died of cancer just three weeks ago. And I've kept my promise to her to adopt Giorgio Jr."

His parents were stunned. "I don't have the words to express myself," his father said, "but we believe in God and that this was the way it was supposed to be. We're happy for you."

Giorgio was glad his parents accepted Giorgio Jr. and he felt even more blessed for all he had; a wonderful wife, loving parents, a beautiful daughter and now a son to carry on the family name. He couldn't ask for anything more.

One morning while Rosa ate breakfast with his parents, Giorgio Jr. walked into the kitchen. He kissed his mother and grandparents and started to sing *Oh Marie.*

His grandfather was surprised to hear him sing. "You sound like your father," he said. "Who taught you that song?"

"My mother did. She loved it."

Giorgio had just gotten up when he heard Giorgio Jr. singing. It brought back memories of when he sang in the nightclub and when he first met Marilyn. She always asked him to sing that song because she knew how much he loved it. He felt that she must have loved him so much more than he knew to have taught Giorgio Jr. to sing that song. He silently thanked her for giving him such a beautiful son.

A few minutes later, he went down to breakfast and kissed his wife, his parents and his son good morning. "I had a funny dream last night," he said. "I dreamed a beautiful woman came to me and said, I love you and I'm very proud of you and your brother. I dreamt about her when I was younger. She was singing and playing a guitar to a bunch of soldiers. But I was surprised because she said she was proud of my brother and me. Is it possible that I have a brother somewhere I know nothing about? I've always felt that a part of me was missing."

Giorgio didn't know that God had more plans for him.

As a child, he used to ask his parents if he had a sibling because he felt like there was someone else in his life. He hoped that someday he'd find out where this feeling was coming from and maybe learn more about his real family. He had so many questions. Who was he? Where was he born? Who were his parents? Why was he an orphan? He felt that only when he had answers to these questions would he feel complete inside. It would be the most wonderful thing to happen to him in his life.

Chapter Three – Joe's story

During this same period of time in 1945, Tom Palmer's ship was on duty in the South Pacific Theater. Suddenly without warning, enemy planes appeared from nowhere and began bombing and strafing the ship, sending it to the bottom of the ocean. Everyone aboard was presumed dead. They searched for survivors and about a week later found Tom Palmer seriously wounded on a deserted island. He was rushed to a military hospital. He had an injury to his hand that was so severe that it had to be amputated. Tom was in a lot of pain, but he knew it had to be done and he'd have to live with the results for the rest of his life.

After spending three months in the hospital, he was released from military duty and sent home to be with his wife and family. They were grateful to see that Tom had made it through the war relatively unhurt. The family did not want Tom to know for the time being that his best friend, Joe Martino, had lost his life in Italy.

After several months, Tom became very depressed-not only did he lose his right hand, his great dream of becoming a professional football player appeared to be over. Then he again started asking about his best friend, Joe Martino, and if anybody had heard from him. The family finally told Tom the truth, which caused an even deeper depression. Tom's wife Lina tried to help him out of his depression but nothing seemed to help. Finally, primarily because of her persistence, he agreed that he needed psychiatric help.

Not long after that, Tom also discovered that his wounds had left him incapable of becoming a father. This feeling of being less than a man only deepened his depression. He felt like his life was through and he began having thoughts of suicide. But a strong loving family did a lot to keep his spirits up. Their deep faith in a loving and caring God helped pull Tom through most of his depression.

1948

Tom's father-in-law John wrote many letters to his cousin Mario in Italy and finally came up with an idea. He thought it might be good for Tom and his wife to adopt a baby since they couldn't have their own. The thought of having a child to raise might pull Tom out of his remaining depression.

One day, Tom's father-in-law, John, received a letter from Mario telling him about the children up for adoption in Italy. They'd been left at an orphanage because their parents had died during the war.

John thought it was time that he had a talk with Tom about his feelings regarding adoption. He invited Tom over one afternoon and spoke about Mario's letter and the children looking for a home.

"Would you be interested in adopting a child?" he asked.

After much thought and after discussing it with Lina, they agreed it was a good idea. These children needed a home and he needed a child. He wanted a boy. He would name him Joe.

Tom and Lina started preparing for a boat trip to Italy to begin the adoption. Lina hoped the baby would help bring Tom out of his depression and that they'd be a family.

They arrived in Rome nine days later. Tom's father-in-law's cousin, an engineer, met Tom and his family and showed them the sights before he took them to the orphanage where they met the administrator who took them to the nursery. Tom searched the room and his gaze momentarily hesitated as he noticed a young boy about four with light wavy hair.

A strange feeling suddenly came over him. He knew there was something special about this child. He couldn't put his feelings into words, but he knew this was the baby they would adopt.

He told the administrator that he wanted that child and asked what his name was.

"Giuseppe," he said.

The administrator told them that it would take several months to arrange all the legal documentation. Tom and Lina decided not to stay in Rome because of Tom's medical condition. They made arrangements for Tom's father-in-law John to stay and bring the child back to America after the arrangements.

Several months went by and during that time, Tom and Lina decorated a room for the child and told everyone about him. They couldn't wait for him to arrive.

The time soon came for John to bring little Giuseppe to America. John had been staying with his cousin, Mario, until it was time to leave.

He had been going to see Giuseppe every few days. He'd brought him toys so he would hopefully learn to trust him. He had a nurse named Nina who took care of him. She had lost a little boy to influenza during the war and Giuseppe reminded her of him, so he became her special charge.

She loved children and couldn't have any more of her own. She knew that Giuseppe was going to leave soon and tried to get him to go to John so it wouldn't be so hard for him to leave her.

When the day came for him to leave, John had to pull him away from Nina, because he wouldn't let go. He'd sob and cry out for his Nana. Only the promise of a plane ride made him stop crying.

"Giuseppe I'll write to you in America," Nina said. "But you have to go now. Your grandfather is taking you to see your new family."

John picked him up and said, "Giuseppe, everyone's waiting to meet you in America. Please don't cry."

John thanked Nina for all her help and gave her fifty dollars.

She didn't want to take the money but when he said, "Please, buy something in memory of little Giuseppe," she acceded.

They stayed with John's cousin for the night and before he left, his cousin said, "Don't forget the mandolin that your father left for you. He hoped that you'd play it in his memory."

John thanked him for letting him stay there.

"It's nothing, you're my cousin. I wish you luck in America with your new grandson."

John called before he left to let Tom and Lina know when he was coming so they could meet him at the airport. Excitement rose as they saw the plane arrive and before long they saw John walk down the ladder with a little boy holding his hand. As soon as they were able, they ran to him, hugged and kissed him, and welcomed him to America. Then they got into their car and rode back to Philadelphia for the wonderful celebration to welcome him home.

Many people attended the party, including Mr. Carlo Martino, Joe's father. He presented Tom with a thousand dollar savings bond for little Giuseppe. "Tom," he said, "you've always been like a son to me and I'll treat you like a son for the rest of my life. I think you did the right thing by adopting this little boy and I thank you for giving him Joe's name. I want you to know how much that means to me," he said as he hugged him.

Carlo's wife Lisa went over to little Giuseppe, picked him up and gave him a kiss, which got her a smile from the boy. Something about that smile made her think of her own son, Joe.

"He smiles like Joe did at that age," she said to Carlo. "What a resemblance."

Everyone had a marvelous time at the party and when it was time to leave everyone congratulated Tom and Lina on their new family and wished them the best.

Because Tom had only one hand, he was unable to hold a job. But he did get a pension from the government, which allowed him plenty of time to spend with little Joe while Lina worked as a secretary.

Starting at age five, Tom would take Joe into the backyard and play football with him. Tom, without realizing it, was attempting to fulfill his own dream of playing football. The time they spent together helped Tom find a new lease on life and helped lift him out of his depression.

There was much joy in the family for Tom and Lina but also with John and Teresa Mare. Each Sunday everyone gathered at their house for dinner. Lina was the only daughter.

Tom's small family didn't live nearby so he didn't see them as often as he saw Lina's.

John Mare and Carlo Martino had arrived on the same boat to America, although they didn't meet there. He came from Santa Lucia, a suburb of Naples. He met his wife on the boat. She had come to America to meet her uncle and to have an arranged marriage. But when she met John, she changed her mind. It was love at first sight.

When she got to America, she stayed with her uncle for a while, even though he was angry with her for not marrying the man he had picked. Because of that friction, she moved to Philadelphia to see John and ended up living with his sister.

John had been a very good tailor in Italy and he found her a job helping him. They got married a few months later. After working in the tailor shop for a couple of years, he opened his own shop called The Santa Lucia Tailor Shop. Teresa worked with him. They made a successful team.

He met Carlo Martino when he came in to have a suit made. During their conversations, they discovered that they had grown up near each other and that they had come over on the same boat, a good reason to start up a strong friendship. Sometimes they'd even play the old songs from Italy on the mandolin.

John sometimes talked about his grandson Giuseppe, who his son-in-law Tom had adopted. "He always listened to me play the mandolin," he told him, "and he's wanted to learn how to play it since he was a little boy."

"Perhaps he was from a musical family," Carlo said. Over the years, Joe was in several recitals at school. He had taken up singing and was really very good.

After one such recital, as they were talking about how good he was, John started playing the mandolin and asked

Joe to sing along with him. "You did so well in the recital but I want to hear you sing these songs."

He taught him how to sing the old songs from Naples that he loved so much. He learned quickly and John was pleased.

"Don't have him play football," he told Tom. "Let him be a singer!"

Joe heard him and said, "Grandpa John, I love football but I love to sing too. When I get older and I can't play football any more maybe I'll sing instead."

John had to be content with that.

One Sunday they went as usual to John's house for dinner. Tom had brought some scotch. "I know you like wine but on this occasion I thought you might like the scotch instead," he said.

"I appreciate that, son," John said, "but remember your mother is making lasagna, your favorite dish. I'm sick so you can eat my portion too."

"That sounds like a good idea. I'm feeling extra hungry today!" They laughed.

"So, what do you want for your birthday?" John asked Joe. He would be twelve soon. "A guitar so I can play with you, Grandpa." John was pleased. "We can play them together," he said. Carlo Martino brought his mandolin to the party and everyone felt nostalgic for the good times they'd had back in Italy. "I can't understand it," Carlo said to John. "Your grandson looks a lot like my son Joe did when he was little. The more I see him, the more I see the resemblance. Could this be Joe reincarnated?" He shrugged. "Ah, but I don't believe in that. It's probably just a coincidence."

John just shook his head.

***

Just after his 59th birthday. John started feeling poorly, but like most men, he kept it quiet. The business was doing well and life was otherwise good—why muddy the waters with something that was probably nothing?

But when the pain became even too much for him to bear, he had no choice but to make an appointment. It was lung cancer and the prognosis wasn't good.

Sometimes during the Sunday dinners, he'd look sad and Joe would try to cheer him up. He'd bring out his guitar and sing the old songs for him. It always made John feel better.

One day Joe asked him, "Grandpa, do you know if I had any brothers or sisters? Because sometimes I feel like there's something missing."

"No, Joe, as far as I know, you were an only child."

Within six months, John was on his death bed, his family around him.

He was lying there talking when he heard a mandolin playing. He smiled. He knew it was Joe. Joe walked out from behind the curtains. He had been trying to surprise him by playing his favorite song, *Santa Lucia*.

John started crying. "Joe, come here," he said. He gave him a big hug and kiss. "Thank you for playing that song, you know it's my favorite. It always brings me back to my childhood and playing with my friends."

"Anything for you, Grandpa," Joe said. "I'll miss you when you're gone and I promise to play that song in memory of you."

John died shortly thereafter leaving his family grief-stricken, especially Joe, who loved his grandfather very much. He even stopped going to football practice because the grief was too much to bear.

The coach thought that he'd quit so he went to the other players and said, "Guys, Joe's grandfather just died and I'm not sure if he wants to come back and play football or not. Look, can some of you, or all of you, go to his house tomorrow night and help cheer him up?"

Tom came to the door when the team showed up the next night. "Mr. Palmer, is Joe here?" one of the boys said. "We were concerned, what with his grandfather--"

"How thoughtful of you," Tom said. "I'll call him for you."

Joe, who was lying on the couch, got up and went to the door. He was surprised to see the whole team. They hugged him and shook his hand and told him how much they missed him.

Joe was overwhelmed by all their concern and started to feel a bit better.

"Go out on the porch and I'll bring some lemonade and cookies," Joe's mother said.

While they snacked, the coach drove up. He hugged him and said, "See how important you are to the team, Joe? We all miss you and we hope to see you at practice again. Even the other students are asking about you. They're concerned, Joe."

Joe never imagined that anyone would miss him so much. With tears in his eyes, he said, "Thank you for coming here tonight and thank you for all your concern and support. I promise you that I'll come back. You've all made me feel so good. It's nice to know people care."

They spent a little more time talking and then it was time for them to leave. The coach said goodbye to Joe's parents. "Thank you for helping Joe feel better," Tom said. "I know he'll be back to school soon and I know how much he appreciated what you did for him."

Later Tom said to Joe, "You made a big impression on people, Joe. See how much they're willing to support you in your time of need."

At that moment, Joe understood that despite everything, life must go on.

The next week Joe went back to school and back to practice. His father usually went to watch him play but this time he didn't. When Joe came home, he saw his father sitting in the living room looking through a photo album.

"How did practice go today?" Tom said.

"Great. Everyone came over and shook my hand and cheered me up. Even some girls said it was nice to see me back."

"That's great, son."

"Thanks, Dad."

"You know, this is a very important day for me. I went to the cemetery to see my best friend. I told you he was killed in the war. It was his birthday today and I brought some flowers for him. I never told you the story of when I played football with him."

"No, you didn't, Dad."

"Well, come on over here."

"This was when we won the high school championship before we left for college," Tom said as he turned a page and pointed.

"Dad, you know your friend looks a little like me, don't you think? Or am I imagining things?"

"Yeah, there's a resemblance. Funny, isn't it though how sometimes we look like complete strangers. You know, we went to college together, at Penn State. I was a receiver and Joe was the quarterback. I was engaged to your mother then and Joe was very happy for me. You know, it's funny, he was always surrounded by girls, but he never loved any of them. I asked him why one day and he said that he just wanted to have a good time and he wasn't ready to settle down. Then we got the news about the war and well, you know the rest. But before we left, we played a last game together. We were losing and during the last thirty seconds, Joe threw a pass to me and we won the game. I'll always remember that, always."

Joe never knew his dad played ball, or that he was that good.

"Dad, if you had come back from the war in good health, you might have gone on to become a big football star."

"Son, your coach says that you have the drive and ability to go on and become a great player and hopefully with no injuries you'll go on to do just that. Or maybe someday you'll decide to become a singer instead. Only time will tell."

"Thanks for sharing that story, Dad. I think I really do want to go on and play football now. This has really inspired me."

Tom coached and played football with Joe until he entered high school. By that time, Joe had made a good impression on the coach.

The coach told Tom that Joe was good enough to become the team's quarterback. Tom's dream could become a reality through his son.

Tom's son, Joe, threw the ball exactly the way his friend Joe did. Was his son a reincarnated Joe? Of course he wasn't, but what if, he wondered.

Joe's football team was pretty much second rate, but Joe was attracted to a cheerleader named Mary Jo Romero.

Mary Jo was a nice Italian girl and her whole family played an instrument. She played the guitar. What she wanted most was to become a physical therapy nurse.

One day after a game, Joe asked Mary Jo if she would like to join him for an ice cream soda. She accepted gladly and they went to the soda parlor. They learned more about each other and what they had in common. Joe told her that he loved music and that he was a pretty good singer. "I was told by my music teacher that I could be a professional singer, but my first love is football. My father taught me and I have a talent for it. My goal is to play professionally. If that doesn't happen, I would either be a coach or try to sing professionally."

Mary Jo smiled. "We're all musicians in my family. It runs in our blood. You gotta meet my father, he plays the guitar. Maybe you could play a duet. You sing, he'll accompany."

Mary Jo invited Joe to her party birthday and while there, Mary Jo introduced him to all her friends and her parents. Her father said he'd seen him play and thought he had real potential.

"I hear you play the guitar," Joe said to Mary Jo's father after they cut the cake. "I'd like to sing a song for Mary Jo and I'd be honored if you'd accompany me."

"I'd love to," her father said.

Joe sang a song he thought Mary Jo would like and when he was done, Mary Jo was obviously amazed. She had no idea that Joe could sing so well. She went over and gave him a big hug and kiss on the cheek and thanked him for the song.

While Joe was eating, Mary Jo's father came over and sat down with him. "You've a got a great voice, Joe," he said. "Anyone else got a voice like yours, in your family, I mean."

"I don't know. I was adopted so..."

"So you don't know who your parents were?"

Joe shrugged and smiled.

"Well someone had to have had musical ability. And you know, if football doesn't work, you can always make a living singing."

"I do think about that because whenever I sing I always feel as good as I do when I play football. My father has always told me that my education should come first, then, afterwards if the opportunity arises, I should try to play professional football. I don't want to disappoint him. He always wanted to play pro football, but he lost his hand in the war. So I guess my dad is living his dream vicariously through me. If I do become a pro, it would make my dad so proud. He's always done so much for me and I just want to help make his dream a reality."

"Joe, you're a smart and loving person. Your heart is in the right place. I hope that your dream will come true someday and that

God will give you the opportunity to play. I'm glad you're my daughter's friend."

Soon afterwards, the party started to end. Mary Jo thanked Joe for coming. He gave her a big hug and a goodbye kiss. He said he enjoyed coming and meeting her parents. Her father came over and shook hands with him. "You're welcome anytime," he said with a big smile.

They saw a lot of each other from then on and their relationship grew when the school year was over, they decided to play music together. Mary Jo played the guitar while Joe sang with some of the band. The band would play at parties and earn money toward college.

One night, Joe felt a pain in his chest and he felt his voice changing. Mary Jo was very worried about him. Joe loved singing as much as he loved football. He would sing all the time. It was an important part of his life.

Joe didn't know what to do when he lost his voice. He told his father what happened. They decided to wait and see but he didn't improve.

Finally, he went to his doctor. "Joe, there's nothing wrong with you," he said. "I can't understand this."

"Sometimes I hear a voice in my head as though it's talking to me, searching for me," Joe said. "This voice would make me feel a little sick. I don't understand why, though. It feels like there's a part of me missing and it's looking for me."

"Joe, forget about it. It's all in your head. Just start singing and playing again and it'll pass."

Joe tried to do as the doctor advised, but he didn't improve, which depressed him even more.

A few days later, he and Mary Jo decided to go to a local carnival. He saw a palm reader booth and decided to give it a try.

The fortune teller looked at his palm. "Your name is Joe?"

"Yes."

"You are very upset now and feel very bad inside. I think for some reason somebody else in your life is disturbed and that's why you feel this way."

"Who could it be? I know sometimes there's somebody else missing from my life, but I don't know who it is."

"Yes, there is somebody else. Do you have any brothers or sisters? I know you're adopted. But I know there is somebody else."

"As far as I know, I have no other family. I came from an orphanage in Italy after the war."

"Joe, there's somebody else that you don't know about, but someday you'll find this person. When you find them, your life will change for the better and you'll be very happy. I wish you good luck and hope that you'll find what you're missing."

Joe was surprised to hear someone was looking for him. He thanked her, paid and left.

When he rejoined Mary Jo, he told her what the palm reader said. She laughed and said, "I think she's lying just to get your money."

"No, Mary Jo, I believe her because I've had this feeling for a long time. That I'm looking for someone and they're looking for me."

"Joe, there's no one out there. Just give it a little more time and it'll pass."

When Joe went home later, he told his father and asked him if there was anyone else.

"As far as I know, you're the only child. No brothers or sisters. But just have faith in God and pray and see what happens."

So Joe prayed and a few days later he woke up and, remarkably so, felt like his old self again. He took a shower and started singing. He felt better and better.

He went to see Mary Jo and sang her a song and laughed and said, "I'm back to the way I felt before."

The band started making arrangements again and everyone was happy to see Joe well.

A lot of people who heard Joe sing asked if he was going to become a professional, he was that good. But Joe always replied, "My priority is my education and then I'm going to pursue my first love--football. If for some reason that doesn't work out, then I'll do whatever God wants me to do."

The summer was good for their band and they made a lot of money which they put into a college fund. When school started back up in September, it was their senior year. Joe would play football again.

He hoped he would do better than he had the year before, and he did. He didn't know why, but he didn't question it either. The fact was, he was a much better player this year, very much so. And when they eventually won the state high school championship, Joe was voted the MVP. Big name colleges wanted him in their programs.

At season's end, the coach threw a party for the players and their families. Joe and Mary Jo had a great time, at least when they could get away from playing—they'd been invited to provide the music.

Joe and Mary Jo's families thought they made a perfect couple and hoped that they would get together. Joe's father said he hoped that Joe would go on to be a great football player and that one-day he and Mary Jo would get married. "I'd be honored to part of your family," Joe said.

When Joe saw Mary Jo in her beautiful red dress at their Senior Prom, his heart filled with joy. Seeing her standing their so radiant and alive and so in love with him, he realized that he loved her and wanted her in his life forever.

Joe's friend Jim was there playing with his band. For Joe and Mary Jo it was probably the last night they would have together before they left for college.

Joe wasn't sure where he wanted to go but Mary Jo was going to California. They promised each other their love would last forever and that they would be together after college.

"I'll miss you, Mary Jo," Joe said. "I hope my love for you will be strong enough to survive when we're apart as it is right at this moment."

They decided to find someplace to be alone. Meanwhile Joe has told his friend, Jim, to go outside and hide in a bush until he got his cue.

Joe walked Mary Jo over to Jim's bush where they sat down. "I'll miss you, Mary Jo. This is our last night together. I want you to know that I'll love you forever. I think we're made for each other."

He took a small ring from his pocket, placed it on her slender finger and said, "This is a symbol of my love for you to remember us by. I'm sorry it's so small but it is just a memory ring."

"I love you the same way and I don't care that it's small," Mary Jo said. "I love the ring!"

She threw her arms around him and they kissed.

Suddenly, they heard guitar music.

"Mary Jo, I have another surprise for you," Joe said. "I've written a special song for you, and I hope you like it. I call it *Lucky in Love*."

When we danced through the night
And I held you so tight
I saw the love for me in your eyes.
In my heart burned a flame
When you told me your name
Our love was such a thrilling
surprise.
Never, never before
Have I been so lucky in love.
Never, never before
Has my life been touched from above.
Darling, darling
Since we met on the dance room floor
I believe in you
And our love so true
Will go on forever more
And together we're lucky in love.

The song made her happier than she had ever been before. Never before had someone written a song just for her.

She kissed him and said, "Joe, this is beautiful. Thank you so much."

Jim came out from behind the bush and she thanked him too.

"Jim, you surprised me. You played beautifully!"

Then they all shook hands and Jim wished them well. He said he and his band were heading for Las Vegas after school and were hoping to hit it big.

Mary Jo and Joe went back inside for a while longer and then Joe took Mary Jo home. Once there he drew her into his arms and told her that he was in love with her. She told him that she felt the same way and that she would never love another man as much as she loved him. They kissed then and as they did, Joe knew that she was the girl for him.

That summer Joe received a lot of scholarship offers. Joe, of course, felt the necessity to hurry through the process, but his father said, "Relax, son, just relax. You've got the whole summer to think about your decision. Enjoy yourself for now."

Joe smiled. "You're right, Dad," he said. "As usual, you're right."

Finally, one day toward the end of summer, he told his father, "Dad, I decided to go to Florida. It's a good school and it's warm. They've always had a good team."

His father was happy with Joe's decision. "I'll be happy to go to Florida and watch you play and get a little sunshine, myself," he responded.

That summer Joe and Mary Jo spent a lot of time together playing music, but they'd be separated in the fall because they were both leaving for college. Mary Jo wanted to become a rehabilitation nurse therapist and had chosen a school in California. At the same time, they promised each other to stay in touch and that someday they'd get married.

About a week before Joe left for Florida, his father was walking in the park. He saw the coach from the high school and said, "Hi, Charlie."

They started talking. "How's Joe doing?" the coach said. "Has he decided where he wants to go?"

"Well, he wants to go to Florida. He wants to be a 'Toro."

Charlie nodded and said, "Smart decision. They're a good team. I think he'll do well. Tom, like I told you before, Joe has a natural ability and the skill to play football. It's the same when he sings. He has this ability to be more than someone else. A year ago when he was running on the track, he had the ability to stay focused. He has the ability in a split second to read the defense, which in my opinion makes him a good quarterback. I think Joe has the ability to go pro when the time comes. You can only teach so much, the rest has to be natural ability. He's the right size and the right weight. Tell him I said hello and please ask him to come see me when he comes back."

"Charlie, remember before I went to war, my friend Joe and I played in high school here. They told him the same thing."

"I wasn't here then but I've heard about Joe Martino and how good he was."

"This son of mine looks like Joe, and sometimes, Charlie, I get the feeling that he is Joe. He seems so familiar to me when he does certain things."

"Tom, I don't believe in that kind of thing too much. You might just miss your friend."

Tom shrugged and said, "Eh, you may be right."

Tom was glad to hear what the coach had said about Joe. He was looking forward to Joe going to college to prove himself.

***

Joe was shown around the campus after he arrived. He liked the campus and surroundings very much and he knew he'd be happy here. They had a good football team and an excellent coach. He felt lucky to have the opportunity to play here. But now he had to prove himself.

The next day all the players got together and had a meeting with the coach.

The coach, a burly man with broad shoulders, a buzz cut and a fiercely competitive nature that shown brightly in his deep brown eyes, hiked up his belt and said, "You're here because you're good, very good, and I can make you better, much better. But this is a team and we're going to play as a team. Is that understood?"

"Understood, coach!" came the in union reply.

"I didn't hear you, girls," the coach said as he cupped his ear.

"Understood, coach," everyone said again, even louder.

The coach smiled and continued. "Now we have team rules, which are clearly stated on your welcome sheets. Live by those rules, obey those rules. If you don't, you will be disciplined. Is that understood?"

"Understood, coach!"

"Okay, great, now let's have the best damn practice any team every had because with this team, the sky's the limit."

The coach saw a lot of potential in Joe, but he felt that Joe needed more experience and practice. So when the season began, the coach made him the second-string quarterback.

The first year Joe only quarterbacked a few games. The coach always encouraged Joe to be patient and with time and practice, he'd be given more responsibility. That year Joe's football team had a record of 6-4, not bad but certainly not what Joe had anticipated.

After the school year Joe went back home to Philadelphia feeling a little disappointed. He thought he'd play more. His father, in an attempt to guide him, told him to be patient, that his time would come. Joe vowed to listen to his father.

The next day Mary Jo called Joe to let him know she was home. Joe, of course, was happy to hear from her.

When they got together, they both felt a strong love. All summer they enjoyed playing music together again and they enjoyed their friends and family. At the end of the summer, they again separated to go back to school.

Joe started a new season, and this time he was the starting quarterback. It was the break he needed and he took full advantage. Following his leadership, the team went on an eight game winning streak. The coach and Joe's father were extremely happy with the way Joe played.

Needless to say, Joe had become very popular with college girls. He called Mary Jo less and less as his popularity increased. The temptation even caused him to overlook the deep love he felt for Mary Jo. He thought that playing around was just for fun. He didn't realize the mistake he was making and how much Mary Jo's love was worth.

As the calls from Joe became less and less frequent, Mary Jo became suspicious. One day she picked up the newspaper and saw Joe's picture with some girls giving him kisses. She called Joe the next day and asked him why he hadn't called her like he used to and if he still really loved her. He reassured her that he still loved her, but he needed space in their relationship.

"Well Joe, that's okay because I need some space too.

There's a man here who's crazy about me and wants to get to know me better."

"Listen, Mary Jo, it's really up to you because right now I can't make any promises."

Joe never called her back.

When Joe finished the football season he stayed in Florida because he liked his new friends and wanted to stay by the beach.

He thought about Mary Jo less and less. Besides, there were plenty of girls around to take her place. But even when he did think about her, he felt a twinge of sadness. He wanted her near, but he hadn't yet convinced himself of that.

Joe's father was upset about him not coming home for the summer and spending time together. He thought that if Joe came home that Mary Jo would come home too. He sensed that the relationship might be falling apart.

One day Joe's father paid him a surprise visit. He took him to dinner because he was worried about Joe's wild streak and thought it might get him in trouble so he wanted to talk to him about it.

Over dinner, Tom said, "Son, I've made a lot of sacrifices in order for you to play football. You know I love you very much and I also love football. I have a feeling your relationship with Mary Jo is falling apart, but it's okay if you're happy with your life. Time will tell who's the right girl for you. I want you to remember that when you're a big star and everything's great, know who you really are and always be yourself. And promise me to always play fair and live a clean life."

"Dad," Joe said, "I know how much it means for you to see me play football and I promise you I'm just having some fun and when the season starts I'll do everything in my power to be the best football player I can be. Look, I don't want to disappoint my coach and teammates and Dad, I don't want to disappoint you and Mom either."

Joe's dad felt content with his response. After dinner, they left the restaurant and Tom told his son he would come back in the winter to see him play.

One night he went out with some friends to a nightclub and had some drinks. One of his friends asked him to sing, so he got up and sang a beautiful love song. He did it so well they asked him to sing again.

A woman approached him afterwards and congratulated him. "If you come to Las Vegas and sing you could make a fortune," she said. "I mean you got the voice, the looks. You're a gold mine."

"That sounds great, but I'm a football player first and in a few weeks I'll be going to training camp."

She didn't want to take no for an answer and she was so persuasive that Joe started to think about it. "Look," he said, "I'll give you a call, okay?"

That night he did start thinking about it. He'd promised his father that he'd play football. He knew if he left he'd break his father's heart. He fell asleep still thinking about it.

That night, he had a strange dream about a young American soldier. "Joe, Joe," he said to him, "what are you doing? You promised your father that you'd play football. You don't want to break his heart!"

In the morning, he remembered his dream, and he wondered if this was some friend of his father's from the war. But he dismissed it as just a dream. It did, however, make him decide to continue playing football.

Later that day he called the woman and said thanks but no thanks. "Maybe one day I'll go to Las Vegas and look you up, but only after I'm done playing football."

September approached and it was time to play again. Joe practiced every day and as he practiced, the coach noticed that Joe was getting better and better. He told Joe that if he continued to play at this level, they might win the championship. Joe tried harder and harder and he was very proud of himself. He had worked hard to get here and he was also glad he was still in one piece, too. Locking horns with 300 pound lineman could end a career in a heartbeat. Thank God, he'd been lucky so far.

A lot of hard practice translated nicely into the creation of a better football team, one that could win the championship. Spirits were high as the season progressed, and as one win followed another, the championship actually appeared within reach.

With Joe at quarterback and following a team concept, the team appeared unbeatable, which made everyone involved feel on top of the world.

Toward the end of the season, The Florida Toro's were favored to win the national title. Nothing could stand in their way.

Before the game, the coach gathered the players around him and said a prayer, asking that they play well and win or lose, they give it their best. He followed that up by asking that, "Please, don't let anyone get hurt."

Everyone applauded and hooped and hollered, which sounded like a hurricane inside the locker room. "Now run out there and bust some heads!" the coach yelled.

The referee gathered the captains in the middle to flip the coin. Joe won the toss and elected to receive. The Notre Dame kicker booted it toward the end zone, but the receiver cut his way to the forty yard line, leaving would be tacklers in his wake. A good start.

In the huddle, Joe called a down and out pattern. "A little fake then cut loose," he said to the receiver. They broke huddle, gathered at the ball and within seconds the play started: Joe stepped back three steps and while the opposition lineman clamored to get to him, lofted the ball sixty yards to the receiver, just a few yards from the end zone. He went in untouched. Seven to nothing, Toro's.

The crowd went crazy and if Joe could have seen his dad, he would have been even happier—his dad had tears in his eyes. Never had he been so proud of his son. It brought back memories of the last game he'd played with Joe.

He couldn't help notice little things that Joe did that resembled his best friend. It was if Sergeant Joe had come back again to finish what he had always wanted to do in his life.

The Toro's were ahead by three points with one minute left in the game. Victory appeared certain. And when Joe threw yet another touchdown pass, victory was assured.

Everybody screamed for joy, but little did the crowd realize that Joe had suffered a career threatening injury. He had to be carried off the field on a stretcher. The Florida Toro's may have won the game but Joe's career seemed in jeopardy.

Joe was immediately rushed to the hospital; his father accompanied him in the ambulance. It was bad news for Joe. A torn cruciate ligament, with medial damage as well. There was a possibility that he would never play football again.

Joe's father started to cry. He realized he had to be strong for Joe so he wiped the tears away and went to his son's room. He assured Joe that he would be okay, that yes, he had sustained a serious injury, but time and God healed all wounds.

"Never give up, have faith in yourself and if it's God's will," he told his son, "you'll play football again. But remember Joe, no matter what happens, I'll always be there for you because I love you."

The next day the headline read, *Joe Palmer badly injured; may never play football again.*

The news created quite a lot of sympathy and sadness, especially among the players and coach. All of Joe's teammates and the coach went to the hospital to give Joe encouragement. Joe was very happy to see them. They showed him the championship trophy and when he saw it, Joe felt his spirits rise—he'd play football again if it was the last thing he ever did.

Joe's father told the players and the coach that the next day he was taking Joe back to Philadelphia for rehabilitation.

Joe's friends and family greeted him when they arrived in Philadelphia. As Joe was wheeled down the ramp, he heard a cheer. They made him feel welcome but in his heart, he felt a little sad about his injuries. He really wasn't sure where he was going from here.

Joe's father was worried because his career might be over, but he tried hard not to let Joe notice his anxiety.

He felt that after working so hard for so long, the fact that Joe was hurt and might not play again had destroyed everything. Joe felt the same way--that he had let his father down. But his father advised Joe to stay positive. "Believe in God and everything will work out."

Joe started physical therapy at the hospital, but it only exacerbated his depression. He told his father that he felt like a failure because he had let everyone down.

And he was particularly depressed about the fact that he let Mary Jo go. She was the most wonderful girl he had ever fallen in love with. And he was certain that she'd married the man she'd told him about.

Joe sought psychiatric help. He told him all his problems, including Mary Jo.

"Joe, it was your fault, but you'll find another girl to love."

"No, I'll never find a girl like her. I loved her and lost her but I know she loved me too."

Joe continued with his physical therapy and because of his depression he saw the psychiatrist for quite awhile. He had lost his zest for life, his girlfriend, and his will to play football. His mother and father were worried.

Every year on his Grandfather John's birthday, he would go to the cemetery with his parents and relatives and play the mandolin in remembrance. His grandfather and grandmother had been dead for many years. This year the day passed without Joe's presence.

One night he dreamt of his grandfather who said to him, "Giuseppe, you don't remember me anymore. Why don't you play your mandolin for me again?"

The next morning, while Joe was having coffee with his mother, he told her about his dream.

"See, Joe," she said, "even your grandfather is thinking of you."

So Joe tried to force himself to do more. He tried to play the mandolin but his heart wasn't in it. He tried to go to the cemetery and to his grandfather's grave, but he just couldn't do it. But still, slowly but surely, he was getting better and starting to come out of his depression.

A few weeks later, he took his mandolin to the cemetery and played for his grandfather. "Grandfather, I'll always come and play for you," he said. "I've been depressed about my injury, but I promise to do better. I'll always remember you in my heart."

Before long, the old Joe was back.

One night he dreamt that he was on a beach walking when a girl ran up to him, hugged him and said, "Joe, Joe, I still love you. But I have people that I have to take care of." He didn't recognize the girl but he thought it might be Mary Jo.

When he woke up, he went down to have a cup of coffee with his father and told him about the dream. "Dad, I'm doing better with my injury and I'll be done with physical therapy soon. After I am, I want to go to California and find Mary Jo. Dad, I know I made a mistake. I thought I could find lots of girls like Mary Jo and I realize now that I couldn't. She's one of a kind and very special. I want to find out if she feels the same way, too. We spent so many years together; I just can't throw that away. I don't think I can live without her. I really want to see her."

"Joe, why do you want to go to California? She's probably married by now with kids. You don't want to ruin her life."

"I want to see for myself. I'll bring her back here if I have to. If you don't want to give me the money, I'll get it from Grandpa Carlo. If I see her and she tells me that she doesn't love me anymore, then I'll come back and forget about her. But I have to find out how she feels about me, if she still loves me or not."

One day Tom ran into Mary Jo's mother, Frances, in the grocery store. They talked for a few minutes and she asked about Joe and how he was doing. She was sorry to hear about his accident. "Joe cries every day because he lost Mary Jo," Tom said. "He believes that she's married to a man she'd mentioned the last time they saw each other."

"Mary Jo isn't married," Frances said with a smile. "She still loves Joe. In fact, Tom, she's coming back home because she heard that Joe was injured and she wants to see if she can help. She applied for a job at the hospital as a physical therapy nurse. She should be starting next week."

Tom was overjoyed and gave her a big hug. "Thank you so much for the good news. But I'm not going to tell Joe yet. It'll be a big surprise for him."

A week later, Tom went to the airport to drop off a friend. As he was watching all the arriving passengers, he noticed a girl who looked like Mary Jo. When she got closer, he realized that it was her.

"Mary Jo, I'm so pleased that you've come home," he said as he gave her a big hug. "Joe talks about you all the time and he's so sorry for all the mistakes he made. I know he loves you and that he's always loved you, even when it seemed like he didn't. He was young and full of himself. You're the only girl who can make him well. He hasn't been the same without you and I know you'll do your best for him."

"Don't worry Mr. Palmer," Mary Jo said. "I love Joe and I'll do everything in my power to make him well. I'll be starting my new job at the hospital in another couple of days. Joe should be in my section, but please don't tell him about my working there. I want to surprise him."

Tom agreed and they said goodbye, promising to meet again when Tom took Joe to the hospital for his physical therapy.

When Tom got home, he had a big smile on his face. Lina asked him why he was so happy.

"Don't tell Joe because it's a surprise, but I ran into Mary Jo at the airport. She came home because she heard that Joe was injured and wanted to help. She's a physical therapy nurse at the hospital and she'll be working with Joe. Isn't that great? Hopefully, they'll get back together again where they belong."

"Oh, that's marvelous, honey. And I certainly won't say anything to Joe."

A few days later at the hospital, Tom said, "I'll leave you here and come back when you're done, Joe. I have a few errands to run if you don't mind."

"No, I don't mind," Joe said as he sat down to wait.

Joe was relaxing in a chair when Mary Jo walked out of a room and said, "Sir, I can help you now. You're next."

Joe looked up and saw the woman of his dreams. He tried to jump up, and almost fell down. He got up and walked toward her. He looked into her eyes and she into his. A minute passed, then two, until finally, neither of them could hold back. They hugged and kissed like the long lost lovers they really were.

"I'm sorry, Mary Jo, for what I did. I never stopped loving you."

"That's why I came back. I love you too and I wanted to be close to you."

They kissed again and everyone in the waiting room started clapping.

Then Mary Jo asked the head nurse if she could have the rest of the afternoon off. The nurse, touched by the situation, gladly gave it to her.

Mary Jo wheeled Joe outside where they met Tom. "Dad, guess who I met!" Joe said.

His father laughed. He knew at that moment that everything would be fine. He saw how happy they were to be together again.

"I'm so happy for you, son. I hope you get well soon. You're getting well will make me very happy."

To celebrate the happy occasion, Mr. Palmer took Joe and Mary Jo to a restaurant for lunch. During lunch, Mary Jo told Joe that she wanted him to get well and continue to do what he loved to do-- play football.

"Honey!" Joe said, "as long as you're behind me, and God gives me strength, I'll play football again."

At that moment, Joe's father gave both of them a hug and wished them a happy and successful new life. With that, they left the restaurant and went to Mr. Palmer's house where they surprised Joe's mother.

Mrs. Palmer was both delighted and happy. She gave her a big hug and welcomed her back into the family.

That night, everybody made plans to get together with Mary Jo's father and mother to celebrate the reuniting of Joe and Mary Jo.

Later that night, Joe and Mary Jo spent some time talking about all the good times they had shared. It brought back good feelings for her and when Joe gave her a kiss, it brought back the old days.

"It's getting late," Mary Jo said. "I have to go home."

She said goodbye to Joe's parents and thanked them for everything.

"I'm so glad you came back," Mrs. Palmer said to Mary Jo. "You've given my son new hope and new strength. I hope with all my heart that you'll be part of this family someday."

"That would make me very happy too," Mary Jo said.

When she got home, Mary Jo told her parents the exciting news. She told them that they were invited to go out for dinner Saturday night so they could all be together like the good old days.

Joe went to physical therapy every other day and with Mary Jo's help, he made better progress than expected.

The next day Joe visited his psychiatrist who saw that Joe was much happier. Joe told him what had happened.

The psychiatrist said that in light of things he didn't have to come so often. "I found the cure for my depression," Joe said. "The girl I love, that I told you about, has re-entered my life and she makes me feel great!"

"I'm happy for you, Joe. I hope I'll see you playing football again someday, too. Let's see you back a few more times, then if you feel better we'll call it quits. But you know I'm here for you any time."

Joe went home and told the good news to his parents, that the psychiatrist said he only needed to see him a few more times. They told Joe that they'd celebrate by inviting Mary Jo and her parents to the house for dinner.

At dinner that evening, they talked about the good old days and how it was a miracle that everybody was back together again.

"I'm so happy that we're all together again," Joe said to Mary Jo's parents. "I appreciate your accepting me like a son. I hope the future for me and you will be even better than the past. I truly love your daughter and I hope someday that we'll get married."

The next day Joe went for his physical therapy and as usual, Mary Jo was there to help. As he left, he told her he couldn't wait to see her tonight.

As Joe walked out of the office, he saw his old friend, Jim.

"Yeah, I'll be home for a few weeks," Jim said. "I'm playing professionally in Vegas, you know. Joe, do you remember when you were in high school, you'd sing a song and we'd have such a good time?"

"It was the best time in our lives. You remember my girlfriend Mary Jo? Well, she's back in my life again and we might get married."

"Hey, that's great. If you do get married, I'll play with my band at your wedding—no charge."

"I'd be glad to have you play at my wedding, Jim."

"I heard that your college coach is going to coach the Philadelphia team."

"Really? Where'd you hear that?"

"The news. He'll be great, don't you think? I mean, he's a great coach."

Later that day, Joe told his father that his old coach was coming to Philadelphia to coach. His father said he already knew about that because, like Jim, he had heard it on the news. "I hope when he comes here that we can invite him out for supper."

"Great idea, Dad."

The coach arrived the following week and Joe called Joe to ask him how he was doing.

"I hope you and I can go out for lunch together, coach," Joe said. "Then we can talk about the old days and the good times."

A couple of weeks later, Joe and his father went to the training camp to watch Philadelphia practice. The coach was happy to see him.

"Wait till after practice," he called to Joe. "We'll talk."

After practice, the coach introduced him to the other players as his second son.

Then the coach gave Tom a big hug and said, "I still believe that Joe can play pro ball. As soon as he's able I'll give him a chance."

"Thank you for encouraging and believing in Joe," Tom said. "This means a lot to the both of us, especially after all the hard work we've done."

As the months passed, Joe's health got better and better but the team didn't perform nearly as well. The coach was very disappointed. Maybe he could convince the owners to give Joe a chance to play the next season.

The next week, the coach introduced Joe to the team owner, Mr. Douglas. "Heard a lot about you, son," he said. I saw you play in college. Too bad you got hurt. If you like what I have to offer, you could sign a contract with me."

The contract, although not as good as Joe would have liked, was decent enough. And there certainly weren't many teams that would even make an offer, not to someone who'd sustained such a debilitating injury. So he signed the contract and shook hands with his coach and Mr. Douglas and left. Better than nothing, he thought.

He went home to tell his father that even though he didn't like the contract, it was a new beginning for him. His father told him he did the right thing and that all he had to do now was to prove himself to the owner.

Joe showed a lot of improvement at training camp. The coach told him that he wanted him to be a third string quarterback. "Don't let that discourage you," he said. "When the time comes, I'll give you a chance to play."

Joe didn't play much the first year, which disheartened him. The team did a little better that season but not good enough to make the playoffs.

Joe's father saw that he was discouraged and asked him what was wrong. "You should be happy; you've got the girl you love, but for some reason you really look sad."

"I'm very confused and I'm not sure I want to join the football team again or do something else, like sing professionally."

"I don't want you to leave Mary Jo and us and go away again. Give football another chance. I think something good will happen if you stay with it."

"Okay, Dad, I'll take that advice because I know we share the same dream."

After a few weeks, training camp started for the Philadelphia Tigers and Joe played better and better. The coach contemplated making Joe his starting quarterback, but decided to wait. After four straight losses, however, the coach had no choice.

Joe got excited about the opportunity to prove himself. His friends and family were all excited to see him play. He played his first game but unfortunately, his team lost. His coach and teammates told Joe that he had done a fantastic job but that one man couldn't carry a team. "Just keep working like you are," the coach said. "You'll see."

Joe got better and better as the weeks went by, and although everyone was impressed by his ability, the team fell one win short of making the playoffs. Everyone was disappointed, including Joe, but the coach told him, "Next season, Joe, you'll see. It's all a learning process and as a team, we're just now learning how to win."

After the 1974 season, the owner called Joe into his office and gave him a bonus for what he said was solid season, something they could build upon. He also gave Joe a new contract at almost twice his previous salary. Joe felt great about the new contract because he wanted to get married and he needed the money.

Joe went home and told his father and mother about the new contract. "You always gave me good advice," he told his dad, "and I think that now is the time to ask Mary Jo to marry me."

"Well, it's about time," his father said.

So the next day, he asked Mary Jo out for dinner at a good Italian restaurant. He asked Jim to be at the restaurant at a certain time to surprise Mary Jo with a song sung by Joe to Mary Jo. Jim said he'd be glad to.

That night Mary Jo and Joe went to the restaurant. The waiter helped Mary Jo take off her coat and then escorted them to their table. She looks so beautiful, Joe thought as he slid out her chair.

"I feel like the luckiest man in the world to have a girl like you," he said as he sat down.

Joe gave her a kiss and said, "I'll love you forever."

"And I'll love you forever too," Mary Jo responded.

Mary Jo saw their parents come in. She was surprised to see them. Mary Jo's mother said, "We don't want to disturb you. We'll just sit somewhere else."

"Nonsense, please, come sit with us," Joe said. "We insist."

"Thanks so much," Mary Jo's mother said as she sat across from her daughter.

The waiter arrived with a bottle of wine. He poured everyone a glass and they said cheers and drank a toast.

Then Jim came over with a guitar. "Jim, what are you doing here?" Mary Jo asked. "Do you have another surprise for me?"

"I guess it's not a surprise anymore," Jim said with a smile.

Joe pulled a red rose from his jacket and gave it to her. "This red rose is the symbol of my love for you. I want you to know that I've appreciated everything you've done for me to help me get better. I love you. And I want to express this love for you in a song written especially for you and this occasion. I call it, *I Will Love You Forever.*"

In my life, I never fell in love,
with anyone but you.
And I know in my heart
You love me too.
Remember the time,
When I took you to the prom.
We danced through the night
And we had a good time.
I know I made you cry
I tried to understand
I know I was wrong
And I sing for you my song.
Your love gives me new life
Your love gives me new strength
And now I know
I can play the game again.
I feel in my heart
My love belongs to you
For the rest of my life.

While Joe sang, he looked deeply into her eyes and held her hand. They were lost in each other's presence. As the song came to an end, everyone in the room applauded. They didn't understand until Joe said to Mary Jo, "Close your eyes, I have a surprise for you."

Joe took a small box out of his pocket and opened it to reveal a beautiful diamond ring. Joe asked her to open her eyes and the first thing she saw was the ring. Then Joe got down on his knee and said, "Mary Jo, will you marry me?"

Her eyes filled with tears and in a loud voice she said, "Yes, I will marry you!" as she threw her arms around him and kissed him.

Everyone in the restaurant applauded again and shouted congratulations. Mary Jo's and Joe's parents hugged and congratulated them.

Several people recognized him and it made him feel that this night was very special.

They went back to her parent's house to celebrate. Her father got out the wine glasses and a bottle of wine.

Then he raised his glass and said, "This is a special night for Mary Jo and Joe. I want to wish them good luck and good health. I'm glad to have such a fine young man as my son-in-law."

The next day Mary Jo's father told her that he wanted to invite Joe's family over for dinner to celebrate their engagement. Joe's parents were happy to accept.

That night, as they gathered around the table, Mary Jo's father raised his glass in honor of the engagement. "I wish my daughter and Joe all the happiness and joy. It's really a miracle that they were able to come together again." Everyone raised their glasses and toasted the happy couple.

Mary Jo got her guitar and they all sang songs together as they had in the past.

Later, Mary Jo told Joe, "I have never loved anyone as much as I love you. When I heard that you were sick, I knew I needed to come home to be with you."

Joe decided to surprise Mary Jo with a trip to Florida to celebrate their engagement. A friend of his from his Miami days was the manager of a big beach front hotel. He had called a few times when Joe was depressed but Joe hadn't felt like talking to him. Now he decided he'd surprise him. He made the plans and he and Mary Jo flew out the next day. When they arrived, they went to the hotel and Joe asked the desk manager if Pete was in. The manager asked, "Are you the guy whose picture is hanging on the wall?"

"That's me."

The manager gave him directions to Pete's office on the 5th floor. Joe, the best man at Pete's wedding, had sung *It's Amore* for him. On a whim, he started singing that song as he opened the door.

Peter rushed over, hugged him said, "Joe, my old friend. I'm glad you're looking and feeling so well. This is a very special surprise for me. How long are you gonna be here?"

"A week. I just got engaged and we're here for a little vacation." He introduced Mary Jo. Peter was very happy to meet her. "Joe was always surrounded with women but he only talked about you and how sorry he was to have lost you. I'm glad you got back together again. I'm going to call Shirley right now and we'll make plans to go out to dinner tonight. Are you staying here in the hotel?"

"Wouldn't have it any other way, Pete."

That night they went out to dinner and talked about old times. They got back to the hotel and went for a walk on the beach. As they approached the hotel, they heard a band playing and a man singing.

"Who's that?" Joe asked.

"He just started this week," Pete said. "He usually plays in Las Vegas."

They went inside to the bar and had a seat. At intermission, Joe went over to introduce himself. "I hear you play in Las Vegas. Do you know a man named Jim Grossi?"

"Grossi? Sure, Yes, I do."

"Well, he's a friend of mine. What's your name?"

"My name is John Morrale. Are you the football player? He talks about you all the time. He says you sing pretty well."

Joe shrugged. "On occasion. Can you do me a favor? I wrote a song for my fiancée to celebrate our engagement. Can you play it for us before we go back home on Saturday?"

"Give me a few days to rehearse and it shouldn't be a problem."

Joe and Mary Jo had a great time seeing Miami Beach and enjoying each others company before they embarked on their new life together and planned their wedding. They had spent some time with Pete and his wife, Shirley, too.

Their last night together they took a walk on the beach before dinner. They stopped at a bench by the stairs and kissed. "Mary Jo, this has been a special time for us this past week," Joe said. "It's been wonderful. I've missed you so much over the past years. Even though I dated other women, I never forgot you. I'm glad we overcame our differences. You'll be in my heart forever."

"Joe, I never loved another man like I love you. I was trying to make you jealous by telling you there was another man when there wasn't. That's why I came back home. We spent many years together in school and I didn't want to lose that. I know you loved me then and I know you love me now. And now that we're together again, we'll never part."

Then they heard the band playing and John Morrale singing, *I Will Love You Forever*. Mary Jo was overcome. "That's your song," she said to Joe. "What a wonderful surprise to have him sing it for us."

Joe was pleased that she liked his surprise. "I wanted to surprise you with it to show you how much I love you."

After it was over, they went up to the restaurant. Pete and Shirley joined them. Joe thanked John for playing the song. "You've a got a wonderful voice," Joe said. And he did.

After dinner, Pete invited them into the bar for a few drinks. Because it was their last night in Miami Beach, Pete had invited some of Joe's old friends to come say hello, but it was to be a surprise. So as they were sitting there, Pete said, "Joe, there's a couple of people I want you to meet at the bar."

Joe got up and walked over with him. As they approached, he saw his old friends. "Surprise, Joe!" they yelled. "Pete told us you were in town and we wanted to come say hello. We always remembered you when you played here. We wanted to congratulate you for playing with Philadelphia. And maybe someday you will win the super bowl!"

"I'm so glad to see you all again," Joe said. "I've always remembered the old times and I'd hoped to see you all again sometime." They shook hands then and said their goodbyes. Then Joe and Pete went back to the table.

"Pete," Joe said, "I was the best man at your wedding and I want you to be the best man at mine."

"I'd be honored to be your best man," Pete said. "I look forward to it. Just let me know when. And now I have another surprise for you. Shirley's expecting our first child and we want you and Mary Jo to be godparents."

Joe was overwhelmed. "Of course we will. And congratulations!"

They filled their glasses and saluted their good fortune. When it was time to leave, they hugged and kissed each other as they said their goodbyes.

"Thank you for showing us such a good time, Pete." Joe said. "It was wonderful. We've enjoyed every minute of it."

"It's been my pleasure. Good luck and have a safe trip home. We'll see each other again at your wedding."

The next morning Mary Jo and Joe flew home. Their parents met them at the airport. Mary Jo promised to tell them all about the trip.

Over the next several days, Mary Jo and Joe started to talk about the wedding date. Joe wanted a mid-May wedding, before the football season started. Mary Jo agreed and they started planning. They found a nice place in a nearby hotel. The manager, who'd heard of Joe, was glad to select a plan. He felt honored to have Joe's business and hoped that he would bring the championship to Philadelphia. "With God's help, I'll do my best," Joe said.

Joe sent out invitations to the coach, owners and some of the football players. He also thought about asking Jim to play at his wedding. Mary Jo heartily agreed.

Jim was glad to hear from him and said that he'd be more than happy to play at his wedding. "Joe, listen, why don't you come here for your honeymoon," Jim said. "My treat, hotel, food, you name it. It's on me."

"Hang on," Joe said. "Hey, Mary Jo, Jim just made us an offer we can't refuse. An all expense paid honeymoon in Vegas. What do you think?"

Mary Jo grabbed the phone. "Jim, oh you're so sweet. We'd love it. Thanks so much! I'm really looking forward to seeing you."

They spent a lot of time preparing for the wedding. Mary Jo took three weeks off from her job to prepare. Things couldn't have happened more smoothly.

Jim arrived in Philadelphia the night before the wedding. Joe and Mary Jo greeted him. Joe took Jim and his band-members to Jim's mother's house where they had lunch.

As they ate, she said that Joe and Mary Jo were the most wonderful couple she'd ever known. "I hope that my son Jim will find a new girl like you."

"Hey, Mom, I'm having a good time in Vegas being single and it'll be a long time before I'll make you a grandmother," Jim said in jest.

Everyone thanked her for lunch and said they'd see her at the wedding tomorrow.

Everyone arrived at the church on time and waited patiently for the bride to arrive. Within seconds, the music started and the ceremony began. The flower girls, so young and sweet looking, walked down the aisle followed by the bride and her father. The groom received the bride and with love in his eyes, they faced the priest and promised their lives to one another.

"You may kiss the bride," the priest said as the vows concluded.

It was a kiss they would always remember, a kiss that began their shared life together as husband and wife.

After the ceremony, everybody wished them a happy marriage, much love, and many children.

Joe's friends, the coach and the owner were at the reception to congratulate Joe and Mary Jo and wish them the best of luck. "Have a good time now," the coach said with a smile. "The honeymoon's over when the children start coming."

Joe could only grin.

Everybody had a grand time eating and dancing and many toasts were offered to the newly married couple.

Tom made a special toast. "We're proud to have been blessed with such a talented son."

Mr. Carlo Martino said, "I wish both of them much happiness and love. I've always treated Joe like a grandson and he's always called me Grandpa. And, you know, I feel like he's my grandson. God bless the bride and the groom!" Then he hugged them both. While he hugged Joe, he thought of his son, Joe. The last time he'd hugged him was when he left for the war. It was the last time he'd seen him.

He turned to the musicians and said, "Please play some good Irish and Italian music. It's traditional in our family."

"Don't worry," the bandleader said, "we play that kind of music a lot at weddings."

Then it was Luigi's turn for a toast. "I salute to this beautiful couple and to my beautiful daughter. I wish them good luck and many bambinos. Joe, you'll always be welcomed in my family. As you know, I have no sons but I've always looked upon you as my son. Now, I want to welcome you to the family." Everybody stood up and applauded.

Salvatore came in with his family and his son, Sam Jr. and they hugged.

Carlo had ordered the food for the wedding, pizza and veal parmigiano, which Sam and his family had set up. They owned a chain of franchised pizzerias. They were retired now, too. Sam Jr. didn't want the pizza business. He'd come a long way from fresh off the boat to where he was now.

When it was time for the first dance, Jim went to the microphone and said, "Ladies and gentlemen, welcome the new Mr. and Mrs. Joseph Palmer!"

After the bride and groom danced, the parents took the floor. Then it was Grandpa Carlo's turn to dance with the bride.

"Thank you so much for your help," Mary Jo said. "Joe thinks the world of you."

"Joe's always been a part of my family and I love him very much."

Then Jim took the microphone. "As many of you know, not only is Joe Palmer a great football player he's also a wonderful singer. And he's going to sing a beautiful song he wrote for a beautiful woman, his bride."

Joe stepped up to the microphone and said, "I call this song *My Darling*." Jim started playing and Joe started to sing.

When I saw you in my dreams

You were sweet and kind

And your smile

Never left my mind.
When I look in your eyes
I realize
I see your love for me in your eyes.
No matter where I go
No matter what I do
I'm always thinking of you.
When we walk through the night
We share the moonlight
And I sing my song for you.
Oh my darling
I'm glad I married you
And you said, Yes, I do
I will share my life with you.

Everyone was amazed, they had no idea Joe was so talented. After he was done, they applauded and told him that maybe he should forget football and become a singer.

The next day Joe and his bride flew to Las Vegas with Jim. A limo took them to the hotel where they spent the night. The next day they traveled around Las Vegas and visited sites of interest.

The next day Jim called Joe to come down to the hotel lobby to see a show. "Got you a spot right up front," he said.

But as Joe and Mary Jo settled in, Jim announced, "Ladies and Gentlemen, I have a special surprise. A good friend of mine just got married. He not only plays football for Philadelphia but he also sings like you won't believe. In high school, he'd sing with the band and everybody loved him. Please, Joe, I know you're on your honeymoon, but would you honor us by singing a love song to your new bride?"

Joe hesitated, but how could he say no? The whole house gave him a standing ovation and his bride had tears in her eyes after he finished his song. He walked to the table and she gave him a hug and kiss and told him she loved him with all her heart.

Not long after, a man walked to their table. "You don't know me," he said, "but I knew your father. We played ball together. I live in Philly. Can you give me an autograph for my grandson? He's a big fan."

"Yeah, sure," Joe said.

"Say hello to your dad for me, all right? Tell him you met Mike the Bull. Your father will know who I am."

The next day Joe and Mary Jo said goodbye to Jim. They'd had a wonderful honeymoon and they thanked Jim for all he had done.

"I'll be in touch," Jim said, "and I'll watch you on TV. Say, Joe, I'd be honored if you'd come here in the off season and sing."

"Thanks, Jim but my priority right now is football and to be close to my wife."

After that, they hugged each other and said their goodbyes.

When Joe and Mary Jo got back from their honeymoon, they were welcomed by the family with a special dinner cooked by Joe's mother.

Afterwards, Joe said to his father, "I met a man in Las Vegas named Mike the Bull. He said you'd recognize his name."

"Oh my God, I haven't seen him for such a long time. We used to play football together. He was one of the most powerful running backs I ever saw." He smiled. "We had some great times together. He'd set me up with blind dates. I met your mother on one of those blind dates. That's why he's so special. Because he introduced me to the girl of my dreams."

***

Joe and Mary Jo spent a lot of time looking for their dream house. After several weeks, Mary Jo saw a beautiful house outside Philadelphia, close to where Joe practiced. It couldn't be more perfect. They moved in right away and worked very hard to make it their home.

One morning Mary Jo woke up feeling sick to her stomach. It went on for a week and she knew, as women do, that she was pregnant. She called out to Joe and told him the good news.

"Let's go out tonight and celebrate," Joe said. "We'll stop by my parents and tell them the good news."

Training started a few days later and Joe felt great. He thanked God in prayer for giving him a wonderful new life.

The coach had a meeting on the first day of practice. "The honeymoon's over now, boys, it's time to knuckle down and play football. I expect nothing less than perfection, and with the new running back that we drafted last year, I see a championship ring on every finger."

The team did well in its exhibition games, which kept the coach happy. And they won the opener in lopsided fashion. But they kept on winning and when the season finished, they'd only lost two games, which qualified them for the playoffs. This team had super bowl written all over it. Joe had a super year, too, and all the sportswriters predicted that Philly was going all the way.

They won their first playoff game by two points-close but still a victory. They won their second game in a walk-over, it was as if the other team forgot to show up, and although the championship game was close, it was clear that Philly was the best team. Now it was on to the super bowl and hopefully, glory that would last for a very long time.

For two weeks before the super bowl the team practiced hard and often, although the coach didn't want to tire them out either. "I just want you guys to stay sharp and focused," he said over and over.

The night before the game, while the players were in the hotel having dinner together, the coach made a little speech. "You guys are playing very well and you know, I don't say this much, not ever, actually, but you're the best team I've ever coached. But remember, this is the biggest game we've ever played, the Super Bowl. A lot of players don't get this opportunity, no matter how good they are. This is a special day for us. Remember, when Joe sang *The Impossible Dream* on the plane home after our games? We hope this becomes the possible dream, to win the Super Bowl. So tomorrow, we're going to play the best game we can play and with a little luck, and God's help, we'll walk away with a big fat ring."

That night Joe had a dream. In it, he saw the same young man in uniform he saw before, who said to him, "My son, don't be worried about tomorrow. Just play as you have been and you'll do well."

Joe felt very optimistic about the game when he woke up. The nerves were gone. Somehow, having that dream and listening to the soldier helped calm him down. He wondered who the man was, but he couldn't worry about it right now.

The coach led them in a prayer later that day, praying that they'd have a good game, one without injuries. After the prayer, everybody stood up and cheered, "Let's win this thing!"

They could hear the crowd cheering as they approached the field. It excited the players and when the game started, they realized it wasn't going to be an easy win--the opposing team had a great defense. Shortly after the game started, Joe felt his confidence grow. Even the coach thought he was playing the best he ever had, which also helped the team play better.

At the end of the first half, Joe and his team were ahead by three points. At halftime, the coach gave his players encouragement and reminded them that they had to be more aggressive. "It's anyone's game, guys, and the only way we're gonna win this thing is to be more aggressive and smarter."

Joe's team fumbled the ball on their first possession of the second half, which resulted in seven points for the opposition. The teams traded scored until, with one minute left and Philadelphia in possession, Joe threw a spiral to the opponent's 40-yard line.

With time running out and behind by four points, the only thing they could do was throw the ball—unfortunately, the other team knew that, too. Joe took the snap, backed up three steps, looked right and then left and found a receiver open in the end zone. He threw a high wide pass and the receiver made an acrobatic catch and came down with his feet inside the line. Touchdown, Philly!

It looked like it might be a winning score, but the other team still had 40 seconds to do something. With only one timeout left, though, it wasn't going to be easy. They started moving the ball like a well-oiled machine and got down to Philadelphia's 30-yard line. Twenty seconds left on the clock. The opposing quarterback dropped back and threw a beautiful spiral into the end zone, and as the crowd gasped in expectation, the safety flicked the ball away. Game over.

Pandemonium broke out on the field. Joe was the hero. Everybody jumped for joy and the crowd went wild. The Philadelphia Tigers had won the Super Bowl!

Joe's father ran up to him and as he was giving him a big hug, said, "I knew in my heart, Joe, that someday you'd win the Super Bowl. I'm so happy for you."

After the game, the president of the league presented the trophy to the owner, the coach and his team. Joe got special recognition for being the most valuable player. He had tears in his eyes. This was a dream come true, not only for him, but his father, too.

The team president arranged a big party for the players and their friends. The first speaker was the team president. "Winning the Super Bowl is the greatest accomplishment I've ever had," he said. "I'm proud of my coach and the players. Now, ladies and gentlemen, I want to introduce to you the coach, Mr. Peter Reed, who did a super job."

The coach approached the mike to the sound of applause, and said, "Thank you Mr. President, for giving me the opportunity to coach this team. I want to thank the players for such a fantastic game. It was a lot of hard work, but the results speak for themselves. My father always told me, 'Hard work and discipline can make you a success in life.' This Super Bowl trophy will make me proud all my life. And I thank my family for their love and support. And God Bless America! Now, without further ado, I would like to introduce you to Joe Palmer, the most valuable player."

Everybody stood up and applauded as Joe went to the microphone.

"First I want to thank the President of the team for giving me the opportunity to play football for his team," Joe said. "He looked past my injury and gave me a chance. His belief in my ability helped win the Super Bowl. This is truly a dream come true for the whole team. And now I'd like to give special thanks to my beloved wife. Her support, love, and encouragement made me decide to play football again after I was sure I couldn't. Thank you, my love, for all you have done for me. I'll love you forever."

Mary Jo ran to Joe, threw her arms around him and told him she would love him forever, too. The crowd applauded.

"I know I made a long speech," Joe continued, "but I know my teammates expect me to sing, like we always do on the airplane after a win. I will in a few minutes but first I want to introduce a special person in my life, my dad. Thank you, Dad, for all the love and support you and Mom gave to me. Dad, I want to thank you for teaching me how to play football. Thank you for believing in me during good and bad times. It was your encouragement that kept me playing. Please, Dad, come up to the microphone."

Joe took his Super Bowl ring off his finger and said, "Dad, you taught me everything I know about football and you gave me the encouragement and support I needed. I might have played the game, but you're the real winner of the Super Bowl."

With that, he gave his dad his Super Bowl ring.

Joe's father gave Joe a big hug and said, "I'm so proud of you, son."

They got a standing ovation.

"Ladies and Gentlemen," Joe said, "I want to sing a song. I'd like to dedicate it to the team. The song is called *The Impossible Dream*."

Mary Jo handed Joe his guitar and he began to sing.

After the song was finished, everybody rose up and gave Joe a huge standing ovation. And their applause was genuine, Joe thought. They actually did admire his singing.

A week later, Joe decided to invite all of his family to his house for a celebration dinner.

Before dinner, they all had a drink together. Joe stood up, raised his glass said, "I owe everything I am to all of you. Winning the super bowl was a great accomplishment, but I didn't do it alone. Two years ago, when I was feeling down and out, I never would have thought that I'd ever be here today. I owe you two especially, Dad and Mary Jo. And everyone else for encouraging me and believing in me that I could do it, that I could get well enough to play again. Sometimes in life, we make mistakes. Sometimes you have to go through the worst to make things better and because of that, we appreciate it that much more. That's what happened to me and I thank God for what I have today. You, Mary Jo, I thought I'd never see you again. But because of our strong love, we got back together. We couldn't be apart. Now for the rest of our lives our love will get stronger and we're having a baby, which will make our love even better. I never expected this two years ago."

Tom got up and said, "Let's pray for the wonderful family that we have and how lucky we are to be here with each other. I also wish Mary Jo and Joe a wonderful future for them and their baby. Joe, I'll always be proud of you and whatever you do in life."

They saluted Joe and then sat down to dinner. Afterwards Tom said, "Don't forget that next week we're invited to the grand opening of Sam's new party house and restaurant."

Sam's party house was called *The Showtime Restaurant and Party House* in honor of Patrick and his wife who had both died about seven years earlier. It was owned and built by Sam's son and Carlo's nephew, Sam Sciarpa, who ran the construction company.

As they all sat down for before dinner drinks and conversation, Sam Sr. surprised Carlo by showing him pictures on the wall of Carlo and Patrick from many years ago when they first started their construction company. "I want to thank you for giving me a job all those years ago and then for naming this the Showtime Party House," he said to Carlo. He showed him a menu. On it was the Carlo special, lasagna.

Carlo laughed. "As long as you make the lasagna the way I do, I accept."

"Yes, just the way you like it," Sam said. Then he said, "I have a story to tell you, one that I've never told anyone before. But first let's salute Patrick, who isn't here with us today. Carlo, I want to thank you again for giving me a job when I first came to this country. Now I'm going to tell you the story of what happened before I came to this country. For two years, I worked on a boat that went back and forth from America to Italy. I was engaged to a woman named Angelina in Naples. I was trying to save up enough money to marry her and to work with my uncle in his pizzeria. That was my dream. But the second time I came home ready to marry Angelina, she wasn't there. She had run away to Rome with somebody else. I had loved her very much and I thought she had loved me too, but she didn't, not really.

For a while, I was very upset and distraught. I started drinking and spent almost all my money. My uncle tried to encourage me to come work with him, but my heart wasn't in it. One day I decided to go back to the ship and make some more money. I told my mother that I'd be back in a year, but I never came back. When I reached New York City, I jumped off the boat and went to my uncles in Philadelphia. After awhile I wrote to my mother and found out she was sick and dying. But I couldn't go back because I was here illegally. It broke my heart that I couldn't see her again before she died. I have never forgotten that. Today I'm an American citizen, which I'm very proud of. I plan to go back to Naples for a visit someday. I'd like to see my family and try to forget the bad memories. So you see, by rights I shouldn't even be here. I want to thank you Carlo and my beautiful wife, Dorete, and my friends and family who love me and gave me their support over the years. And remember, don't be strangers. I expect you all to come here once in awhile and have dinner on me."

Everyone applauded and said salute and wished him good luck in the future with the restaurant. Then they ate and drank and had a good time.

"You know, I've been invited to be on a talk show in New York," Joe said. "I'm going with Mary Jo. We're going to make it a mini vacation before the baby arrives."

Everyone wished him good luck and said they'd watch him on TV.

After the party was over, Joe said to Sam, "I wish you good luck with your restaurant. I'll be back. The food was wonderful."

"If it's not too much trouble," Sam said, "I'd like an autograph to put on the wall and one for the kids. And you know, you can come in any time and have dinner on me."

"Remember, Sam, Grandpa Carlo is like part of my family and you are too. I'll do anything I can to help you with the restaurant and make it a success. Perhaps I'll even come and sing for you sometime."

"I'd appreciate that. I wish you all the luck on the talk show."

A few days later Joe and Mary Jo drove to New York for his appearance. They planned to arrive a few days early to relax. The hotel was already reserved. They had a great time taking in the sights, The Statue of Liberty, The Empire State Building, The Chrysler Building, even Broadway. Time flew by and before they knew it, it was time to go to the studio for the show.

Joe was a little nervous as he waited his turn in the wings. The show started and Daniel gave his monologue. Then he said, "Tonight I have a special guest. He's the winning quarterback and the MVP of the Super Bowl. Ladies and Gentleman, I want you to welcome Joe Palmer from the Philadelphia Tigers. I know he plays great football but I hear he sings, too, and maybe, with some coaxing, he'll sing for us tonight."

Joe came out and sat down. "Thank you for inviting me to be on your show, Daniel. I'll be glad to answer any questions you have."

"First I want to congratulate you on a great game. It was fantastic to watch. I also heard some story about you singing on the airplane after the games."

"Yes, I do. Helps keep my teammates loose."

"Did this have anything to do with you winning the Super Bowl?"

"Daniel, we won because we're a good team with a genius coach who's like a second father to me. We've all worked hard to get to where we are today. And Jimmy Taylor at running back didn't hurt—he did a fantastic job. I nicknamed him Jim the Bull, I mean at six four and two fifty he's hard to bring down. I promised him that every time he ran for a hundred yards he'd get invited to my house for lasagna. He loves my mother's lasagna and he's always asking for second helpings! That's what helped us win, well, plus all our hard work. And you know, maybe it was our destiny to win, that it was supposed to be."

"Joe, if you sing like you play football, we're in for a real treat."

"Daniel, that wasn't part of the deal," Joe said jokingly. "That's going to cost you a little bit more money."

"Well, if I like your singing, you got a deal."

Joe smiled and said, "I'll sing the song I wrote for my wife, Mary Jo. It inspired me to do so much more with my life. I was very selfish and I almost lost her. But she loved me so much that she never wanted any other man in her life. When she heard I was injured a few years ago she came back home to take care of me. She's the inspiration because she loved me and believed that I'd play football again. I owe everything to her. I love her very much. The song's entitled, *I will love you forever*."

As usual, his singing surprised everyone who had yet to hear him.

Daniel got up and hugged him when it was over. "Joe, I said I'd give you a few more bucks if I liked your singing, well, I loved it."

"Glad you liked it, Daniel, and tell you what, just take that extra money and give it to the association for handicapped kids. I believe in giving something back to those who are less fortunate, especially kids."

"Thank you for being on my show, Joe, and for singing that wonderful song. I wish you great success next year and we'll all be pulling for you to win the super bowl again."

Joe left the stage to raucous applause.

The next day Joe and Mary Jo left for home. They wanted to spend a lot of time together before he went off to training camp. He really hoped he'd have another good year and he was thankful that he hadn't been injured. Knock on wood, he thought as he pondered next season and all those 300 pound linesman bearing down on him.

The coach's speech was fairly predictable. "We won the super bowl last year because we didn't have many injuries and because we've got lots of talent. I hope this year will be another Super Bowl year."

Everybody yelled in agreement and the coach said, "Let's play ball!"

The season arrived quickly. It was, Joe thought, as if he'd never left the playing field. They won the first five games, but during the sixth game one of those burly 300 pound linemen Joe often worried about, hit him so hard he didn't think he'd ever get up. "Stay down, Joe," his coach said as Joe tried to get up—to no avail. "Let the docs take a look at you."

Tom rushed from his seat and rode with Joe in the ambulance to the hospital. X-rays found that he had a severe concussion. They'd have to see what happened over the next few days.

Joe improved over the next three days, but the doctor told him he probably shouldn't play football again. Joe told his father that he had to play because the team needed him. Joe said he wanted a second opinion. But the second opinion didn't differ—if he played again he risked serious damage, maybe even worse. But even though the doctors advised against it, Joe insisted that he was going to play again.

One Sunday afternoon Tom said to him, "Come on, let's go for a walk in the back yard."

He put his arm around Joe and said, "Remember when you were little and I'd throw you the football? You did what I always wanted to do, play football professionally. You won the Super Bowl. You've made me the proudest father in the world. Now with your injury, if you should play again and get hurt, I'd be the saddest father in the world. You have a beautiful family that you love dearly. So my question is; why do you want to take a chance on your health? You have enough money to live comfortably for the rest of your life. Like I told you before, everything in life is timing. There's a time to use good reasoning and common sense. The way I see things now, Joe, it's time you retired from football and dedicated your life to your wife and baby. They sacrificed a lot for you and they need you. Now is your time for them."

After thinking for a few minutes, Joe said, "Thanks for the advice, Dad. I know you're right but, Dad, it's my decision and mine alone."

They went back into the house and Joe told his dad that he'd make a decision in a couple of days. His father said, "I hope you'll do the right thing for your family because they all love you, Joe."

A couple days after their meeting, Tom was rushed to the hospital. The doctor said that the sickness he'd contracted during the war had returned and gotten worse. It was affecting his lungs and he only had about six months to live. "I can't give you an exact date, Joe," the doctor said, "but it won't be too long."

Joe was devastated. He thought about his retirement and it finally became real to him. If he retired, he could be with his dad for his final days. There really was only one choice.

His father was discharged from the hospital a week later. Joe picked him up and brought him to his house for dinner so they could spend some time together.

During dinner, Joe told everybody that he planned to retire from football. Even though he loved the game so much, he believed in his heart that it was time to quit. "I realize that spending time with my family is more important than making more money. I have enough to live on for the rest of my life," he said.

Everyone gave Joe a big hug and encouragement.

A week later, Joe met with his fellow players and the coach. At that meeting, he told them about his decision to retire.

"This is a very hard decision for me, but I realize that at this time my family and my health are the most important things. I will truly miss each and every one of you and I'll miss you, coach. You've been like a father to me. I'll go to every game, count on it."

The coach, speaking for himself and the team, said, "We all respect your decision and wish you and your family the best. We will all miss you. As a coach, you made me very proud."

Joe left the building with a saddened heart but he knew he had done the right thing.

Now that he was retired, Joe spent every moment he could with his father. He took him for walks, to the movies, out to dinner. They spent a lot of time just talking. He planned weekend vacations with just the two of them. At times when he looked into his father's eyes, he felt that he knew that his time was almost over. He always made sure to tell his father how much he loved him and how much he appreciated him having adopted him and giving him a good life. "If it wasn't for you encouraging me, Dad, I never would be the man I am today. Happy, successful, with a good family and no financial worries."

Joe wanted to do something special for his father. He had always driven a Cadillac but never a new one, always used. So Joe went to a dealership and bought a car for him. He made arrangements to pick it up in a week.

He also wanted to surprise his father with a weekend in Atlantic City because he knew his father loved to gamble. So as they left the house that morning he told him he had to stop by a car dealership to look at a car. After they arrived, Joe went inside, got the keys and signed the papers.

While he was doing that, his father was looking at a beautiful maroon Cadillac next to their car. As Joe came out, he said, "Joe, look at this car, isn't it a beauty?"

"Yes it is." He smiled. "And here are the keys to it. See if it starts."

"Joe, are you crazy? Are you stealing this car?"

"Dad, it's yours, I bought it for you. You deserve this after all the things you've done for me my whole life."

Tom was overwhelmed and with tears in his eyes, gave Joe a big hug. "Thank you, son, this is a wonderful gift."

"Let's drive this to Atlantic City and have fun," Joe said. "We'll have someone pick up my car and take it home."

While in Atlantic City, they took in a lot of nighttime entertainment. They had a great time together.

One afternoon Tom said to Joe, "Joe, you've given me so much joy during your life. I'm very proud of you. If I die tomorrow, I'd be a happy man knowing that you've accomplished so much."

Joe gave his father a hug.

Joe thought about having a banquet to honor his dad. His birthday was coming up—a perfect time. He'd get some of the coaches and players together from high school and college. He called everyone he knew and set it up.

The next week Joe told his father he was going to take him for a special surprise for his birthday. They walked into the restaurant and everyone stood up and said hello to Tom and wished him many more birthdays.

Tom was very surprised to see all the coaches and many of the players he knew. He hugged everyone and shook their hands. As could be expected, he'd been feeling incredibly depressed, but this outpouring of affection touched him deeply. The Tigers coach said, "Tom, that ring looks good on your finger. Not too many fathers have the privilege to wear a ring like that."

"Thank you for helping my son win the super bowl," Tom said. "I'll always remember this. I feel like I won the super bowl myself!"

They had a great dinner, filled with laughter and conversation and the general feeling that times like these should never end. Afterwards Tom asked Joe to sing a song. "Remember when you used to sing on the plane."

"I'll be happy to sing for you," Joe said.

On the way home, Tom thanked Joe for the special surprise. "I can't thank you enough for tonight. I love you, son."

In his heart, Tom felt that time was running out for him. But he'd always remember this night and how good his son was to him. He felt that he was his own child even though he wasn't. He couldn't have asked for a better son. He only wished that he could have been his real father.

A few weeks later Tom complained of not feeling very well. The pain was excruciating. Joe called the ambulance and had his father rushed to the hospital.

The doctor told them he only had a little time left. The family gathered around his bed to say goodbye. Joe was holding one of his hands and Lina the other. They tried to cheer him up, but Tom felt he'd be leaving soon—the pain was so bad, he just wanted it to end.

"I'm glad I married you," he said to Lina. "And Joe, I'm glad I adopted you. These are the two best things I ever did in my life. Both of you have given me so much joy and happiness over the years. I was very proud to fight for my country. My father would always tell me, 'Tom, this is a great country to live in.' My father was from Ireland and he loved this country very much. He came to Philadelphia as a young man and used to take me to see the Liberty Bell. He'd say this was the symbol of freedom in America. If you work hard and try to be honest, you can become a great success. I always remembered that."

Then he took the super bowl ring from his finger and gave it back to Joe. "Thank you for letting me wear this ring. It meant a lot to me. But I'm giving it back to you because my time is over. Don't be sad for me. I've had a good life and now it's time for me to go. Remember when we played football in the back yard? I always told you what a great player you were and that maybe one day you'd win the super bowl and you'd laugh at me. But guess what, you did! Whenever you look at that ring, I hope you'll remember me. Never feel sad for me and always remember all the good times we had together. God bless you, Joe, and take good care of your mother. She's a good woman and loves you very much."

"Dad, I promise I'll take care of her always. And know that I'll love and remember you for as long as I live."

"Tom," Lina said, "I fell in love with you the first time we met and you'll always be in my heart."

"Honey, could you give me some water?" Tom asked.

Lina poured some water for him and he said, "This tastes so good."

Then he laid back, closed his eyes and passed away.

They had the viewing the next day. Many good friends, team members, coaches and the owner of the football team paid their respects. They all lined up to give Joe their sympathy. Tom was well liked by everyone who knew him.

The coach said, "Joe, your father was a great man. He felt like a brother to me."

Joe embraced the coach and thanked him for such a nice compliment.

At the service, Lina asked Joe to sing *Ava Maria*. Someone else had been scheduled but Lina said to Joe, "When you were young you'd sing *Ava Maria* so beautifully. Your father loved the way you sang it and I know he'd love to have you sing it again for him one last time."

Joe agreed and went to the piano. He sang *Ava Maria* with such emotion that everyone was overcome with tears.

After the service and the burial, they went to Sam Sr.'s restaurant to have a meal in Tom's memory.

After they had eaten, Sam Jr. made a speech. "Joe, you lost your father who you

loved so much. He was a great man. Your father was a good friend to me too, he treated me like his son and I thought of him like my own father. We always had a good time together. Whenever I wanted to see you play, he always got me tickets. He was generous like that. I'll always remember him."

Then Joe presented Sam with a picture of himself in his uniform with his father standing next to him.

"Thank you. I'll hang it on the wall and when people ask me about it I'll tell them about you and your wonderful father."

Overcome, Joe got up and hugged Sam. "Sam, thank you for your kindness. This means so much to me. You'll always be like a member of my own family."

"Joe, you're welcome here anytime and dinner is always on me in memory of your father."

Carlo Martino told Joe, "Your father was like a brother to my son and I feel like I've lost another son."

"Thank you, Grandpa," Joe said. "I love you like you were my real grandfather."

Then the time came for everyone to say his or her goodbyes and farewells. Joe and his mother thanked everyone for coming.

Now that his father was gone, Joe felt a terrible emptiness inside. He had lost one of the most important people in his life, his dad, his best friend and his teacher.

Joe spent a lot of time with his mother after the funeral talking about the family business. His mother relied on Joe to take care of everything. Joe helped his mother and he helped take care of his pregnant wife. Planning for the baby's arrival kept everyone full of hope, joy and excitement.

Joe and Mary Jo spent a lot of time together preparing for the arrival of the new baby. They decided that if it was a boy he would take Joe's father name.

A couple of months later Mary Jo went to the hospital and gave birth to a baby boy. They named him Tom. The baby was born healthy but after three days, the doctor noticed something unusual. The diagnosis--a slight case of mental retardation. He felt though that with proper medication and time it would not be too great a handicap.

Joe and Mary Jo were shocked about the diagnosis. But they realized that no matter what, they'd have to accept what God had given them. They all believed that their faith in God would pull them through. "We're going to dedicate ourselves to making this child as loved and as happy as any other child," Joe said.

The next night during dinner, Joe said to Mary Jo, "We have a lot of things to overcome for the sake of the baby, but with the help of God I know our son will be all right. Now that I'm retired I've decided that I'm going to dedicate my time helping handicapped children like our son by raising money."

Joe promised himself that he would open a foundation to help handicapped children and that all the money he raised would benefit the foundation. It was a new challenge for Joe, which gave him a new life goal. And maybe, just maybe, it was the way it supposed to be.

Mary Jo loved the idea. She told him that his heart was definitely in the right place. She reminded him of how much she loved him which made Joe feel lucky and blessed to have such a loving family.

With his father gone and Joe himself now in retirement, he decided he couldn't just sit around and do nothing. Everyday, as he looked at his own son, he was reminded of how he wanted to help other handicapped kids. But he wasn't sure how to go about it.

One night he had a dream. He dreamt about his father who said, "Joe, God gave you another talent, to sing. I think you should use that talent for a good cause. Because of your own son being handicapped, singing to raise money for other handicapped children who don't have as much would be wonderful. Sometimes we do things for the money and other times we do things because it's the right thing to do."

When Joe woke up, he told Mary Jo and his mother about his dream. He'd been looking for some way to raise money for the kids and this was the way, he could feel it.

"This is what I want to do, "he said. "Dad told me to sing and raise money for handicapped children and that's what I'm going to do."

A few days later Joe got together with a group of businessmen who highly endorsed his idea. They told him to talk to someone at a TV station about getting airtime to host a show in order to raise money for his foundation. Joe liked the sound of that.

He found a TV station that was willing to sell him airtime so he talked to the manager about his idea. When the manager saw that it was Joe Palmer, the famous football player, he was quite surprised and welcomed him warmly. He called in his staff and everyone told him what a wonderful career he'd had. They also told him they felt bad that he wasn't playing football anymore. Their adoration made Joe feel great.

"Thank you for the great welcome," he said. "I have another goal to accomplish now and that's why I'm here today."

He went on to describe his plan to help handicapped children. "I don't know if you realize that besides playing football, I also sing and play the piano. I want to raise money for handicapped children because I myself am the father of a handicapped child. I don't need the money; I want to do it for the kids. This is my new life's mission."

"Joe," the manager said, "if you can sing as well as you play ball, you'll raise a lot of money for your kids. And because I've heard you sing, I suspect things will work out great. I'll find a time slot and let you know the time and date."

Joe thanked everyone concerned and they all told Joe they'd do the best they could to make sure that he achieved his goal. Joe shook hands with everybody and went home with the good news.

Mary Jo saw the big smile on his face. "What?" she said.

"Great news, honey, the TV station loved my idea and they'll let me know what time slot they'll have available for me to play."

Mary Jo beamed. "Joe, what you're doing for the handicapped kids is wonderful and I'm really proud of you."

The following Sunday Joe's in-laws invited them to dinner. After dinner, he shared the great news--that he was going to be on TV. He addressed his father-in-law for the first time as Dad. He asked him if he would play his guitar with him and Mary Jo to make it more entertaining. He also thought he'd be more relaxed and comfortable if he played with people he knew. They both agreed and were happy that he'd asked them. He asked them if they could start practicing the next night. He wanted to be ready when the time came. They agreed to meet at seven the next evening.

The next night they got together and practiced. They all thought it sounded good. "I can't believe I'm going to be on TV," Mary Jo's father said. "It's never too late to be a star!"

They practiced every night and got better and better. One night Joe got a call from the station manager telling him that he had a one-hour spot the next Sunday from 7 to 8 in the evening. Everybody was excited but also nervous. It was finally coming true!

As Sunday approached, and despite their nervousness, they all felt confident in what they were going to do. They had all played in front of large crowds before and knew what to expect.

They arrived at the TV station two hours before the show. They were greeted by the station manager who showed them where they would be performing and where to put their equipment.

Then the station manager introduced Joe to Mr. Robinson, the director of the Institute for Handicapped Children. Joe had a rush of strong feelings for him. He gave Mr. Robinson a sturdy handshake and said, "I'm so glad to meet you. I totally believe in what you stand for. I believe that we as a team can help a lot of handicapped children."

"I wish you the best of luck with your show and I hope you bring in a lot of money!" Mr. Robinson said.

Before they knew it, it was show time.

"Ladies and Gentlemen," the station manager said into the microphone, "I want to present a man from Philadelphia. A man who helped win the Super bowl. Most of you have already heard of him. It may surprise you to know that as well as being a great football player; he also sings and plays the piano. Tonight this superstar has a new mission--to raise money for handicapped children. It's my pleasure to introduce the Super bowl champion, Joe Palmer!"

Joe took the microphone from the station manager and said, "Ladies and Gentlemen, it's a pleasure to be here and sing for you. As you've heard, I'm here to help raise money for handicapped children. I've started a foundation that'll give help and money to those who need it. I'm doing this because I'm the father of a handicapped child. I know how much they need special help and that, of course, takes money. I'm not making money off of this. All the proceeds will go directly to the children. And now I'd like to sing a song that I hope you'll enjoy. It's dedicated to all my fans and the people of Philadelphia. It will always have a special place in my heart. *God Bless America*."

The phones rang off the hook with donations after the song ended. The people of Philadelphia loved Joe's singing and his cause, and they opened their wallets to show him how much. His show was a success and everybody was delighted and encouraged Joe to keep up the good work. He raised more money than he had ever imagined. Afterwards, it came to him that maybe he could do this in other cities as well.

A lot of people called Joe's house the next day to congratulate him. They were surprised that he could sing so beautifully.

Mary Jo took a call from a woman named Ann who wanted to talk to Joe about something important.

"Mr. Palmer, you don't know me and I'm sorry to disturb you. My name is Ann Morgan. First, I want to congratulate you on the beautiful show you did last night. Myself, my husband and my two twin boys were very impressed. You're my son's hero. Between your football playing and your singing, they think you're a very special person. Last year they both played football. They're both eleven. Recently my son David was diagnosed with leukemia. We're having a hard time dealing with it, as you might well imagine. We don't know if he'll live another year. I have a big favor to ask of you. This Saturday is David's birthday. He'll be twelve. He's still in the hospital. We're going to invite some of his friends from the football team and have a small party for him. Mr. Palmer, do you think you could come and sing happy birthday to him? As I said, you're his hero. I know you're a busy man so I'll understand if you can't."

Joe, overcome with emotion, said, "Ann, call me Joe. And thank you for calling me. It'll be my pleasure to come to the hospital and sing for your son. It's what I love doing. I'm devoting myself to helping sick and handicapped children in any way I can. What time do you want me there, and where do you want me to go? And let's not tell anyone. We'll make it a surprise for the kids."

They talked about the details for a few more minutes and then hung up. Joe told Mary Jo the story and what he was going to do to make the day special. She was very touched.

That Saturday Joe went to the hospital. Ann's husband George was outside the room waiting for him to arrive. He had the birthday cake and handed it to Joe. Then he lit the candles. He made sure the time was right and then Joe entered. As he came through the door, he started singing.

Happy Birthday to you

Happy Birthday to you

Happy Birthday, dear David

Happy Birthday to you

The children were, of course, surprised and elated. David knew right away that it was his hero, Joe Palmer. "It's Joe Palmer, its Joe Palmer," he started yelling at the top of his lungs. "This is the best day of my life!"

Then it was time to blow out the candles, which David did. Joe gave him a big hug and wished him happy birthday.

"Mr. Palmer," David said, "thank you for coming to my birthday party. This is the best present I've ever had!"

Joe was touched. "I'm glad to be here, David. You're a brave young man. I promise that next year on your birthday you and your family will be my guests at a Philadelphia Tigers football game."

He brought out a bag, took out an autographed picture of himself in his football uniform and gave it to David. He also gave one to every kid there. He gave David a signed football and wished him happy birthday.

"David, May God Bless you and give you health and happiness and may all your dreams come true. Please call me any time you want and we'll talk."

Ann and her husband stepped outside with him. They hugged him and thanked him profusely for coming to the party. "David and all of us will never forget you and what you have done for us," Ann said. "You've made it a special day for him."

"It was my pleasure. Really. What about your other son, Joshua? How does he feel about David being sick?"

"Joshua quit football since David got sick. He's very upset. We tried to encourage him the best we could, but each twin responds to the other when something is wrong and this was no different. The doctor said there's nothing wrong with Joshua but he feels guilty about being well when David is so sick."

"I hope everything turns out well for you and that David gets better. Please call me if there's anything else I can do."

He said goodbye to them both, got into his car and drove home. On the way, he wondered if what happened to the twins might have happened to him too. Maybe I've got a twin out there, too, he thought. Just too many coincidences for there not to be. He decided that one day he'd go to Italy and find the orphanage where he was adopted and start looking for his twin.

He told Mary Jo about what had happened. "This is the best thing I've ever done. I wish I could do more."

She kissed him and said, "Joe, I love you. You're the best man I've ever met."

Unfortunately, a few months later they heard again from Ann. David had just died but she wanted to thank him again for what he had done. "David said he'd never forget his special birthday present, and he didn't."

"Ann, I want to sing *Ava Maria* for his funeral service. Would that be okay?"

"Thank you, Joe. David would like that."

"Let me know the time and place and I'll be there."

The service was held later that day. When the time arrived, Joe sang a beautiful *Ava Maria* that brought tears to everyone's eyes.

After the service, Ann and her husband thanked him again for all he had done.

When Joe went home, he told Mary Jo, "Honey, I feel good about what I did for that boy and his family. This is something I want to keep doing, helping others. When I was little, I used to go to my Grandfather John's tailor shop. I'd see how he treated his customers, like family. He'd say, 'Giuseppe, remember to do something good for people and you will be rewarded.' This is what I've learned today. That if I do good things, I'll be rewarded. He always gave me good advice. It's his birthday next week so don't forget, we'll be going to the cemetery to see him."

The following week, as they did every year, they picked up Grandmother Lina and went to the cemetery to celebrate Grandfather John's birthday. On the way there, Joe said to them, "I never told you this before but one day I overheard him praying. He said, 'God, I know pretty soon I'll be coming to see you. Thank you for sending me to Italy so long ago to bring my beautiful grandson Joe home to America. He has given me so much joy in my life. I'm very impressed by his talent. And especially that he would learn the old songs from Italy for me. I hope he'll keep growing in the right direction in the ways that I have advised and will one day fulfill the destiny you have for him.'

"Grandma, I loved him very much and that's why I always celebrate his birthday in remembrance of him."

After they arrived at the cemetery, they put some flowers on his grave and said a short prayer. Each person took a moment to remember him and hoped that he was well where he was, and watching over them.

One day Mary Jo took the baby to the neighborhood park. A lot of people congratulated her on the show. They told her to tell Joe to keep up the good work and that he was doing a great thing for the kids.

Hearing everyone's reactions made Mary Jo very proud of Joe. She went home and told him all about it. The encouragement inspired Joe to try the same thing somewhere else. He wondered where he could go next with his show.

Then, unexpectedly, Joe got a call from Jim in Las Vegas. The timing was perfect. Jim said he hoped all was well with him and his family. He said he had gotten a call from his mother who had told him about the wonderful show Joe had put on for the handicapped children and about how well Joe could sing.

"My mother said you had a wonderful voice and that your TV show raised a lot of money for handicapped children. Joe, if you come out here to Las Vegas for about a month, we could raise a lot of money with my band and your voice."

"Thanks for the offer, Jim. Let me talk it over with Mary Jo and see what she thinks."

"Let me talk to her for a few minutes."

Joe gave Mary Jo the phone.

"Mary Jo," Jim said, "what do you think about Joe coming to Las Vegas and doing a show?"

"Jim, it does sound good, but I have to talk it over with Joe first."

"Okay, take your time. Whatever you both decide will be fine with me. Call me back when you decide."

"Joe, I know this means a lot to you," Mary Jo said after she hung up, "and I know that a city like Las Vegas can raise a lot of money for you. But I'm going to stay here. I have little Tom to take care of and I think it's better I stay home to do that. But I'll miss you and I know you'll accomplish a lot of great things."

Joe gave her a kiss and thanked her for her love and support.

Joe called Jim and told him he'd accept his offer to play there.

"Great, listen, let me talk to the casino manager, I'm sure he'll be delighted."

Joe talked to Mary Jo about it and he agreed to go meet with them.

"I'll have a limo pick you up at the airport and take you to the casino," the manager said. I'm glad you're coming."

Joe was taken to the hotel that Sunday. At the same time, another limo was waiting to pick up a passenger.

A man left the hotel and the chauffer opened the door for him. But before he got in, he looked over at Joe and waved. Why's he waving at me, Joe wondered. Then he went inside the hotel. The man was Giorgio Fiorino, in Las Vegas for a one-night concert. For some reason when Giorgio saw Joe, he remembered his mother telling him how proud she was of him and his brother. He'd waved because he actually felt like he knew the man.

Joe went inside the hotel to meet Bill, the manager. He told him he'd just seen a man leaving in a limo and wondered who he was. "That was Giorgio Fiorino," the manager said, "the tenor from the Metropolitan Opera House in New York. He was here for a one-night concert. You know, you two bear a strong resemblance."

"You think so?"

"Yeah, yeah, I do."

For some reason Joe felt a connection with him. He needed to know more about Giorgio Fiorino.

Jim and his band also welcomed him and told him they were glad to see him again. Then Joe went to the manager's office. They talked and the manager said that Joe could sing there for a month with Jim's band backing him up. "I'm looking forward to it," he said.

They arranged for him to start in a week. That would give the band and Joe time to practice. Joe agreed and talked to his wife about it.

She was delighted with the idea. Joe said he'd do it for just a month. He didn't want to be away from his home and family longer than that.

The week fairly flew by and soon it was time for the grand opening of Joe's act. He and Jim and the band thought they were ready. Joe felt a little nervous, he had never sung before so many people before, but Jim told him not to worry. He had a great voice and everyone would love him.

Jim and his band came out first and played a few numbers. Then he went to the microphone and introduced Joe. "Ladies and Gentlemen, we have a special guest here tonight. A close friend that I went to school with in Philadelphia. Not only will some of you recognize him as a world champion football player but he's also got a great singing voice and plays the guitar. It's my pleasure to introduce you to Joe Palmer!"

Everyone started clapping. The audience's reaction encouraged Joe and gave him the confidence he needed to sing his best. He thanked the audience and said, "Thank you very much, you're very kind. I want to dedicate my first song to the wonderful country that we live in. *America the Beautiful.* As you know, I'm singing here to help raise money for handicapped children. I hope you'll enjoy it."

Joe sang the song with so much emotion that when he was finished the audience stood up and gave him a standing ovation. Their adoration made the rest of his concert that much easier.

The night was a total success and he raised a lot of money. After the show, he went into the lobby and people gave him a lot of checks. They also wanted his autograph.

Some people jokingly asked him if he was singing to make more money, but Joe replied, "I'm doing it because I love to sing and because I have a handicapped son who I love very much. I'm going to put the money into a fund for all handicapped children like my son. It's something that I've always wanted to do. And you have my word that every penny will go to help handicapped children."

One night when he was at the hotel having dinner, the manager approached Joe and said, "Congratulations. Everybody loved your singing. I'd like you to sing for me next month, too. What do you think?"

Joe shook his head. "I promised my wife I'd sing for the summer, and that's it. Sorry."

"Well, if you ever change your mind, the invitation is always open."

One night Mary Jo called the hotel looking for Joe. The manager told her that he was on stage singing and he would give him the message when he was done.

After the show, the manager gave Joe the message. Concerned, Joe called home. Mary Jo almost never called him.

"Honey, is everything okay?"

"Everything's fine, but I have a big surprise for you. First, I have to apologize to you. You used to tell me that someone was missing from your life and I didn't believe you. Well, I just found out that you have a brother named Giorgio Fiorino, the famous opera singer. And that Grandpa Carlo really is your grandfather."

Joe was overcome. "Is this true? Are you certain?"

"Yes, Joe, it's true."

"Honey, how did you find out?"

"By chance Grandpa Carlo met a man named Rino Forte. He came to the house and saw a picture of your Grandpa Carlo's son, Joe, and realized he knew about him and your mother."

"How could this happen? That he came to America and met Grandpa Carlo?"

"Joe, when you come home you'll find out what happened."

Chapter Four – Rino Forte

Rino was only eleven when he was wounded during a German attack. His mother took him to a convent manned by nuns, which was also used as a makeshift hospital.

One night Rino overhead a conversation between Maria, the mother of twin boys, and a nun, Sister Theresa. The sister asked Maria who her twin's father was and she said he was an American soldier, Sergeant Joe Martino from Philadelphia.

Rino's health eventually got better and he was able to leave the convent, but he was still deeply disappointed because he'd learned that he would walk with a limp for the rest of his life. It prevented him from playing sports, which he loved to do. His mother tried to encourage him to use his other talents, like playing the piano, which he had promised his father he would do while he was away in the war.

Rino was made fun of at school because of his limp. He'd cry as he watched his friends play soccer because he couldn't join in the fun.

When his mother asked him what was wrong he'd tell her.

"God has given you a special talent, to play the piano," she said as she looked into his eyes, "and if you work hard and try with all your might, someday you'll be somebody and those laughing children will applaud you."

At that moment, his five-year-old sister, Lisa, came through the door.

"We're all going to get together at church and we're going to pray to God for your father to have a safe return from the war in Russia," their mother said. "When he does return he'll be proud of how well you play the piano."

They prayed for his father's safe return, but the only answer they received was from the Italian government who hadn't heard anything and who warned that he might be dead. But in her heart, his mother felt that he was still alive, that one day he might return.

Their mother continued to apply for help from the government and they eventually decided to give her a sorely needed pension.

As the years went by, Rino became a good student in both the classroom, and in the music room—he played the piano beautifully.

Despite that, his relationship with the opposite sex was at a standstill—it was his bad leg, he decided. What else could it be?

One night at dinner, his mother noticed a sad look on his face and asked him what was wrong.

At first Rino didn't want to talk about it. Then Lisa, who loved Rino very much, told him he should be honest with his feelings because family was all they had.

"We'll be there to support you no matter what," she said.

So Rino opened up and told them that every time he asked a girl to go out with him, they always had an excuse. "I know it's because of my limp, even though they don't say that."

"Remember that your last name is Forte," his mother said boldly. "It means strong, and you have nothing to worry about. It's time for you to go to Rome to study the piano. I have a grant from the government to help you pay for the schooling. My son, someday you'll find a girl who'll love you for the way you are. And I also have faith that someday you'll be a famous pianist."

At eight years old, Lisa was half Rino's age. She did well in school and especially excelled at art and fashion drawing. Her teacher was very impressed and asked her what she wanted to do in life. She said that she wanted to design beautiful dresses.

Her mother had a sister who sewed to help support herself. They decided to go into business together to help support both families. After school, Lisa helped out by doing some of the sewing for them. They got a lot of their business from the nearby American air base. She did a fine job and they made good money. The business thrived for five years, until Lisa turned thirteen when the American air base decided they didn't need to send their things out anymore. They had to find another way to make money. Lisa did what she could, she designed wedding dresses and because she had an eye for detail and fashion, they got a lot of business.

During that time, Rino played the organ for Father Antonio in the church. In the summer, he played in hotels for tourists to make extra money. His dream was to save enough money to go to the conservatory and study the piano.

A guest congratulated him afterwards. "My name is Mr. Morelli," he told him, "you have surprising skill. This isn't the place for you. You should come to Rome and go to the conservatory. I'll introduce you to the administrator and we'll see what we can do. I'm certain you'd qualify for a scholarship."

"I'd love that," Rino said. "That's why I'm playing here, to save money so I can attend. I'll talk to my mother about it."

His mother gladly gave her consent, but she was sad too, because it meant Rino would be far away. Still, she knew about his dream and wanted to help him fulfill it.

Rino went to the conservatory with Mr. Morelli and met with the administrator who, amazed with his talent, arranged for him to take lessons from their best teacher. The teacher was very impressed—he'd never had a student who had so much talent. The boy had great promise.

His mother made arrangements with a cousin in Rome who agreed to let him stay with him until he found a place of his own. He worked hard at the conservatory and continued his studies until he turned twenty-three.

After graduation, the conservatory customarily sent its graduates on concert tours in Italy to gain experience. Rino invited his mother and sister to his first concert. Afterwards, his mother told him that his father would have been happy that he was following his dream.

Rino went on to play more concerts and as his expertise grew, so did his name recognition. He had become a star.

One day, while at the conservatory to visit his teacher, he saw a young woman, a soprano, singing while his teacher played. She had amazing range and power.

"Wonderful, just wonderful," he said after she'd finished.

"This is Stephanie Romano from New York City," the teacher said. "She's come to Italy to learn Italian and to study opera. She studied at the Eastman School of Music in Rochester. When she graduated, her teacher recommended that she come here to Rome to continue her lessons."

"It's nice to meet you, Ms. Romano," Rino said. "Your last name is Italian."

"Yes, I'm of Italian descent. My grandfather was from Rome. I always wanted to see the country and now I have the opportunity."

"If there's anything I can do to help you, please don't hesitate to ask."

"Thank you very much, I appreciate that."

Eventually, they became friends and went out for coffee and sometimes dinner. Rino helped her with her Italian and the different aspects of Italian life. Sometimes he, Stephanie and his friend, Luigi, would put on concerts and play together. Over time, Rino began to develop feelings for her. And why not? She was talented, beautiful, Italian. How much better could it get? And the best part was--she didn't seem to mind his limp at all.

Stephanie noticed that Rino was falling in love with her, but unfortunately, she didn't feel the same way. She liked him very much, but love was another matter entirely. She had a reason why she couldn't fall in love with him, though. She knew she was leaving soon to go home and didn't want to get involved with anyone.

Stephanie decided she had to talk to him about this and invited Rino for coffee the next day.

"Rino," she said as soon as they sat down, "I have something very important to tell you."

"Yes, Stephanie, I'm listening."

"Rino, listen carefully. I appreciate everything you've done for me. Helping me with my singing and learning the language, I can never repay you. I'll never forget that. I hope you'll always be my friend. But I don't have the same feelings for you. I know that you're falling in love with me, but I can't love you back like you want. This is not a good time for me. I'm sorry about that because I truly care about you. I hope someday that you'll meet a woman that will love you the way you deserve, but I can't be that woman."

Rino didn't know what to say. After a few moments, he said, "Stephanie, I have a lot of respect for you as a person and that will never change. Yes, I was starting to fall in love with you and I'll always love you in some way. Thanks for telling me. I hope we can still be friends. As always, anything I can do for you, just ask."

Stephanie was very relieved. She didn't want to lose Rino's friendship.

From that moment on, they stayed close friends. Some people at the conservatory thought they were having an affair because they were always together. Rino heard the rumors but he didn't care what they said. He was happy with the way things were.

After a two year stint, it was time for Stephanie to go back home. She had learned everything she could. She spoke fluent Italian and she was a highly-trained operatic soprano.

The night before she left, Rino, Luigi, and her teacher took her out to dinner and toasted to her future success. "We wish you good luck and success. We're sure you'll do well in your career and we hope you'll keep in touch."

"Thank you all very much," Stephanie said. "I'll never forget everything you've done for me. I promise to come back and see you all again when I can."

Rino took her to the airport the next day. She was leaving for Germany to tour before going home.

"Stephanie, I wish you good luck with your tour," Rino said.

"Rino, I love you like a friend and I'll always remember you and what you've done for me. I'll keep in touch. I know someday you'll become a great pianist."

Rino would never forget her and that he almost fell in love with her. Of course, he hoped that one day he'd meet the right woman, but so far, he hadn't had much luck. His big dream now was to tour outside of Italy and become more well known.

A few weeks later, he got his wish. The conservatory made arrangements for him to go to Vienna to play. He was excited and looked forward to it. He went with Luigi and they had tremendous success. They spent a few extra days touring the country and then came back home to Rome and a huge celebration. At thirty-three, his career was well on track.

***

Lisa's story continues.

As Rino was beginning his adventures, Lisa had just turned 18. She had spent the last few years making wedding dresses and designing evening gowns. She had started to make a name for herself in Anzio. But her dream was to go to school and learn how to truly be a fashion designer. Eventually, she wanted to own her own store.

One day, while she was having her shoes repaired, she met Sergio, the store owner's son. They struck up a friendship and started going out. Eventually, they fell in love.

Lisa's mother didn't like Sergio very much, though. "He's such a womanizer, always flirting with the girls behind your back," she said more than once. "He's not the man for you."

But Lisa felt that he'd settle down once they were married.

One day that summer, Sergio met a beautiful French girl named Michelle, in Italy on vacation. He thought she had a lot of money so he started spending a lot of time with her. When her vacation was over, she invited him to come to Paris with her. He gladly accepted.

Lisa was of course, very upset and hurt when he left. She thought he had loved her and that they had a future together. Her mother was right, though--he was just a womanizer. She tried to comfort Lisa. She told her that one day she'd meet the right man for her, but it was hard for Lisa to trust a man after that.

Sergio came back to Anzio three months later. It hadn't worked out. She wasn't as rich as he thought and they didn't love each other. He went to see Lisa realizing that he still had feelings for her. He knew he hadn't treated her right and wanted her forgiveness. But Lisa was finished with him. "No, Sergio, I won't take you back. I loved you once, but it's over."

Lisa felt that the best thing for her to do was to leave Anzio. Over the years, Rino would often come home to visit and she'd occasionally go to Rome to visit him. This time she decided to go back with him and attend a two-year fashion school. After school, she tried to get a job at one of the fashion houses. Her teacher had been very impressed with her talent and thought she wouldn't have a problem.

Mario Argentieri had a fashion store in Rome and whenever he needed help, he'd go to one of the fashion schools. He happened to come to Lisa's school and as luck would have it, her teacher highly recommended her. Mario decided to visit her in Anzio to see exactly the kind of person she was.

He went to her house and knocked on the door.

"Are you Lisa Forte?" he asked when she opened the door.

She simply nodded.

"My name is Mario Argentieri. I need some help in my store in Rome and your teacher recommended you. I'd like to hire you. But first I have to ask, was your father a chef in a hotel in Rome during the war?"

"Why yes, he was."

"I ate there many times and your father and I became fast friends."

The reference to Lisa's father made Lucia feel better about Lisa going to Rome.

"Don't worry about your daughter," Mario said. "I'll keep an eye on her."

"Let me think about it," Lisa said. "Can I call you in a few days with my decision?"

"Of course."

Lucia felt reassured. She had developed a heart problem and couldn't work as much as she wanted to. With Lisa gone, her finances would suffer, but she'd do anything to help her children fulfill their dreams.

Rino came for the weekend and Lisa told him her news. He was, of course, happy for her. It was decided that she would live with Rino in Rome. Hopefully, she thought, I can leave the bad memories behind.

Sometimes on the weekends, Lisa and Rino would travel the forty miles to Anzio where they would spend time with their mother. She always made dinner and said a special prayer for their father's safe return.

Mario was impressed by her talent. He realized that he had a very good designer working for him and planned to have her help improve his store.

After she had been there about two years, he told her about a fashion show scheduled for the summer. "I want you to be in charge of that show," he said.

She was a gifted seamstress and designer and he'd received a ton of compliments about her fashions. He thought she'd do well and this was an excellent opportunity for her to shine.

One day a businessman named Nino came to the store and introduced himself. He was instantly attracted to Lisa. During the conversation, he gave her a lot of compliments. From then on, he made it a point to come to the store whenever he made the trip and look for Lisa.

One day, just before the show, he asked her out. She didn't really like him, but she was polite in the way an employee of a store is polite to a customer. He was too old for her anyway.

Seeing her determination, Mario finally had a talk with Nino in an attempt to convince him to let her alone.

He threw up his hands and said, "Okay, okay. As you wish."

As coincidence would have it, a fortune teller approached Lisa inside the store and said, "Please, give me your hand."

After looking at her palm, she said, "Someone will come into your life from far away and you'll be married. You'll fall in love and be happy."

"I don't know anyone like that," Lisa said.

"The day will come and then you'll know."

With the arrival of summer came the fashion show. Lisa had worked hard on making it a success. People came from all over the country and even from America.

Gene Rosenberg, from America, was one of those people. This was his third trip.

Each time before he left, his father Izak would say, "If you have time, see if you can find Alexander's family and see what happened to them."

Izak and his family came from Russia during the 1916 Russian revolution. His parents owned a tailor shop and designed clothes. The revolution of course, made them fear for their lives. They had no choice but to leave the city. They wanted to cross the border into Czechoslovakia where they'd be safe. Before they left they knelt and said a prayer goodbye.

When they got to the border, it was almost closed. As they got near, some Russian soldiers started firing on them wounding Izak's father and brother. He tried to help them but they couldn't walk. His mother told him to go, that they'd be okay, to save himself. But he didn't want to leave his family behind. His mother kept begging him to go so finally, he kissed them goodbye and ran. His father yelled to him as he left, "Ben shelanu rootz, anachnoo ohev ata lech im elohim!" (Our son, run, we love you. Go with God!) He was lucky enough to get to the border without being hurt.

He never looked back so he never knew what happened to his family. The only thing he remembered was what they had said to him when he ran for the border. He went to the nearest big city where he found a job as a tailor. There he met his wife, Sarah. They worked very well together. After all they had suffered, they were happy to be together and to be alive. They stayed there until 1926 when Izak decided they should move to Rome.

He started working with some other Jewish people and because of his skill, and with their help, he was able to buy his own store.

He and his wife would go to a nearby hotel restaurant for dinner on the weekends. They liked the food very much and would always compliment the chef. One day he asked the waiter if he could meet the chef.

The chef, whose name was Alexander Forte, was quite pleased. He liked to see satisfied customers. "My name is Izak Rosenberg," Izak said. "I've lived in Rome for three months. I love this city very much. I'm a tailor and I own a clothing store. If you ever need anything for you or your family, please come to my store and I'll take care of you."

They started talking and found out that they liked the same things, which fostered a lasting friendship. On occasion, they'd go walking and see the ancient sights of Rome.

In 1930, Alexander married a young woman named Lucia. Izak gave him his wedding clothes as a present. The same year, Izak had a son named Gene and in 1932, Alexander had a son named Rino. Sarah and Lucia became good friends and Izak helped them as much as he could. Lisa Forte was born in 1938.

Germany had occupied Italy in 1939, and then started to invade several more countries in Europe. In 1940, the Germans started deporting Jews from occupied countries to concentration camps. At first, the Italian Jews thought they'd be safe but unfortunately, that wasn't true.

In 1941, Alexander was called to join the Italian Army and to fight against Russia. A week before Alexander was to leave, Izak went to the hotel for dinner. "Izak," Alexander said to him, "I love you like a brother. But I've heard from friends high up in the Army, that the Germans are going to come to Rome and take all the Jewish people to concentration camps."

"I can't believe that'll happen to us," Izak said. "What will I do with the store?"

"Your life and your family are worth more than your clothes. I talked to my priest and he's going to help you. He's going to hide you and your family in the church until things are better. But don't wait too long to see him."

After a few days, Izak began to believe him. He'd heard rumors and he was frightened. He told his friends that they had to leave too, but only a few believed him.

He took his wife and children and some friends to the church. He brought as many clothes as he could to give to the priest and others.

Izak went to the hotel for the last time when it was time for Alexander to leave for the war. They tried to go for a walk but they saw SSI military trucks entering the city. Izak was frightened. "Stay with me," Alexander said, "I'm in uniform and they won't bother us."

Fortunately, they got back to the hotel safely. "Stay here," Alexander said, "the priest will come to the hotel tonight to take you to your family. Izak, we've been friends for a long time. I hope someday I'll come back and we'll be good friends again."

"Alexander," Izak said, "thank you for everything you've done for me. I wish you good luck and I hope we meet again."

Izak knew the chances of Alexander coming back from the war weren't good. With tears in their eyes, they hugged each other goodbye.

Izak and his family stayed in the church until the war's end three years later. Then he and his family went to America to live. He started a tailor shop and became very successful.

As Gene got older, he helped out in the store and eventually, they ran the store together.

Every year for the first few years, Izak would call the hotel restaurant and see if they had heard from Alexander, to no avail. Finally, the Maitre'd said, "Izak, I'm sorry but we heard that he was killed in Russia."

Izak, understandably, was very sad. One night he had a dream about Alexander. "Izak, I'm happy now," he said. Izak took that to mean that he was still alive somewhere.

Finally, it was time for Gene to go to Rome for the fashion show. His father Izak had died in his sleep recently and he was despondent. He'd thought about canceling his trip but his mother encouraged him to go. His mother told him that he might find an Italian girl who was good at design to help out in the store. "She might be a good candidate for a wife, too," she added with a grin. "Gene, maybe you can find out what happened to your father's friend Alexander, who helped hide us during the war."

"I'll try, Mother, if I have time."

When he left for Rome the next day, he felt like he was going home. He hadn't been back for a long time. He remembered what it was like when he was little before the war. He treasured those memories.

When he arrived, he went to his hotel, changed clothes and then went to a restaurant to eat. It was the same restaurant his father frequented. The maitre'd was named Julio then. When he arrived, he asked if Julio still worked there. "In the office," came the blunt reply.

A man opened the door to the office and Gene asked, "Excuse me, but is your name Julio?"

"Yes, it is. Can I help you?"

"Yes, you can. My name is Gene Rosenberg. My father used to come here many years ago. He was good friends with the chef, Mr. Forte."

"Yes, I remember him very well. And you're little Gene. I'm happy to see you again. How's your family?"

"My father passed away recently but my mother's fine. I'm here for a fashion show. I was wondering if we could get together some time before I leave."

"I'd like that. Sure."

"Do you know by chance if any of the Forte's are still around?"

"Mr. Forte was killed during the war but the family lives in Anzio now. I hear Rino is going to the conservatory of music here in Rome to be a pianist. Maybe you can look him up."

"I'll do that."

The next day Gene went to the fashion show and met Mario. They'd met a few times before. He was impressed by the show and all the new designs. He complimented him on how well the store was doing, but he was very taken with a certain designer and asked Mario who he was.

"*Her* name is Lisa," Mario said, "and she's been working for me for awhile. She's very talented, isn't she? In fact, she put on this fashion show."

"Really? Well, I'd very much like to meet her if I could."

"That can be arranged."

Mario asked her and she said yes. She was very flattered to think that a man from New York wanted to meet her.

"I've known him a long time and he's an honest man and a gentleman," Mario said.

She could have supper with him the next evening. Lisa came to the dinner with Rino, who wanted to see what kind of man he was. Even though he was younger, he felt very protective of her.

Gene was disappointed when he saw Lisa with a man—he wondered if he was her boyfriend or maybe even her husband. When Lisa introduced him as her brother, Rino Forte, he couldn't believe his eyes.

"My name is Gene Rosenberg and I live in New York City, although I was born in Italy. I have to ask you Rino, but did your father, Alexander Forte, work as a chef in a hotel here?"

"Yes, my father used to work there. He died during the war."

To their surprise, Gene hugged Rino and then Lisa. "I know you're wondering who I am and I know you don't remember me, but I remember you both. I remember when your father and mother used to come to Rome to my father Izak's store to buy clothes. Then we'd have dinner at the hotel."

"I remember now," Rino said. "Lisa was a baby and too young to remember."

"My mother and father in America never forgot what your father did for us," Gene said. "Before he left for the war, your father went to my father and said he heard they were going to export the Jews. He said I've made provisions with the priest that he'll hide you and your family in the church. My father didn't believe him but he sent my mother and me there to hide just in case. He had a store to run. But one day he heard that it was true, so he went to the church and was reunited with his family. They stayed in hiding for three years until the war was over. My parents never forgot your father and what he did. I'm sorry that I didn't get a chance to thank him for my father. How's your mother?"

"She's well," Rino said. "I'm sure she'd love to see you and hear how your family's doing."

Gene turned to Lisa. "I'm afraid I'm neglecting you. I wanted to meet the woman who put on such a wonderful fashion show. I'm very impressed with your ability. I have a fashion store in New York City and I would very much like you to design dresses for me. Rino, you wouldn't have to worry about her, she'd have a solid future."

"Thank you for the compliment," Lisa said with a big smile on her face. I'd love to design dresses for you. There is a problem, though. I can't leave my mother behind. She depends on me. I'd have to talk to her first."

Rino agreed with her and said, "Gene, I like the idea of my sister going to America and having a better future. I'm studying piano and I'm going on tour soon, so I don't see my mother as often as my sister does."

"I'd like to talk to your mother about my intentions and assure her that I'm a good man and mean no harm to her daughter."

Rino nodded.

The next day they left by car for Anzio. Their mother Lucia was happy to see them but surprised to see a stranger.

Rino introduced her to Gene and said, "This man came from America for the fashion show Lisa put on and wants to talk to you about her future. His name is Gene Rosenberg. Does that name sound familiar?"

Puzzled, Lucia said, "Yes it does. I've heard that name before."

"Do you remember when you and Father used to take us to Rome before the war to buy clothes and then out to dinner?"

With tears in her eyes, Lucia said to Gene, "Yes, I remember now. Your father was Izak Rosenberg and he ran the clothing store. He and his family were the ones that Alexander saved during the war. Oh my God!"

She started crying and hugged Gene.

"I've always wondered about you and your family and what happened to them after the war," she said. "We heard that you went to America and that was all."

"My father recently passed away, but my mother and I have always remembered how good your father was to us. In fact, she reminded me before I left that I was to see if I could find out where you were while I was here."

"In honor of this special occasion, I'm going to make a special dinner for you tonight, my famous pasta Alfredo."

"Please don't let me put you out."

"No, I insist. It's the least I can do."

After dinner, Gene said, "Signora Lucia, your daughter has a great talent. I own a fashion store in New York City. I'd like her to work for me. She'd have a good future doing something she loves to do. Someday she could even be a partner. The problem is that your daughter doesn't want to leave you behind, because she thinks you won't be happy without her. That she's the only one left to watch over you."

Lucia laughed and said, "That's true, I love her very much and at this time in my life I don't want to let her go."

"I respect your feelings. It's not an easy thing to be parted from your daughter. "

"Why doesn't your wife help you with your store?"

"I don't have a wife because I've never found the right woman."

"Well, to be honest, right now I do need my daughter. She's all I have and my health isn't good."

Gene smiled. "I understand, I do, and I'll be in touch with you and your daughter in case you change your mind."

Gene thanked her for an excellent dinner and Lisa, and Rino for their hospitality. He gave Lucia a big hug and Lisa a gentle kiss on the cheek as he got ready to go.

"Give my best to your mother," Lucia said.

Gene said goodbye and asked Rino to take him to the hotel.

After he left, Lucia said to Lisa, "I think this young man has feelings for you. I saw the way he looked at you. He's a handsome man, and he might be the man for you."

"From what my boss told me about him, he's a gentleman and I do have good feelings about him. Maybe in time I'll get to know him better."

In the car, Gene said, "You have a good mother and a very talented sister, Rino. If I can help you in any way, please feel free to let me know."

Rino thanked him and said, "As I told you, I'm gone a lot playing concerts. My sister helps mother as much as she can. That's another reason why my mother doesn't want Lisa to leave."

"If your sister comes to New York, we'll send you all the money you'll ever need."

"Thank you for your generosity. I'll keep that in mind."

After they reached the hotel, they shook hands and said goodbye.

"I'll be in touch with your sister because I always call the store and talk with Lisa's boss," Gene said.

Gene's mother was waiting for him at the airport. She was delighted to see him so happy. He hadn't been this happy for a very long time.

"Mom, I found the Italian girl that you always talked about," he said with a smile. "She's a genius in fashion design and very beautiful. And mother, I have another surprise for you. She's the daughter of the family father saved during the war when the Germans were trying to deport all the Jews from Rome. Her name is Lisa Forte."

"Oh, I have so many good and happy memories about that family," she said. "It would be so nice to see Lucia again.

"I'm sure she'd love to see you again, too."

Gene called Rome every few weeks and talked to Mario to see how things were going. It was his way of getting to know Lisa a little better.

Eventually, he asked her if she had a boyfriend.

"Many men are interested in me, but I'm not dating anyone seriously," she replied.

So I've still got a chance, Gene thought.

"Look," he said, "when you think of it, drop me a line just to let me know how the family's doing. Okay?"

"Of course," she said with a smile in her voice.

On her birthday, Gene called Mario and asked him to buy a bouquet of flowers and a bottle of perfume and have them delivered to the store for Lisa. He thanked Mario profusely and Mario said he was happy to help.

The perfume and flowers very much surprised Lisa, and made her very happy. Especially coming from Gene.

She told her mother about the gift and her mother said, "It was very nice of him to remember you on your birthday. I do like him and I trust him. I think he'd be good for you, Lisa. He comes from a good family."

"I think I have feelings for him, but he is Jewish and we're Catholic. Is that a problem, Mom?"

"What counts is what a man has in his heart, not his religion because we believe in only one God. I know his family and they're good people."

Lisa smiled. Maybe she *should* have a relationship with him, she thought.

Gene called her every week, even if only to say hello. He was in love—and that had never happened before. He wanted to do everything in his power to convince her to marry him someday and bring her to New York. He felt she was the right girl for him, both as a wife and as a partner in his business.

In Italy, a good designer is called a woman with a golden hand, mano di'oro.

One day Gene called Lisa's work and Mario answered. He asked how Lisa was doing. Then he said, "Tell her somebody important wants to talk to her."

When she answered the phone, Gene said in Italian, "Comesta mia bella princess."

Lisa wondered who it is, but when she realized it was Gene, she laughed and said, "You surprised me. I've never been called a princess before. It makes me feel special."

"I'd also like to compliment you on the clothes you've been sending to my store. A Jewish lady asked me who made these beautiful dresses and I told her they were done by a beautiful lady with a golden hand. I tell people you have a golden hand because you design and sew so well. Someday, Lisa, I hope to bring you to America."

Lisa, happy to hear the compliments about her clothes, said, "Gene, my mother loves you. She thinks you're a gentleman. Who knows, maybe someday I might come to America. I trust you won't take advantage of me, though."

"Maybe I'll come back to Italy for a vacation in a few months. I want to get to know you better, Lisa."

"That sounds like a wonderful idea, Gene."

They called each other every week. Gene always asked about her mother and her brother, Rino.

During this long distance courtship, her mother started feeling a little weak, but she was still doing well. Rino was also becoming even more well known with his music.

Every Saturday Gene went to Temple with his mother. If the Temple ever needed anything, Gene and his family always helped out.

One day Gene was getting ready to call Lisa when she surprised him and called him first.

"Gene, I have some bad news. They took my mother to the hospital. She has a bad heart. The doctor said she needs an operation but they're not sure if she'd survive it because she's so weak. They're hoping to make her stronger before the operation in a few weeks. She has to stay in the hospital until then. She thinks she's going to die. Gene, her last wish is to see me married to you."

"I'm so sorry to hear about your mother," Gene said. "You know, I was going to wait, but now that she's so ill I have to say something. Lisa, I'd like you to be my wife. I know this isn't the best time, but I've been in love with you for a long time."

"Yes, Gene, of course I'll marry you, I love you, too. We'd have to be married in the hospital, though. My mother is just too weak too travel."

Gene was terribly saddened by the news. He truly loved her mother.

"My brother Rino knows the priest well," Lisa said. "He likes music. I know he'll come to the hospital and marry us."

"I have to talk to my Rabbi. He'll have to come to Italy and marry us, too."

"Don't wait too long, Gene. Her health isn't good."

Gene made an appointment the next day to see the Rabbi.

"Gene, what a pleasure," the Rabbi said. "You look well. I want to thank you for you and your family's support. We really appreciate it."

"Thank you. But I have a big favor to ask of you, Rabbi. You've always said to me, Gene you're thirty-three years old. When are you going to get married? Rabbi, I've finally found the girl of my heart. She's a fashion designer. I want to marry her and have her be my partner in life as well as in my store."

"I'm happy for you, Gene, very happy. You finally found a nice Jewish girl."

"Well, no, not exactly, Rabbi, I'm sorry. I would love to marry a nice Jewish girl, but she's an Italian girl from Rome."

The Rabbi sat up straighter and clenched his jaw. "Have her come to America and convert to Judaism and I'd be happy to marry you," he said in monotone.

"She can't come here, that's the problem. You've known me since my Bar Mitzvah. Now I'm in love and I want *you* to marry me."

"Gene, she's in Italy. Do you want me to come to Italy and marry you? She's not even Jewish!"

"I'll pay for your airfare and put you up in the best hotel in Rome."

The Rabbi crossed his hands, looked away and said, "Gene, you put me in a very delicate situation."

Gene said, "You know, Rabbi, I love this girl very much and I also think she will help me in my business since my father passed away. Plus she's the daughter of the man that saved our family during the war."

When the Rabbi heard that, he felt obligated to help him. He felt that this was the right and moral thing to do. The Rabbi smiled and said, "Okay, I'll do it. You and your family have always been good to the Temple."

"Thank you, Rabbi. Our only problem is that we have to leave as soon as possible. Lisa's mother is very sick, so time is of the essence."

The Rabbi promised to be ready as quickly as possible.

Gene called Lisa and told her the news. "Did Rino talk to the priest and tell him about your mother and her last wish?" he asked.

"It wasn't easy but Rino convinced him. Because my mother is sick and it is her last wish, he'd feel bad if he didn't fulfill that wish before she died. So it's set. Rino talked to the hospital administrator and they've set aside a special room for us to be married in."

"Mario will be my best man."

"Rino said that at first the administrator said that this is a hospital, not a church. But Rino was very persuasive and he finally said okay."

Five days later, Gene, his mother and the Rabbi flew to Rome. "I'm sure Lucia will be surprised to see me," Sarah said. "I'm looking forward to seeing her. It's been a long time since we've met. I'm only sorry it has to be under these circumstances."

Lisa and Rino met them when they got off the airplane. Then they went to their hotel, freshened up, and got ready for the wedding.

The priest arrived a few hours later and met with everyone. The Rabbi said as best as he could in Italian, "This is all very unusual for me, to come to Italy and marry someone of a different religion in the hospital. But I accepted the challenge."

"It is unusual," the priest said, "but because I've known Rino and his mother for so long, I wanted to grant her wish to see her daughter married to Gene before she died."

Lisa had made her own wedding dress and she looked stunning. She met Gene's mother, Sarah, at the hotel along with the Rabbi.

"Lisa, what a beautiful gown," Sarah said. "I've never seen such a dress. Gene told me you were a wonderful designer and there's the proof."

When they arrived at the hospital they got on the elevator, each of them decked out in wedding finery. Everyone stared at them because of the way they were dressed--no one had ever gotten married in the hospital before and it was all a bit unusual.

When they arrived at Lucia's room, the doctors and nurses all wondered what was happening. But Lisa's mother was well pleased, and that was the only thing that mattered.

She was so happy, deliriously so. With tears in her eyes, she said, "You look so beautiful, Lisa. My one wish was to see you and Gene married."

Then she noticed Sarah, but at first, she didn't recognize her. "Lucia, Sarah said, "you don't recognize me? I'm Sarah. Remember your husband saved our lives during the war?"

Lucia remembered then. She motioned her over and gave her a hug and a kiss. "I'm sorry I didn't get a chance to see you before all this. I truly meant for us to get together and talk about old times before now. But now it seems we won't have that time. I am glad to see you, though. It's wonderful that your son is marrying my daughter. I'm glad for them both and now I won't have to worry about her."

"Don't worry about your daughter," Sarah said. "She'll be in good hands. I'll treat her like my own daughter."

Lucia was moved into the special room where the ceremony would take place. Rino had hired Luigi to play the wedding song on his violin and flowers of all colors and varieties dotted the room.

The Rabbi started the ceremony in the Jewish tradition. When he was finished, the Priest performed the Catholic ceremony. By then, Gene couldn't wait to kiss the bride.

Lucia called the priest to her side and thanked him for fulfilling her last wish.

"Thank you for coming," she said to the Rabbi. "You have fulfilled my last wish, which is to see my daughter married to Gene. If something happens to me tomorrow, I'll die happy knowing that Lisa and Gene are together and that she's well taken care of. I know she'll be in good hands."

Everyone was getting ready to leave when Lucia called for the nurse. She wanted a glass of water.

After she'd finished, she said, "I feel good right now. My wish was granted."

It became all too apparent within the next few minutes that she wasn't going to make it much further. The Priest came over and gave her the last rites and suddenly she was gone. Everyone was saddened that such a happy event took such a terrible turn.

They held her funeral two days later. It was a very sad honeymoon for Gene and Lisa. But at the same time, they were glad that her mother got her wish. After the service, they went out to eat at a nice restaurant Rino had found.

Over the next week, Gene and Lisa showed the Rabbi the city of Rome. He was very impressed and hoped that one day he could come back.

Before they knew it, it was time go back to New York City. During dinner the last night, the Rabbi said to the Priest, "Some day you have to come to America to see me. I'll show you around just as you've shown me. We've had a new experience in life today. With times changing we have to try to please the people in our life. I'm glad we were able to grant Lisa's mother last wish. This is my first visit to

Italy and the first time I've married someone in a hospital. I'm sure this is new for you too, but I'm sure we did the right thing. God will be glad that we did something so good."

The priest agreed, and after dinner was over, they all shook hands and hoped to get together again, God willing.

"If you come to America one day," the Rabbi said, please make sure you stop by and see me. This experience has given us a better understanding of the changing future."

"This experience will stay with me for the rest of my life," the priest said.

Lisa was sad to be staying behind, but she knew that it would soon be time for her to go to New York, too. She had to get her Visa in order. She went to the airport with Gene and the Rabbi and said goodbye to them both.

"Lisa, I love you and I'll miss you very much," Gene said. "I can't wait until we're together again. Rino, take care of yourself."

The next day Lisa went back to work at Mario's House of Fashion. She was excited about going to America but at the same time, she was a little sad about leaving her brother in Italy.

She asked her brother if he would come to America.

"I'll try my best to come when I can arrange it because you're my only sister and I want you to be happy," he said.

Lisa gave him a hug.

Gene called daily because he couldn't wait for the day he and Lisa would be together in America. He knew somebody in the Embassy who could help speed up the paperwork.

Three and a half months later the visa finally came and Lisa was ready to leave. She asked Rino to come with her. "I'd love to," Rino said, "but I've got so many commitments. I promise you that as soon as I possibly can, I'll come see you."

Rino and Mario took Lisa to dinner before she left. They made a toast, wishing her a happy marriage and good health. "And we'll see each other again in America," Rino said as he raised his glass high.

"I'm sorry to lose you because you feel like a daughter to me," Mario said, "but I understand that you have to start your own family. Don't forget to call me now and then."

Lisa hugged them both and said, "You'll both be in my heart."

The next day Rino and Mario took Lisa to the airport. Their eyes were full of tears of joy as Lisa boarded the plane. She assured them she would call as soon as she could to let them know she was safe.

As Rino and Mario were driving back home, Mario said, "I know you have family here, but you're always welcome in my home whenever you want because I know you lost your father and your mother and now your sister."

Rino felt a deep sense of gratitude for Mario's invitation.

"I'll stay in touch and when time allows, I'll spend time with your family," Rino said.

"Your mother always wished you would find a nice wife, to be happy, and have a nice family."

Rino couldn't help but be reminded of his limp and the derogatory affect it had on the opposite sex. He rubbed his leg unconsciously and smiled at Mario.

"You're a talented man," Mario said. I'm sure you'll find a woman who appreciates you for who you are."

"I'm leaving for a concert in France soon," Rino said, "but I'll call you when I get back."

Several weeks later Rino was having lunch with his friend Luigi at a small cafe. Two men, one young, one older, were having lunch close by. Rino recognized the young man—it was Rocco. They played soccer together before he got hurt. He was one of the kids who had teased him.

After they finished eating, Rocco and the older man got up and walked over to his table. The older man, Mr. Barone, was Rocco's father.

"Mr. Forte, I'd like to congratulate you on your recent concert. I'm a big fan of classical music and it was wonderful!"

"Thank you, Mr. Barone."

"Rino," Rocco said, "I, uh, I want to apologize for my behavior when we were little. I didn't know any better. I don't know if you knew, but I got injured… I can't play anymore. So I understand what you're going through."

Rino looked at him a second and said, "I accept your apology, Rocco. Please, sit down and join us."

"On one condition," Mr. Barone said, "that I pay the bill as a token of my appreciation for your wonderful concert."

"Sure," Rino said, "that's very kind."

"Rino, I have a favor to ask you," Mr. Barone said afterwards. "I have a daughter, Angela, thirteen, who loves music. She plays the piano very well but I'd love for her to take lessons from you. If that would be agreeable with you, of course."

Rino was flattered. "Mr. Barone, I'm very busy, but as a favor to you…" He smiled. "I like young talent. I'll teach her until I have to leave the country for a concert."

"Angela will be so happy. She was at the concert and she really enjoyed your playing."

They shook hands. "Bring your daughter to the Conservatory tomorrow at ten and I'll meet with her."

Angela was very anxious to meet Rino. She played for him and he was very impressed by her talent. They made arrangements for Rino to teach her once a week at her home.

Several months later, she invited Rino to a birthday party at her parent's summer villa outside Rome. There was much food and merry making and everyone had a good time.

Later that afternoon she invited Rino to come to the stables and watch her ride her horse. He sat by the fence and watched.

Then she showed him how she could jump. Rino was impressed. "Can you jump higher?" he said.

"This horse can jump over the moon," she said, smiling.

But this time the horse stumbled; she fell off and hit her head.

Rino ran over to her. He thought she was dead—she was so still, so quiet. He put his ear to her mouth—was she breathing? He couldn't be sure. "Help me, anyone. Please," he yelled. Stable hands came running. "We need an ambulance," he yelled. "Hurry."

She was rushed to a private clinic where the doctor ran tests. She was in a coma. She had a 50-50 chance of coming out of it. Everyone was devastated. Rino, of course, felt guilty. He had encouraged her to jump higher.

Angela's parents and family came every day to see her. Sometimes the family priest came with them. They talked to her hoping she could hear them, but nothing happened.

Rino found her father and mother praying with the priest.

"Signora," he said, "I'm very upset by what happened to Angela. I feel like it's my fault. She's like a sister to me."

"Rino, don't blame yourself," Mrs. Barone said, "it's not your fault. Sometimes these things happen. She's under God's care now. There's nothing more we can do but pray."

Rino went home and decided to take a day off. He went to see his manager. He told him what had happened and that he felt like he should cancel his French tour.

"No, Rino," his manager said, "you can't cancel that tour. It's very important to your career. You have to go. Look, think it over and let me know next week."

"Fair enough."

That night Rino had a dream. He heard a voice calling, "Rino, Rino, don't worry. Everything will be all right. She loves music, play for her."

Play for her, he thought when he woke up. But how? Wait, Luigi. He went to Luigi's house and told him about what had happened.

"Of course I'll help you," Luigi said. "When do you want to go?"

They went the next day. Angela's parents were in the room. Rino introduced Luigi to them.

"Signor and Signora Barone, this is my friend, Luigi. He plays the violin. Angela loves music so much that I thought we'd play her favorite aria for her. Maybe, just maybe we can get through to her."

The Barone's hugged him and said, "Rino, do whatever you think will help. It's a wonderful idea."

Luigi played *Nesun Dorma (None Shall Sleep)* by Puccini. He played beautifully but Angela apparently, didn't hear a note.

"Thank you and Luigi for helping," Mr. Barone said. "We'll see what happens. She may still respond."

Rino went home and started thinking. He believed very strongly in the voice who told him that she was going to get well.

The next day he went to Luigi's house again. Luciano, a tenor that they both knew from the conservatory, was also there. Rino told him the story.

"We have to try again," he said. "I really think the music helps."

"I can sing," Luciano said. "What do you think? Do you want me to see what I can do to help?"

"That's a great idea," Rino said.

They went back to the hospital that very afternoon, and as before, her parents were there. Rino introduced Luciano. Mrs. Barone was surprised to see him. She knew his mother.

"Thank you for coming, Luciano," she said. "We appreciate it very much."

"Anything I can do to help."

Luigi played *Nesun dorma* again and Luciano sang. He had a truly wonderful voice. Rino asked them all to hold hands and pray.

While they played and sang, Dr. Salipante was talking to the clinic director. He had just returned from his honeymoon in America. He was telling him that he had also seen his cousin in New York. "I was very impressed by the new technology. The team of doctors he works with are wonderful. I told him how impressed I was and that I hoped to take some of his ideas back to Italy. In fact, my cousin offered me a job if I wanted to come and work with him. I could make more money, but all my family and friends are here and I don't want to leave them. Italy is my home."

"We're always interested in learning new things," the director said. "Please, what exactly have you learned?"

Before he could answer, they heard music accompanied by a beautiful tenor voice. "Where's that coming from?" the director asked.

They called a nurse. "We have another concert today," she said. "You've been away. A young girl is in a coma and her friends decided to play some music to see if it would help."

"Interesting," the director said. "Let's have a look."

Meanwhile, just as Luciano had finished singing, Angela's eyelids fluttered. "It's a miracle! She's awake!" her mother yelled.

About a minute later, with the director and his friend standing in the doorway, Angela opened her eyes and in a groggy, barely audible voice, said, "I had a wonderful dream. I heard such beautiful music that it made me want to wake up and find out where it was coming from."

She focused on Rino and Luigi, a weak smile on her face. "Thank you, it was so beautiful. And thank you to your friend. What a beautiful voice."

The doctors called the nurse. "Tests, we need to run some tests," they said in unison.

Mr. and Mrs. Barone hugged the three men and thanked them profusely for their help. "Thank you so much for coming up with this idea, Rino. Who knows how long Angela would have stayed in her coma without your help."

"Anything for Angela. I know how much she loved music and I thought that it would help." He thought about the voice from his dream and how prophetic it had been.

A few minutes later, Dr. Salipante came back and said, "Rino, it certainly doesn't follow medical prodigal, but I have to believe that your music was an inspiration."

"Is it unusual that a patient wakes up with no ill effects?" Rino asked.

"To tell the truth, I've never had this happen. But a lot of things that happen that are beyond our control and apparently, in the hands of God. By the way, I just have to congratulate you on your wonderful concert last month. I really enjoyed it, especially your duet with the violinist. Was that him playing in the room? I hope someday you'll give another concert. I know I'll be there."

"Thanks for the compliment. I'm glad you enjoyed it. I'm going to Paris for a concert shortly and then on to Russia. After that, I'm going to America to see my sister. When I'm done with all that, I'm giving another concert here in Rome. I'll send you tickets."

"America? Where in America?"

"I'm planning to see my sister in New York. I haven't seen her in a long time."

"I think you'll enjoy New York very much. I was just there on my honeymoon. I saw my cousin in Rochester, too. He was surprised to see me. We went to New York for a week and then Niagara Falls. I spent the last week with him at his practice observing him in his office and in the hospital. Rino, I wish you a good trip to America. I'm sure when you come back you'll tell me all about it and we'll have some good stories to tell."

Rino shook his hand and thanked him. "I feel much better about leaving now that I know Angela's better. I'll see you when I get back."

Later that week the Barone's took Angela home and a relieved Rino was able to go on his concert tour. He planned to keep in touch with the family during his tour and afterwards.

Rino had a few misgivings about his concert tour—the French could sometimes be very critical, but they loved his music. The reviews were excellent. He had fulfilled his goal of being one of the top pianists in the world.

He was to leave for home the next day but he told his manager, Mauro, that he wanted to stay an extra day to tour Paris. So they rented a car and traveled all around the city. They went to the Eiffel Tour and marveled at how anyone could combine both strength and beauty in such a marvelous way. He bought a little souvenir for Angela, a miniature of the tower. For Rino, Paris was a city full of energy. He could live there, he thought.

While they walked in the park below the tower, they found a little trailer with some gypsies selling fortunes. One young woman approached him but he wasn't interested. Too much mumbo jumbo.

"Rino, go ahead," his manager said. "Let her read your palm. Maybe it won't come true but there's no harm in it. That's how I met my wife, through a fortune teller. She said that I'd meet a special woman and that I would fall in love, and I did."

Rino shrugged and said, "Ah, what's the harm," sat down and held out his hand.

"I see a lot of good things in your life. Some time soon, you'll meet a special lady who you'll fall in love with. I see something else in your life, too. You'll meet someone who'll be very important to you. I see something else, something big. You'll meet a man who'll become very special to you. You'll change his life with knowledge that only you hold."

Rino shook his head. He didn't usually believe in this kind of thing, but for some reason he didn't entirely dismiss what she'd said. He thanked her and gave her a huge tip.

Rino told his manager what she'd said. "It's funny but I don't know, what she said had a ring of truth."

"An open mind never hurts. Just like what happened to me. It all came true. But then again, sometimes it doesn't always happen the way we would like."

On the way home, Rino thought about how special his trip had been. He fervently hoped that someday he'd be able to come back. There was so much more to see. He thought about what the gypsy said. Could something like that really happen, he wondered. He smiled. Only time would tell.

When he came back, some of his friends threw him a big dinner party. He asked Mario to join him in the celebration. He went to the Barone's house afterward. They were very glad to see him again. Angela was doing well and he surprised her with his gift. He told them all about his trip over dinner.

"Thank you for coming over, Rino," Mr. Barone said. "As you can see, Angela is doing well. We'd love to have a party to celebrate. I hope you and your friends will come."

"I'd love to." He paused, then, "I'm sorry I won't be able to continue teaching her, I've got some tours coming up. If you don't mind, I've got a friend, a very talented friend. He can take over where I left off."

"I understand," Mr. Barone said. "If you recommend him, I'm sure he'll be a big help."

They had a drink together and before he left, Rino made a toast. "I wish Angela continued good health."

At his apartment later, Rino got a call from his sister, Lisa.

"I miss you and I can't wait for you to come to America," she said. "I've got some good news. You're going to be an uncle! If it's a boy we're going to name him Gene, but his middle name will be Rino."

Rino welled up—how could he not? He wished he could be there with her, but he had commitments. "My agent got me a tour in Moscow," he said.

"That's wonderful, Rino, just wonderful."

"I really want to be there, you know that, don't you?"

"Of course I do. We'll see each other soon enough."

As soon as he hung up, he thought about going to the American Consulate and doing the necessary paperwork required for an Italian visa. If he did it ahead of time, he could be ready to go to America when the time arrived.

The next day his agent told him that the Moscow tour would happen within the next six months. At thirty-eight, his career has finally taken off—Moscow, he thought, the seat of classical music, home to so many legendary classical composers. And maybe while he was there he could look for his father. Or at least find some clue about what happened to him.

"That's wonderful news," he told his agent. "After the tour I'm going to America to see my sister."

"Sounds like a good idea. You never know how this tour is going to go."

Rino prepared for the upcoming Moscow tour like a man possessed. He practiced constantly, to the point of exhaustion. He'd be prepared even if it killed him.

A month before he was supposed to leave, Angela's father came to see him. "We're having a small party for Angela and I'd like to invite you and your two friends."

"We'll be there. We wouldn't miss it."

"Good. I look forward to seeing all of you and I'm sure Angela will as well."

Judging by the number of cars, the party was going to be a grand affair. Rino rang the bell and the maid answered.

Before they walked in, Luciano said, "You both go ahead; I'll be there in a few minutes."

Angela greeted them as they entered the huge and well-appointed living room. "Thank you so much for coming," she said as she hugged them. "I've missed you both." She pulled away and looked around. "But where is Luciano?"

"He's coming. He should be here in a few minutes." "I'm really looking forward to seeing him again."

Suddenly they heard *Nesun Dorme*—Luciano had rarely been in better voice. Angela ran over to him, "Luciano, I'm so glad you're here!"

"My little princess, I'm pleased to see you and looking so well." He gave her a hug and kiss. Then he gave her music to *Nesun Dorme*, which all three had signed and written, "To our little princess, Angela. We love you and wish you good luck in the future with your playing."

Then Mr. Barone introduced them to his guests and family. His son Rocco came over and thanked Rino and his friends for helping his sister get well. Other guests came over and complimented them, too. Then Dr. Salipante and his wife were introduced. He was glad to see Rino and the others again.

After dinner, Mr. Barone made a toast. "Thank you all for coming here tonight. This party is in honor of Angela and her continued good health."

Then Angela got up and said, "Thank you for coming. Now with your indulgence, I'd like my friends to accompany me."

Everyone followed her into another room and watched as she sat down at the piano, flanked by Luigi on his violin and Luciano. They played *Nesun Dorme*, Angela's favorite song.

Everyone enjoyed the concert and applauded loudly when they were done. They were all glad to see Angela back to her old self.

Then Mr. Barone got up and said, "I believe there's a reason for everything. As you all know, I'm a professor of science at the university. I never believed in miracles until it happened to Angela. The doctors had helped her as much as they could. The music was an inspiration. I believe it was by divine intervention by way of Rino and his friends. I'm a very wealthy man and I'm in good health, but I would have been the poorest man in the world if Angela had not recovered from her accident. She's everything to me. But she did recover and now I have a full life again. This experience taught me that sometimes we have to go through bad things to appreciate all the good things in our life. Rino, Luigi and Luciano, I thank you again for all you did."

Everyone wished Angela well and thanked the three men.

"Mr. Barone," Rino said, "thank you for this wonderful evening. I'm glad Angela is doing so well. I'll keep in touch. After my tour I'll come by to see how things are going."

"I hope your Moscow tour is a great success. I look forward to seeing you again."

April in Rome is one of the most beautiful times of the year. Spring can't wait to express herself and the trees burst with a vibrant new green. Flowers bloom in every available pot. Everyone was out walking and enjoying the warmth.

That evening, while Rino was walking with his friend Luigi, enjoying the warm night air in the Villa Borgese, Rino said, "I'd like to take you with me to Moscow, but I can't. You've been a good friend, especially when you helped me with Angela after her accident."

"You don't have to thank me; we've been friends for a long time. We'll get together after you get back. Speaking of Angela, how is she? Have you heard from her?"

"Her father stopped by my house the other day to thank me again. She's doing great. They want us to come for dinner sometime."

"That sounds good," Luigi said. "Just let me know when."

"After the tour I'm going to America to see my sister. I've been looking forward to this for a long time. I got my visa quite a while ago."

As they walked, they saw two girls approaching. One had a limp, like Rino.

She smiled at him. When he looked into her eyes, he saw a special look. He knew that she liked him. He remembered what his mother had told him. "Someday you'll find a special girl to love you."

"You have a nice smile," he said.

She smiled and then both girls laughed as they walked past.

Rino was smitten. "Let's turn around and see where they're going," he said to Luigi.

But they were nowhere to be seen. They walked awhile to see if they could find them, but to no avail.

"I liked that girl," Rino said. "Maybe I'll see her again someday."

"Don't get your hopes up. They could have been tourists."

Rino thought about the girl all night. Sure, he'd only seen her for a moment, but there was just something about her, something mysterious and very appealing. He even dreamed about her walking in the park with him again. For the next few days, he went back to the park every night about the same time trying to see if she was there. Eventually he decided that if fate willed it, then so be it. But if not, well, there was nothing he could do about that.

The following week, Rino went to the American consulate. When he went inside he went up to the front desk and the man sitting there. The man said, "May I help you?"

Rino said, "I need to apply for a passport."

The man said, "Please join the line until it is your turn."

Rino stood and waited and then it was his turn and he went into an office where he saw a beautiful young girl sitting behind the desk. She looked familiar to him. She said to him, "What can I do for you?"

She had recognized him right away as the young man from the park.

Rino said, "I need to apply for a passport to see my sister in America."

She said, "Let me get the right forms and I'll be right back."

As she got up and went over to the cabinet to get the papers, Rino saw that she walked with a limp and he immediately knew she was the girl from the park. No wonder she looked familiar.\

Rino said, "Excuse me but we met in the park a few weeks ago."

With a smile she said, "Yes I am."

Rino said, "I never thought I would see you again. I've been looking for you every night at the park hoping to see you again. It must be destiny."

She blushed and said, "I've been doing the same thing. We must have missed each other."

Rino said, "Let me introduce myself. My name is Rino Forte and I'm a pianist at the Rome Conservatory."

"My name is Rita Riley."

Rino was very impressed with the way she expressed herself in Italian and her kind spirit. He asked her what part of Italy she was from because she spoke Italian so well. She laughed and said, "Actually I'm from Philadelphia in the states."

Rino said, "I congratulate you for speaking so well, I thought you were a native." Then they sat and filled out the paperwork he needed for the passport.

Then Rita said, "I will process this and you will get a letter in the mail telling you when to come to the consulate and pick it up." Then she said shyly, "By the way, I really love your music. I went to a concert you gave several months ago here in Rome."

Rino knew then that this woman was different from the other women he knew. He said to her with a smile, "I see that you walk with a limp just like me."

She shrugged and said, "I've learned to live with it and accept it."

"Listen, I know this is very forward of me and perhaps too soon, but I would like to invite you to have dinner with me tomorrow night."

"I'd love to have dinner with you," she said with a beautiful smile.

"It was a pleasure meeting you and I'll see you tomorrow night," Rino said. Then he shook her hand and then kissed it and left.

The next night Rino arrived a little early at the Cabernia De'Mercanto. "Welcome Mr. Forte," the maitre'd said. "We have your table waiting."

Rino had requested a special table with special lighting, which the Maitre'd had arranged.

"Anything for you, Mr. Forte."

The table arrangement included flowers, candlelight and a bottle of wine.

The Maitre'd smiled and said, "You must be expecting a special guest."

"Yes, I am. A very special lady."

Rita entered the restaurant then. Rino greeted her with a smile and the bouquet of flowers. He paused a moment then kissed her hand. She gave him a smile and a gentle kiss on the cheek. For whatever reason, maybe the kiss, Rino felt closer to her than he had ever felt to any woman.

Rino poured two glasses of wine after they sat down, asking the sommelier if he'd mind.

"But of course, sir," the sommelier said.

"I usually don't drink wine," Rino said, "but for this occasion I'll make an exception because I'm with a special woman."

"Me, too," Rita said simply.

They both started to laugh and saluted each other with their wine glasses.

After the waiter took their orders, they engaged in conversation.

"How long have you been working for the American Embassy?" Rino asked.

"About four years. I love my job."

"I must say again that you speak Italian so beautifully."

Rita smiled and said, "Thank you. I have to give credit to my grandfather for that. He was born in Naples, but he's lived in America for over half a century. I've always heard him speak Italian and it inspired me to learn the language. I studied it in college. After I graduated, I was offered a job at the American Embassy in Rome. It wasn't easy in the beginning because I missed my family and friends. But I've never met so many nice people. I began to love what I do and now I'm traveling around the countryside learning about it and of course trying all the wonderful foods. I miss my family but I try to get back every summer to visit. I always love coming back to Italy, though, the country I fell in love with."

"You fell in love with Italy but have you ever fallen in love with an Italian man?" Rino said with a smile.

"I've dated Italian men but I never found a man caring enough to accept my handicap."

Rino touched her hand. "I've had the same problem all my life. And I think when two people have the same handicap, they understand each other better and have a special relationship, which my mother always said would happen. She said someday you'll meet that special person who will accept you for the way you are."

Rita looked into Rino's eyes with compassion and said, "That's what I've been searching for all my life. A person like you who accepts me the way I am."

The waiter arrived with their dinner then, a meal they both enjoyed, but not nearly as much as one another.

After the meal, Rino said, "I have a sister who lives in New York City. I haven't seen her in a while and she's going to have a baby. Her husband owns a fashion store. They moved there about four years ago. They were married in a hospital in Rome by a priest and a Rabbi because that's the way my dying mother wanted it. She died ten minutes after the ceremony."

Rita, obviously very touched by the story, said, "I wish I would have known your mother before she died."

"She would have liked you very much."

"When are you planning to go to America?"

"In the summer, I hope. I haven't got any concerts planned right now, but a friend asked me to sit in for him so I'll be playing in Florence this weekend. I'd be delighted if you came to it."

"I'd love to come and I'd really enjoy hearing your music again."

The next day Rino visited Mario's House of Fashion to see his old friend. He told Mario he had met a wonderful lady who worked at the American Embassy. He also invited Mario and his wife to come to his concert. "I'll introduce you to Rita afterwards," he said.

Mario was delighted.

Everyone was amazed by Rino's performance. Afterwards everyone went backstage and wished him the best of luck in Moscow.

"Your performance was beautiful," Rita said and gently kissed him on the cheek.

"I appreciate the compliment, but the kiss, well, that's even more appreciated."

"You play so beautifully," Mario said, his wife beside him, "and I think your mother in heaven would be very proud of you."

He gave Rino a big hug as did his wife. Mario looked at Rita and said, "This must be the special lady you talk about so much."

"Yes, a very special lady."

Mario's wife kissed Rita on the cheek and said, "It's a pleasure to meet you. We've known Rino for many years and he's a wonderful person."

"Tonight it's my pleasure to take you and Rita to whatever restaurant you prefer," Mario said, "to celebrate your success tonight and your future success and, of course, to get better acquainted with Rita."

Rino and Rita accepted the invitation and decided on a restaurant they liked. The Maitre'd recognized him. "Welcome, Mr. Forte," he said, "how can I be of assistance?"

"A table for four would be great."

They followed him over and sat down. Everybody ordered something different and then Mario said, "Let's salute for the future success of both the concern and your relationship with this beautiful lady with a glass of wine."

"Salute!" everyone said. Then Rino told Mario he would be leaving for Moscow in a few weeks.

"Get in touch with me when you get back," Mario said. Rino promised that he would.

After dinner and before they left, Mario turned to Rita and said, "It was a pleasure to meet you. This has been a special night for all of us. Remember that you're always welcome in my store and if there's anything you need, don't be afraid to ask. I'd love to make a special dress for you as a gift from my wife and I and Rino."

"That'd be just wonderful," Rita said. "Thank you."

"Thank you for your generosity and hospitality, Mario," Rino said. "I'll call you when I get back from Russia."

Rita invited him in when they got back to her place. She gave him a glass of whiskey and they toasted to his success. Rino looked into her eyes and she into his. The love was unmistakable. He drew his mouth close to hers and kissed her, and when she threw her arms around him and kissed him with all the passion she could, they both knew what the future held.

"I have special feelings for you," Rita said, "and even though I want to make love to you I think it would make sense to wait until we know each other better. I hope you understand."

"I understand. I really do," Rino said. "I'll miss you when I'm in Moscow but you'll always be in my heart."

They saw each other as much as possible before he had to leave. He met Rita's friends and they did a lot of talking. They'd go for walks and sometimes they'd go to the Villa Borgase.

"You know, Rita," Rino said, "I believe sometimes we don't make our own destiny, that destiny makes us. The reason I say that is that the night I met you I had a prior engagement that was cancelled at the last minute. If I'd gone, I probably never would have met you. We were destined to be together."

"Rino, I believe that too. Sometimes you just can't explain what happens in life."

Rino, inspired by meeting Rita in the park, decided to write a song for her.

One day while they were talking, Rita mentioned that her birthday was just a week away.

"That's funny," Rino said, "my birthday is a few days before yours. Another coincidence?"

Rino decided to make the day special for Rita. He arranged a special dinner for her. He asked Luigi to play his violin for them and Luciano to sing the lyrics to the song he had written. Luciano was flattered. "Anything for you, Rino," he said.

Rino picked Rita up at her apartment and brought her one big beautiful red rose. When she opened the door, he said, "I bring you this rose in honor of our love."

"It's beautiful, thank you very much."

Rino took her arm and they walked to the restaurant where they were led back to a special table. The Maitre'd brought over a bottle of champagne and poured. They made a toast and saluted. Then Luigi appeared playing his violin. Rita was again, impressed. She loved the melody. Then Luciano sang the lyrics to *L'amore Di Primavera. (Springtime brings me luck and love).*

Una sera di primavera ho incontrato l'amore.

Il mio cuore vorra

Per la mia felicita

La primavera m'ha portato fortuna

La primavera m'hapertato l'amore

Per ogni cuore inamorato

E l'ora di cantare

E l'ora di amare

Venite tutte bimbe belle
In questa serra,
Venite a cercar l'amor.
Venite bimbe inamorata,
In questa sera di primavera

Rita was overcome. She leaned over, kissed Rino and said, "Rino, thank you for making all of this so special. It's a beautiful surprise and I'll never forget it."

"Rita, I'd do anything for you. You're the girl of my dreams. I wrote this song just for you."

"Rino, I love you."

Rita drove Rino to the airport to catch the plane to Moscow. She said she would be waiting for him when he returned. He gave her a big kiss and hug and said, "You're the first person to make me feel loved and I promise I'll be back as soon as I can."

Rino came to a realization on the flight to Moscow. His love for Rita had actually affected his playing. The passion he felt for her translated onto the keyboard like magic. What a wonderful way to become a better musician, he thought with a smile.

A few hours into the flight, he fell asleep and dreamt of his father. "You're a wonderful pianist and I'm very proud of you," his father said.

He had a good feeling about the dream, that he would one day see his father again even though he knew he was dead.

The theater director was waiting for him with a limo. He gave him a big welcome and then they went to the hotel.

When they arrived, the chauffer helped him out and said, "My name's Alex." He said a few words in Italian and Rino looked him in the face and said, "You look like an Italian with your wavy black hair."

"I'm proud to be of Italian descent and someday I'd love to go to Rome for a visit," Alex said.

Alex also said that he and his father owned a restaurant and asked if after the concert he'd like to come and have a complimentary dinner.

"Thanks, Alex. I'll see what happens after the concert's over," Rino said.

That evening when Alex went home, he told his father that he had met a man named Rino, a very talented concert pianist, and that even though he had a limp, he carried himself in a professional manner.

His father was surprised to hear that he had a limp.

"We'll all go to his concert tomorrow," Alex said.

Deep down inside Alex Sr. wondered if this was his son, Rino, that he had left behind in Italy. He felt a tug in his heart when he heard about the limp. It saddened him deeply. At the moment, he didn't want his family to know that Rino might be his son.

The next night the entire family went to the concert to watch Rino perform. Everyone was totally amazed with his performance, especially Alex Sr., who plainly saw that this man was indeed his son.

"Why are you crying?" his wife asked.

He looked into her eyes deeply and said, "Honey, I have to tell you a secret. The gentleman playing the piano is my son. The one I left behind with my daughter."

Olga's eyes went wide with surprise and at the same time, her heart filled with joy. "Honey," she told Alex, "why don't you invite Rino for dinner and tell him who you are."

Alex agreed and asked Alex Jr. to ask Rino to dinner.

During intermission, Alex Jr. went into the dressing room and invited Rino to dinner. Rino asked his manager if his schedule was free tomorrow night and he said it was.

The next night Alex Jr. picked up Rino and his manager and drove them to the restaurant.

When he arrived, Rino introduced himself to the family and when Rino shook hands with Alex Sr. something deep down inside gave him a feeling he had never felt before. He didn't understand it, but when he looked into Alex Sr.'s eyes, and he heard him say, "Bonvenuto", he felt he had heard this voice before, but he just couldn't place it.

The years had changed his father. He was gray and bald. And in his heart, he really felt that his father had passed away.

Everybody enjoyed a special dinner made by Alex Sr., which he had made in Rome many years earlier. He was very anxious and worried intensely about how he would tell Rino that he was his father and even more, why he never came back to Italy after the war.

With his hands shaking, Alex Sr. pulled a picture from his wallet and showed it to Rino. "Do you recognize those people?" he asked.

Rino just stared at it awhile. Then tears came unbidden to his eyes and with his lips trembling, he said, "Oh my God! You are mio papa!"

Their eyes met and deeply locked on each other for a moment as the tears began to flow. Suddenly they couldn't resist giving each other a big hug.

The entire family cried tears of joy and celebration. Rino hugged the half-brother and half-sister he had never met before. He was so filled with happiness and joy.

Alex Sr. told his waiter to bring the best wine in the house to celebrate the special moment.

After dinner, Alex Sr. asked Rino to join him for a walk. On that walk, he said to Rino, "Let me explain to you why I never returned to Italy. After I'm done, you can tell me whether you want to see me again. By the way, how are your sister and mother doing in Italy?"

"My mother died two years ago and my sister married Gene Rosenberg, the son of your best friend, Izak. Mother always loved you and believed you were alive somewhere."

Alex nodded and said, "Why do you limp?"

"War injury. They hit the house where we lived. We were lucky to survive. At first, I was very depressed because I couldn't play sports like the other guys, but mother always encouraged me and made me realize that I could use my other talents. Her inspiration has kept me strong and made me what I am today. My deepest hope was that one day my father would see me play at a concert. I never thought that dream would come true but it has. One part of me feels so happy and full of joy and another part of me feels very sad because you never wrote us or came back."

Without warning, Alex Sr. grabbed Rino and hugged him. "Rino, my son," he said, "you're right, but listen to me very carefully." He pulled away and looked at him. "I was wounded very badly outside Moscow. The enemy thought I was dead. After awhile, a young lady showed up, ran back to her house and told her mother about me. The mother used herbs to stop the bleeding and heal my wounds. After several weeks, my health and strength came back a little. I still couldn't get out of bed but what was worse, I couldn't remember anything. The two ladies fed me milk and bread and cheese from their farm. When I got well, I realized that there was no man in the house because the woman's husband was in the Russian Army. So I helped them with their daily chores. As I helped them survive, I realized I had strong feelings for the daughter. Her name was Olga. She had blonde hair and a sweet smile. She was very kind to me and we talked a lot. If not for her, I wouldn't be here right now. One day we were by the river where she'd found me. We lay down in the grass and our eyes met and, well, we made love. She got pregnant that night. I was confused because I didn't know what to do. I was supposed to return to Italy. When the baby was born, it forced me to make a decision, either stay in Russia or go back to Italy. I decided to stay in Russia. I knew that the Italian government would take care of you and your mother, and I didn't have the heart to leave Olga and the baby because she had saved my life. Then I changed my name to Alex Fortechez because I was afraid that the Russians would put me in jail after the war. Rino, my son, you need to realize that even though many years have passed, I always loved you. I'm your father and I'm very proud of what you've accomplished in your life. You've fulfilled what I always told you before I left for the war. I know you're leaving for Italy tomorrow. You have to be the judge of whether or not you'll forgive me for what I've done, but remember that whatever decision you make, I'll always love you as a son."

They hugged and although Rino had mixed feelings, his father's story touched him deeply.

Rino said goodbye to his half-brother and sister. They hugged each other and said, "Today is a wonderful day. How often do you see a brother you've never met? We're very proud of what you've accomplished in your life. I hope we'll meet again someday."

At the hotel, he told his manager what his father had told him.

"Rino," his manager said, "it's up to you whether you want to see your father again but remember, your half-brother and sister love you like family already, now that your mother's gone and your sister's in America. If you can find it in your heart to forget the past and look to the future and restore your relationship with your father, who loves you deeply, you can have a new and loving family."

"Maybe you're right, maybe in time I might find it in my heart to forgive my father and maybe I can start a new relationship with him."

He was very surprised to see his father and family waiting at the airport the next day to say goodbye.

"Rino, you'll always be in my heart," his father said.

His brother and sister told Rino that they would always love him and were looking forward to seeing him again.

After his plane touched down, Rita greeted him with a big kiss. They got his luggage and then drove to his apartment. "I have a wonderful story to tell you but right now I need to rest," Rino told her.

After a good night's sleep and as they were sitting down to breakfast, Rino said, "I'm going to call Mario and ask him to come over. I think he should hear this, too."

After breakfast, Rino said, "I had a wonderful time and I played well. The people loved my music but the big surprise, well, that's what I want to share. For the last thirty years, I thought my father was dead. But, you know, even I can't believe it, but I found him in Russia and I ate in his restaurant and I met his new wife and family, my half-brother and sister. It was the most shocking experience of my life."

"I don't believe it," Mario said. "I thought he was dead, too."

Then Rino told the story of why his father never came back to Italy.

“I’ve known your father since he was a young man,” Mario said, “and he was an honest man. Sometimes things happen that we don’t expect and we react in a way that seems unusual. You have to make a decision. If I was in your father’s situation after what you told me, I might have done the same thing. I can’t tell you what to feel except to give you my honest opinion.”

“I have to call Lisa,” Rino said. “I’m planning on going to America and telling her the complete story.”

After breakfast was over and as he was leaving, Mario said, “Nice to see you back again. Just know that whatever you decide is fine with me.”

Rino went back to the conservatory in Rome where he received a big welcome from his colleagues. Then he prepared for his visit to see Lisa. Rita was going to arrange to get a passport so they could go to America together. She was born in Philadelphia and every July she went home to visit her family. She’d be glad to meet Rino’s sister and then they could go meet her family. Rino was anxious to see his sister and her two children he’d never met.

About a month before Rino left for America, Lisa and Gene were celebrating their 5th wedding anniversary. They decided to invite the Rabbi and his wife for a special dinner. Lisa was going to make lasagna with cheese because she knew how much he liked it.

At that dinner, the Rabbi asked for a little bit more because it was so good.

“My father was a chef and he taught me how to cook,” Lisa said.

After dinner, they had a little wine and said, “Salute! And many more to come.”

“I think I made the right decision to come to Italy to marry you two,” the Rabbi said. “And don’t forget, whenever you make lasagna, be sure to invite me!”

They laughed.

For Gene, marrying Lisa was the best thing that ever happened to him. She was not only his wife, but also his business partner and a genius designer. Her customers respected and admired her. The store was doing much better because, too. Everyone always asked for a dress by the woman with the golden hands. Gene would laugh and say, "That's my beautiful wife."

She was so good, they started exporting her clothes to Italy where they were sold by her old boss, Mario, who always said he'd come to America one day to see them.

They had two beautiful children, little Lucia and little Gene Jr. that Grandmother Sarah was crazy about. She took them to the Temple several times a week. She had promised her old friend Lucia that she would treat Lisa like her own daughter and she did. She was proud of Lisa for being a good mother and a great wife to her son.

Even the Rabbi was happy that Gene had found a wonderful girl and had a happy marriage.

Little Lucia, who was four, always said, "Comesta," to the Rabbi. The Rabbi laughed and was very happy to see that she was learning Italian.

Finally, the day came when Rino and Rita were to leave to see Lisa. After a seven-hour flight, they landed in New York City. Lisa and her husband and children were waiting for them.

Lisa cried when she saw Rino. And Rino felt tears in his own eyes as he said, "I love you and I missed you very much." He turned and introduced Rita. "This is my good friend and fiancée, Rita. She came to visit her family in Philadelphia."

Lisa was very happy to see her brother had a nice girlfriend. The kids and Gene all hugged Rino and Rita. "Welcome to New York," they all said.

"I've made reservations for a great dinner in the best restaurant in New York for you," Gene said.

Lisa liked Rita; she knew she would be very comfortable around her. "I'd like you to spend a few days with our family before you leave because I'm having a big celebration for my brother. A lot of people have heard about him and his music and they really want to meet him."

"I'd very much like to stay, but I have to call my parents and explain to them why I'm not coming home as planned."

"If you want, why don't you ask your parents if they'd like to come to New York City for the celebration? I'd love to meet them."

Rita called her parents and asked them if they wanted to meet her boyfriend's family and they happily accepted.

Rita also asked her grandfather if he'd come. "Thank you, but I'm not feeling well," he said. "Besides I don't travel much anymore."

"I'm sorry to heart that," Rita said, "but remember that I love you and I'll see you when I come home in a few days."

Lisa and Rino were delighted to hear that her parents were coming to the party.

The next day Lisa took Rita to a fashionable department store. "I have a present for you and I hope you'll accept it," she said. "Please, pick any dress you want. Don't worry about the price. It would make me very happy."

"That's very nice of you," Rita said. "Thank you very much. I'm sure Rino would love to see me all dressed up."

Rita's parents arrived the next day. Lisa and Gene greeted them at their home in Long Island.

Rita introduced Rino. They were very glad to meet him. "We heard a lot of nice things about you and your music," her father said. "My father's very anxious to meet you. He was born in Naples, you know. He loves Italian music."

"I'd very much enjoy meeting your father," Rino said.

They went to the mall and to the celebration. A lot of people were waiting to be introduced to Rino--he felt very honored by the attention—it made him feel special.

After talking to and meeting so many appreciative fans, everybody sat down to have a delicious dinner.

After dinner, they asked Rino if he'd play something. Rino was delighted. "A few classical pieces, maybe," he said.

As usual, Rino's talent overwhelmed his audience.

After he was done, everybody stood up and gave him a big round of applause. Rino felt very proud and it was good to see all his guests and fans having such a great time.

After the celebration, everybody started to leave and Rino thanked them for coming. Lisa and Gene invited Rita's parents to spend the night at their home, which they gratefully did.

The next day, after everyone enjoyed breakfast together, Rita, her parents and Rino left for Philadelphia. Before he left Rino told his sister, "Just a few days in Philly, sis, then I'll come back and spend time with you."

Rino said goodbye and thanked Lisa and Gene for all they had done and then they were on their way.

Rita and her parents arrived in Philadelphia after a two hour drive. They met her grandfather, Carlo Martino who was waiting for them.

They had a pleasant dinner and after dinner, Carlo asked Rino to have dinner with him the next night. Rino graciously accepted.

Carlo met them at the door the next evening and gave everybody a big hug before he showed them the house and its treasures--he was a very rich man.

After the tour, they all sat down and enjoyed a beautiful dinner. Carlo made a toast, "Rino, you're welcome in my house and I'll be very happy if someday you marry my granddaughter. I'd be very happy to celebrate your wedding day if God wills it."

"Mr. Martino," Rino said, "I'm sure you have a long life ahead of you."

Rita's parents left after dinner. Rino and Rita stayed. Carlo and Lisa took them into the living room to have a cup of espresso.

"After the war I decided to come to America because I had a brother in New York who has since passed away," Carlo said as they settled in. "I was a mason in Italy. I met my wife on the boat on the way to America. She was from Ireland and I think my father-in-law liked me because we were both masons. Well, we became partners and after he passed away, I took over the company and," he looked around and smiled, then looked back at Rino and Rita, "as you can see, business has been good." He took a drink and continued. "Then I retired, just like that. I sold the company to my nephew and grandson, Sam Junior. They've done a great job keeping the business going. I also had a son who was killed during the war."

He picked up a photograph and showed it to Rino. "This is my son, Sergeant Joe Martino."

Rino looked at the picture and said, "I'm sure I've heard that name before." He thought a moment, then, "Sure, when I was in a convent as a child. I was wounded when the Germans bombed my house." He crossed himself.

"By the grace of God I survived. That's why I limp. I was lying in a bed next to a lady who had just had twin boys. Her name was Maria. A nun asked her who the father was and Maria said the father was an American soldier named Sergeant Joe Martino from Philadelphia. He'd promised her that when the war was over that he'd marry her and take her to America. The nun asked Maria if the sergeant knew that she was expecting. Maria said no because it happened just before he was sent to the front. The nun asked her what she wanted to name her sons and she said she'd name one after his father, Giuseppe, and the other after her father, Giorgio. But I never knew what happened to the twins or Maria. I assumed that she met up with her Sergeant and went off to America."

"Carlo," Lisa said, "in the last letter Joe wrote to us he mentioned a girl named Maria and that he was deeply in love with her.

Carlo was overjoyed to hear that he had two grandsons. He hugged Rino and said, "I never expected to hear this. You're like an angel to tell me this."

He turned to his wife and said, "I'm in bad health, but with the help of God I'm going to go to Italy to the orphanage to find out who adopted my grandchildren. Now I have a reason to live, to see my two grandsons."

"I'm not sure you can travel in your condition," his wife said.

"I don't care; I want to know my two grandchildren before I die."

"Rino," he said, "you have to do me a big favor. You have to take me to Italy to the convent where the twins were born."

Rino looked at Rita then back at Carlo. "I've only got two weeks vacation, but I can work something out."

Carlo smiled broadly and shook Rino's hand vigorously. "Grazie, Grazie," he said.

Rino called his sister the next day and explained the situation to her.

"Sure, I understand," she said. "Do what you think is right, Rino."

Carlo got out his passport, made reservations and before long they were on their way to Rome. While they were in the air, Carlo prayed to God to give him strength and hope to find his grandchildren.

Mario greeted them at the airport and took them to his house for dinner and rest.

They drove to Anzio and to the convent the next day. A nun greeted them. "I'd like to talk with Sister Teresa," Rino said.

They waited a few minutes before they heard her footsteps along the stone floor. She was a tall, attractive woman in her seventies, with small features, save for large, green eyes. Her smile comforted them.

"I've heard you play," she said to Rino. "Divine, simply divine." She looked skyward then looked back at Rino. "How may I help you?"

"This is Mr. Carlo Martino," Rino said as he felt a blush circle his collar.

"I've heard that name before," she said as she smiled at Carlo.

Carlo said in Italian, "I understand, sister, that you were the nun who cared for my two grandsons and that you also knew their mother, Maria. I think she told you the two boys belonged to my son, Sergeant Joe Marino."

"Yes, I did know Maria before she died and I did take care of the children for a little while."

Carlo's eyes filled with tears of joy. "I'd like to donate $20,000 to your convent for whatever you need to show my appreciation for the good care you provided my grandchildren."

"That's very generous, Mr. Martino."

Carlo nodded and smiled. "Sister, if I may," he said, "where is she buried? Maria, I mean."

"She wanted to be buried outside the convent near the chapel where Joe, your son, promised her that he would marry her after the war. I put flowers on the grave every now and then because she was a good friend and she sang like an angel."

"May I?" Carlo said.

"Of course."

They went outside, knelt by the grave and said a few prayers. "I'm glad that you were able to show my son so much love when he needed it the most during the war," Carlo said.

"I'm sure you want to know what became of the children," Sister Teresa said.

"Oh, yes. Very much."

"We had them for six months until the Mother Superior decided that we had too many orphans, so we took some of them to a bigger orphanage in Rome where they would get better care. I'm sorry, Mr. Martino, but during the war that was the best decision we could make for the children. We hoped that someday a good family would adopt them. I heard one of the boys, Giorgio, was adopted by a family in Venice. Now it may just be coincidental, but the famous opera singer, Giorgio Fiorino is also adopted, although I'm not sure if that's the same man. I've often wondered if it is him, though."

"Oh my God!" Carlo exclaimed, "could he be my grandson? Sister Theresa, you have to take me to Rome to find out who adopted my two grandsons and if indeed, one is Giorgio Fiorino."

Sister Theresa paused, then, "Certainly," she said. "Just let me ask the Mother Superior."

It took less than an hour to get to Rome. And when they arrived, they went straight to the orphanage where a very friendly nun greeted them. They asked to talk with the Mother Superior. The nun said they should wait in the waiting room. After a few minutes, the nun escorted them in the Mother Superior's office.

Sister Theresa introduced everyone and said, "Mr. Martino came all the way from America to find out who adopted his two grandsons, Giorgio and Giuseppe. They were brought here from the convent at Anzio during the war."

The Mother Superior looked at Carlo and crossed her hands on the desk. Her frown caused Carlo's heart to race. "We don't normally give out that information," she started, "but in this case I'll make an exception because you're the grandfather and we know Sister Theresa very well."

"Can I have the files on the boys?" The Mother Superior said to her secretary, standing in the doorway.

The files provided the information they'd come for-- Giorgio had been adopted by a man named Giorgio Fiorino from Venice, whom they knew. The other boy had been adopted by a man named Thomas Palmer, who lived in Philadelphia.

Carlo was very surprised. In a big and happy voice he said, "I don't believe it. The man who adopted Giuseppe was my son's best friend. Wow, this is the best surprise of my life. I've always felt some connection to him and now he's my real grandson. I've seen him play football. His name is Joe Palmer! This makes me the happiest man on this earth. I have another grandson that I met while I was vacationing in Venice many years ago. He sang to me on a gondola and I was so impressed with his singing that I gave him ten thousand dollars for his education. That was Giorgio. My wife said he resembled my son who had passed away during the war."

Carlo turned to the Mother Superior and said, "Thank you, Sister. This is far more valuable than all my money. I now know that I have two famous grandsons. And I promise you, Mother Superior, I'll bring those grandsons here in person for you to meet."

Later on, Carlo called his wife with the good news. "I'll call you with more details when I come home tomorrow. Make sure everybody's there to hear the news."

Epilogue

Rita greeted them in Philadelphia the next day. "What's the big news?" she asked. Carlo told her everything.

"My god," Rita said, "I've got two famous cousins."

When they got to the house, Lisa and Carlo embraced for a very long time. Then they went into the house and he told everyone the whole story.

"After meeting Rino, I was finally able to learn what happened to my son, Joe. I also learned that I have two famous grandsons. I never expected this, never. Now I want everybody to come with me for a surprise visit to meet my grandson, Joe Palmer."

Joe's house was about a half hour away. Joe's wife was surprised to see so many people pull in the driveway.

After she opened the door Carlo grabbed her in a happy embrace. "Why are you so happy?" she said.

"I just learned that your husband, Joe Palmer, is my grandson!"

Tears fell from her eyes as she hugged Carlo and his wife.

"I'd love it if Joe were here," she said, "but he's in Las Vegas. He's got a job singing there, can you believe it? He's trying to raise money for handicapped kids."

"That's wonderful," Carlo said. "I'm sorry that I missed him, but what he's doing is much more important."

The next night Joe's wife called the casino looking for Joe. "He's right in the middle of his set," the manager said.

"Can you give him a message for me?"

"No problem."

"Have him call me as soon as possible. It's very important—not life threatening, I don't want to give you wrong impression… It's just very important."

"I understand."

Joe called back about an hour later. "What's going on?" he said.

"I have a big surprise for you. Carlo Martino has discovered that you're his grandson!"

A pause, then, "Are you sure? How is that possible?"

"I'll let Carlo explain."

Carlo took the phone and said, "Joe, my grandson. I've known you for a long time, since your stepfather Tom adopted you from Italy, where you have a twin brother. You're both the children of my son, Joe, who died in the war. Your mother's name was Maria. Joe, I'll explain everything when you come back home. Your brother sings at the Metropolitan Opera in New York. I'd like it if we could all go meet him."

Overwhelmed, Joe said, "Grandfather. How do you know that?"

"I met a man named Rino Forte, he's Rita's boyfriend. They're visiting from Italy. I was telling him about Joe and when I showed him a picture, he said, 'I know that name'. And then he told me a wonderful story. But I want to tell you that story in person."

"I've always loved you and respected you even before I knew you were my grandfather," Joe said. "It makes me so happy to know I have a twin brother. I always felt there was something missing and now I know what it was. I'll be home tomorrow night. Please let me talk to my wife."

"Honey," Joe said, "I can't believe what I'm hearing. I wish my father was here. I already had a feeling that something or someone was missing in me. And now I know that it was my twin brother who was missing. And you won't believe this, but I think I saw him when I first came to Las Vegas. I felt then that I had to know more about him."

After Joe hung up, he called the hotel manager and asked to talk with him in his office.

Joe walked into Bill's office singing, tears running down his cheeks.

"Joe," the manager said, "you're supposed to be singing in the casino, not in my office. What's going on?"

"My wife called and gave me the most amazing news I've ever had. It's worth more to me than all the money in the world. I know I have a handicapped child, which makes me sad. And I realize that life sometimes makes you happy and sometimes it makes you sad. The great news I heard today makes me happy because I discovered who I am. I was an adopted boy from Italy. God blessed my stepfather, Tom, who brought me from Italy when I was a baby. He loved me like his own son and taught me the game of football. He said the way I threw the ball reminded him of his friend who died in Italy. And now I understand why because I'm his friend's son. It's too bad that Tom died before I could tell him that. I've also found out that I'm a twin and that I have a brother who sings at the Met. His name is Giorgio Fiorino. That's why people told me I looked like him. I had several dreams about him but I never knew I had a brother because my stepfather never knew either. I also found out that the man I talked to on the phone is my grandfather. That's why I have to leave. I have to go back to Philadelphia. Jim, I promise you that I'll be back someday with my brother, Giorgio, and we'll sing together in the casino for you."

Bill was amazed. "It sounds like something you'd see in a movie. Fact *is* stranger than fiction, after all."

But Bill knew this was the real thing. He gave Joe a big warm handshake and wished him good luck. "I hope you're going to see your brother in New York."

"Thank you, Bill, for everything."

He decided to go down to the bar for a drink to help him relax.

When he got there, he saw his ex-teammate Mike with his wife. Mike offered to buy him a drink and gave him a huge hug. They talked about the good old days and how much they missed them.

"I heard that you sing in the casino and I also heard that you collect money for handicapped kids," Mike said. "I think it's a wonderful and selfless thing you're doing."

"Mike, I love singing and this gives me great pleasure just like playing football gave me great pleasure. And you know, it's something that I really believe in. It's too bad I'm leaving tomorrow. Do you remember when you went to New York last year and you saw that Italian opera singer and you told me he looked a lot like me? I had a feeling we were related. Well, I found out who that singer is. Are you ready for this, my twin brother!"

"What?"

"Yes, he's my twin brother. Isn't that amazing? That's why I have to leave right away. I have to meet with my family and my brother in New York City."

"That's great, Joe. I'm very happy for you. Keep in touch and let me know how things are going."

Joe took a plane to Philadelphia the next morning. His wife met him at the airport.

When he got home, Joe's mother gave him a big hug and said, "Joe, my son, this is a big surprise for me, but I'm really glad I found out who you are. You're the son of your father's best friend. His name was Giuseppe, just like yours. That's why you'd always walk and throw the football like your real dad. Like he was reborn in you."

"You'll always be my mother," Joe said. "Where else could I have gotten so much love?"

Joe called Carlo. When he answered, Joe said, "Hello, Grandfather. I just got home. I can't wait to meet you because I've always suspected that you really were my grandfather."

"I love you, my grandson. This wonderful news has given me the strength to continue."

"Why don't you and everybody else come over for dinner tonight?"

"I'd love to."

Later, when Joe looked out and saw them coming, he ran outside and embraced Carlo.

"Grandfather, grandfather! I'm so happy to see you!" he said.

Carlo introduced him to Rino and Rita. "Joe, Rino told me the story about your mother. He knew you and your brother when you were born. Rita's my granddaughter and Rino's fiancée."

Joe gave Rino a warm hug and said, "Some day you'll have to tell me and my brother the whole story. For now, let's go inside and enjoy a good dinner together."

During dinner, they talked about meeting Giorgio in New York City. Joe also wanted to visit the graves of both fathers. Carlo liked that idea very much.

After dinner, they took a ride to the cemetery and Joe paid his respects to his father. While they were there, Joe's mother said, "Tom, you were right when you thought your son would walk and talk like your best friend, Joe. It's too bad you're not with us to enjoy this moment."

Then they visited Joe's grave. "Joe, I'm so proud and amazed that your son has inherited your genes and your dream of playing football. He became a great champion. You'd be proud of him."

After they visited the cemetery, everybody went home and made plans to leave for New York City the next day.

The next morning Joe called Carlo and asked him if he was ready to leave.

"Joe, I really don't feel well," Carlo said. "You know I have a heart condition. I'm afraid that the excitement has left me a little weak. Your grandmother's concerned. She doesn't think I should go."

"I'm really sorry to hear—"

"But I pray to God that He'll let me because I'm really looking forward to meeting your brother. I'll go to God happy if he lets me see him before I go."

"Then--"

"To heck with it, let's go!"

Rino called Lisa and told her they were coming. "I should be going back to Italy, but something's come up. I'll explain it all when I see you. I'm coming with Rita and her grandfather, Carlo and Joe Palmer."

"That's great. Call me when you get here and I'll make dinner for everyone."

***

They reached Gene's and Lisa's house two hours later. They received a warm welcome and Rino introduced Carlo as Rita's grandfather and Joe as Carlo's grandson. Gene was very happy to meet them both. "I was a great fan of yours when you were playing football," Gene said. "It's great having you in my house."

As they were called to dinner, Rino said, "You know, Gene, I'm supposed to be back in Italy but I got an extension because something unbelievable happened. Joe here is Giorgio Fiorino's twin brother, the tenor who sings for the Met. And I have a surprise meeting with him."

Gene shook his head in disbelief and said, "A couple of months ago I went to one of his concerts. You know, I thought he had Joe Palmer's smile."

"I always felt like something was missing from my life," Joe continued. "And I'm glad I found the missing part."

"I think when Giorgio finds out he'll be very surprised."

After a good dinner and good conversation, Carlo called Giorgio. Rosa answered the phone. "Hello?" she said.

"This is Giorgio's grandfather calling," Carlo said, his voice filled with excitement.

After a brief silence, Rosa said, "I'm sorry but Giorgio just got home from Italy. His grandfather died. I hope you're not going to ask him for money."

"No, of course not. Look, I went on vacation in Venice a long time ago, and he sang for me in a gondola. After that, we had some coffee together and I gave him money for his education. And the incredible thing is, I've recently found out that he's my grandson."

"Oh my God, you're Carlo, the one he always talks about. You know, I've been trying to contact you the last few months to thank you for giving him that money. I very much wanted to meet you, too. What a surprise. Why don't you come over to the house right now. Giorgio's in New York City rehearsing for a play, but he'll be back when you get here."

"We'll come right over."

She gave him the address--not more than ten minutes away.

Ten minutes later, Carlo rang the bell. Rosa answered.

When she saw Carlo, she gave him a big hug and called him Grandpa. Carlo welled up when he heard that.

When she saw Joe, she said, "Oh my God, you look like Giorgio."

"Well, he is my twin brother," Joe said with a grin.

"Everyone, please come inside and sit down."

"This is Rino and my granddaughter, Rita," Carlo said. "Rino's the one who told me the story about their being brothers."

"Rino," Rosa said, "You're a very successful pianist. Giorgio said he really wanted to meet you. Boy, won't he be surprised."

While everyone settled around the table, Giorgio's son and daughter came in from the backyard. When he saw Joe, the son said, "I thought you looked familiar when I saw you on TV. I always told my dad you looked like him and he always laughed and never paid much attention."

Then he hugged him and Joe said, "I'm your real father's brother and this is your grandfather, Carlo."

"I'm glad to have a Grandpa and an uncle," he said. "This is really good news."

Carlo hugged him back and with tears in his eyes said, "Thank you, God. I have a beautiful family I never knew I had. It's a miracle."

"You know, Joe," Rosa said, "Giorgio read the article in the newspaper about you retiring last year and it said you'd come a long way from being adopted. Well, it made Giorgio really believe that you two might be related. He was going to Italy to find out more, but then his mother died and he couldn't. All he knew was that he was adopted from an orphanage in Rome. He went to the orphanage and they agreed to look in their files, but he couldn't find out what he wanted to know. He was very disappointed.

"Giorgio was always telling people about the great generosity you showed him," Rosa said to Carlo, "but he couldn't get a hold of you because he couldn't remember your last name. But he always believed that one day he would meet you. Now, with you being his real grandfather, a missing piece of his life that he was always looking for will have been found. I have to ask, though, how do you know that you are his real grandfather?"

"This gentleman's name is Rino," Carlo said, "and he told me a story, that's how I know."

"I was an eye witness in the room when the twins were born," Rino said in Italian. "I'll tell the whole story when everyone gets together."

"Rino, I can hardly wait to hear it."

After they finished their drinks, Rosa called Giorgio in New York City. The office manager answered the phone and Rosa asked for Giorgio. He was, however, in the middle of rehearsal and couldn't be reached. But the manager said he would give him a message when he was finished.

"We'll wait for the call," Rosa said.

She made coffee while they waited and they talked and got to know one another better.

After a half hour, the phone rang. Rosa answered it. It was Giorgio. "Honey, is everything all right?" he said. "I still have another hour of rehearsal."

Rosa laughed and said, "Giorgio, I have great news for you."

"Did I get a big contract from somebody?"

She laughed and said, "No, no! You had better sit down for this. Are you sitting down? Remember the gentleman that gave you the money for your education?"

"Like it was yesterday."

"Well, I just found out that he's your real grandfather."

"Oh my God! Are you sure?"

"Is it all right if we come over to the conservatory?"

"Sure, sure, of course."

After he hung up, he asked the secretary to make dinner reservations for more people at his favorite Italian restaurant.

When he went back to the rehearsal hall, he was so excited that his maestro asked what he was so keyed up about. "Remember the story I told you about the man who gave me money for my education? I tried to find him but I couldn't remember his last name. Well, I just heard that he's my real grandfather and he and my wife are on their way here right now."

The news only enhanced Giorgio's performance and just before it was over, his wife and everyone walked in.

He ran over, kissed his wife, and gave his grandfather a hug. He looked at his brother, Joe, who certainly did look like him and they hugged each other with great joy and with tears in their eyes.

"We've finally found each other," Joe said. "The other half of ourselves that we've been searching for."

"You know this gentleman, Rino?" Rosa said.

"I know of him and I'm very happy to finally meet him in person. You're a wonderful pianist, Rino, and the concert you did in Moscow was truly amazing. I've always wanted to meet you."

"Thanks," Rino said. "I've always wanted to meet you, too."

Carlo held Giorgio and Joe by the shoulders and said, "Rino is the one who knows the whole story about when you were born. You're the sons of my son, Joe Martino, who died in the war."

"I made reservations for dinner and you can tell me the whole story then," Giorgio said.

Giorgio invited some members of the orchestra and the director. Then Rino said to him, "Is it okay if my sister and her husband join us?"

"I didn't realize you had a sister living in New York City," Giorgio said.

"My brother-in-law owns a fashion house there and my sister Lisa works with him."

"Oh my God!" Rosa said. "Lisa's your sister, Rino? I buy all my clothes from that store. I'd really like it if she could join us for dinner."

Rino called Lisa and asked her and Gene to come to dinner. "I know you're probably busy, but I'd like you to join us for dinner because I have a big surprise. There are some people I want you to meet, including the famous tenor, Giorgio Fiorino."

"That sounds marvelous. I'm sure Gene and I can make it. We should be there within the hour."

Giorgio arrived in a limo with his brother Joe, Carlo and their guests.

The Maitre'd greeted them and then escorted them to a table in the back room. He couldn't help but notice how much Joe looked like Giorgio. "Mr. Fiorino," he said, "is this man related to you?"

"Yes, he is," Giorgio said with a big smile on his face. This is my long lost brother and this other gentleman is my grandfather. And this is definitely the best night of my life!"

"In honor of this special occasion," the Maitre'd said, "let me give you some champagne on the house and I'll make sure you have the best dinner of your lives. You've been a very good customer; it's the least we can do."

A few minutes later Gene and Lisa came in and Rino introduced them to everyone. Lisa went over to Rosa and gave her a big hug. "This is such a wonderful surprise for me," she said.

"Me, too," Rosa said. "I love your clothes."

A few minutes later, the champagne arrived and everybody made a toast. Carlo raised his glass and said, "Salute! I want everybody to know that tonight is the greatest night of my whole life because I've been reunited with the two grandsons I never knew I had. I want to tell you a short story about my grandson, Joe. I went to his high school graduation. I went to his wedding and his retirement party. I did all that before finding out that he was my real grandson. I loved him before I knew we were related. And now that I do know, I'm filled with great love and happiness."

Then he turned to Giorgio and said, "It was just a coincidence that I went to Venice ten years ago and took a ride on a gondola. And it was just coincidence that I heard a young man with a beautiful singing voice. I was so impressed that I told him, 'I was born in Sorrento. Would you sing the song *Come Back to Sorrento*?' He said he would and after he finished I had tears in my eyes, it was so beautiful. I gave my wife a hug because it brought back so many memories of when we were young. After we got off the boat, I asked him if he would join us for cappuccino and he said yes. That's when I gave him ten thousand dollars if he promised to use it to help further his singing career. My wife thought I'd lost my mind, but he reminded me of my son, Joe, and I felt that with the right help, he had a wonderful future. Now here it is ten years later and I know I did the right thing. And the fact he's my own grandson has made me sure of it.

"This joyous occasion fills my heart with love and great happiness. I'm glad to have all my friends here to celebrate with me. So, ladies and gentleman, after this great dinner my good friend, Rino, who's going to marry my granddaughter, Rita, is going to tell us all the story of Joe and Giorgio. He's the person responsible for bringing us all together here tonight."

Later, after dinner, Rino got up and said, "Thank you all very much for this warm welcome. I'm going to tell you a miraculous story. It all started when I met this beautiful woman, Rita, my fiancée. She works in the American Embassy in Rome. She asked me if I knew anyone in America and I told her about my sister, Lisa, and her family who lived in New York City. I was very impressed with how well she spoke the Italian language and asked her where she was from. Imagine my surprise when she said she was from Philadelphia. She said she went home to visit her family and her special grandfather Carlo for two weeks every summer. I liked her very much and we eventually started dating. We decided to go together so I could meet her family. We were engaged by then. Once there, I met her parents and then her grandfather. We had gone to his house for dinner and while we talked, I noticed a picture of a young man in uniform. I asked him who it was and he said, 'This is a my son, Sergeant Joseph Martino who was killed in the war. Hearing that, I was reminded of when I was a child. I'd been hurt in the war and I was in a convent. I overheard a young woman named Maria who was talking to Sister Theresa. She had just had twin boys and was telling the Sister about their father, Joe Martino, an American soldier."

He turned to Carlo and Rita. "Just think, if I had never met Rita none of this would have happened. All of this was forgotten until I saw that picture. When I told Carlo, he asked me to go back to Italy and to the convent and see if I could find out anything. I told him I would and the three of us, Rita, Carlo and me left for Rome. When we got there, we went to the convent in Anzio and met with Sister Ann. She told us that all the children were sent to Rome. She was so intrigued by the story that she decided to take us there herself. Once there we met with the Mother Superior. Mr. Carlo was very persuasive and she finally agreed to tell us who had adopted the boys. Giorgio was adopted by Giorgio Fiorino and Joe by Thomas Palmer from Philadelphia. And we know what happened from there. Joe was adopted by his father's best friend and raised as family."

Everyone stood up and applauded and raised their glasses in a salute. "This is the greatest moment in my life," Carlo said, "being here with you both and with all my friends and family."

"If you all have the time, I would like to share a story about my father," Rino said.

Everyone applauded so Rino continued. "When my father left for the war he went to Russia with the Italian Army. Before he left, he told me that I had to promise him to continue to practice the piano so that when he came back from the war I would be an accomplished player…"

And so his story continued and when he was done, everyone applauded as he thanked them for listening. Then his sister Lisa gave him a hug and a kiss on the cheek and said, "I know the way you must feel and I would have acted the same way you did. I'm glad Papa is alive and well."

Giorgio asked his brother Joe and his grandfather to spend the night at his house in Long Island. They accepted and Rino and Rita spent the night with Lisa and her husband.

At breakfast the next day Giorgio decided to invite his brother Joe over with his wife. They decided to have a big get together with all their friends. Carlo said it was a great idea, but he asked if it could be held in Philly because of his health.

Carlo asked Rino if he could stay another week for the party. Rino nodded and smiled. "For you, Carlo, anything."

Joe said he'd make all the arrangements because he had all the connections in Philly.

Papa Carlo wanted them to have it at his big house in the country and he wanted to invite everyone. "My grandsons," he said, "I want to spend the weekend with both of you. This is a special day for me. And in honor of the occasion, I want to make a special dish that my mother taught me how to make in Naples."

"Okay, Grandpa," Joe said. "We'll be there, and we'll bring our familites, too."

Carlo wondered if this would be the last time they'd be able to get together. The doctor had said his heart wasn't going to last much longer and he wanted to spend as much time as possible with his two new grandsons.

Giorgio called his father in Italy to tell him the news, that he now knew who he was. "Papa, I have something wonderful to tell you. Do you remember long ago in Venice when that man gave me ten thousand dollars just for singing for him? Well by sheer coincidence, I've met him again. And I found out that he *is* my grandfather."

Giorgio's father was astounded. "How did this happen? How did you meet this man again?"

"It's a long story, Father."

"I'd like to meet this man. You know it's been hard for me to get around ever since your mother died. But I'd like to come to New York and meet him. I've got lots of questions. I'll make the arrangements and come as soon as I can. I think I'll bring Christina, too. I'll call you with the times."

After he hung up Giorgio told Rosa about the call.

Two Saturdays later, Giorgio, Rosa, their two children, Lisa and Gene and their two children, Rino and Rita, Joe's mother Lina and Papa Carlos's daughter, Josie all went to Philadelphia for the party. They were going to stay in Papa Carlos' house for the weekend. They arrived around noon. Rino and Lisa had to leave right after the weekend.

Carlo was up with the cook the night before. She was assisting him with his special lasagna, and making sure there was plenty of good wine available.

Everyone gathered in the living room and had a wonderful time. The children were running around screaming and playing and everyone else was trying to talk over the din. Papa Carlo held up his hand. "I have something to show Joe and Giorgio," he said.

He gave them a picture of their father, Joe, and his stepfather, Tom Palmer, in their football uniforms. He told them the story of what a great friendship they had.

"It's too bad that Tom isn't here," Lina said. "He would have loved to have heard this story and to have been here. And to have known that he had adopted his best friend's son."

Joe and Giorgio smiled at each other, glad to see their father's picture and how much they resembled him.

When it was time for lunch they went into the dining room and sat down. The wine had already been poured. Papa Carlo got up and said, "Salute, everyone. This is a special day for me. To be here with all my family, my children and grandchildren. This makes me feel very blessed."

He took Lisa's hand and asked her to stand next to him. "I met and married this beautiful Irish girl a long time ago. I know when you meet someone and fall in love, it doesn't matter that you can't speak their language. I've loved this woman for the last fifty years. My father-in-law, Patrick, liked me the first time he met me on the boat. He'd been in the war too. World War One. He liked me because I was just like him, a hard worker. And he felt I was the best man for his daughter. It didn't matter that he was Irish and I was Italian. We both wanted a better life. We worked together when we came to America. I treated him like my own father, my best friend. And he always said that when he was in Italy he'd heard of lasagna but he'd never tried it. We always had corned beef and cabbage at his house. I told him I'd surprise him one day with something that he had never had before.

"One Sunday after I'd built this house, I invited him over for dinner and made him lasagna. It was made with fresh goat milk for the ricotta which, as many of you know, makes it sweeter. I had a friend who had goats and I got the cheese from him. I made it the way my mother taught me. He loved it and when he came over he always begged me to make it for him. I remember when I was a small child in Italy, we'd have the ricotta cheese made from the goat's milk. We also had goat's milk with bread for breakfast every day. One day the goat died and my mother started to cry, saying, 'We have no milk for the children now.' One of the neighbors came by and heard her. 'Dona peppina' (don't worry) he said. 'I'll loan you my cow until you get another goat.' I always remember that when I have ricotta. But today is a day for celebration and in honor of it, I've made my famous lasagna. And I have a friend who made ricotta with goat milk specially for me. So enjoy!"

It was the cook's cue to come out with the huge platter of lasagna. It smelled heavenly.

The doorbell rang just as everyone started to eat. The maid went to the door, opened it and saw a taxi outside. Giorgio's father and Christina stepped out. They were supposed to be on the plane that afternoon, but they'd arrived early to surprise them.

When they walked into the dining room, Papa Carlo said, "Giorgio, this is your father and sister?"

He nodded and hugged him and his sister. Carlo shook his hand and said, "Bon Venuto to America. Pia Cere (nice to meet you). You've come at a good time. As you see, we're just sitting down to lunch. Please join us before the food gets cold."

Everyone praised Papa Carlo's lasagna. Giorgio's father said, "This is excellent. I haven't eaten lasagna like this ever. What's your secret again?"

Carlo laughed and said, "The ricotta cheese made from goat's milk. It makes it sweeter."

Everyone enjoyed lunch and afterwards they had expresso coffee.

"Mr. Carlo--" Giorgio started.

"Please, call me Papa Carlo."

Giorgio smiled. "Papa Carlo,I want to thank you for your gift so long ago. It made such a difference in my life."

Carlo laughed. "I'm sure you thought I was a crazy man. I know my wife did. I'd never done that before. But I felt that there was something about you, that I needed to help you."

Carlo's wife laughed. "You laugh now, but you didn't then. But it's all worked out the way God wanted, I'm sure."

Mary Jo got up, went into another room and got her guitar. When she came back she started playing some old Italian songs. Everyone sang along.

Carlo felt like he was back home in Naples. It brought back so many happy memories and he had tears in his eyes. Little Giorgio started singing. He sang just like Carlo remembered Giorgio sang when he was little, the same wonderful tone, the same energy that seemed so unforced. He went over to him and hugged him. "Thank you, Giorgio," he said.

And then to everyone he said, "I have the most wonderful, talented family. This has all made me very happy today. I'm glad I've lived long enough to enjoy all of this. I have something else special for Joe and Giorgio."

He brought out a picture of their mother and showed it to them.

Before Joe left Maria that final day, he'd had a friend take a picture of them together and one of just her with her guitar. She had the picture with her when she was in the convent. After her death the Mother Superior kept it until Carlo came along.

"She was a beautiful girl as you can see," Carlo said.

Joe and Giorgio were overcome. This was their mother and she was playing the guitar. They'd obviously gotten their singing ability from her. They passed the picture around and everyone was amazed that it had survived for so long.

The picture brought back a flood of memories for Rino. "That's a wonderful picture of your mother," he said. "I spent a week or so at the convent during the war. Even though things were grim, your mother always made everyone smile with her singing and playing. For a while we'd forget about the war and just be happy. Everyone always said to her, 'Maria, canda, canda' (sing, sing) when they saw her coming because they enjoyed her so much. Even the doctors and nurses. She was a breath of fresh air. The day before I was discharged I saw Sister Theresa bring both of you over to her and put you into her arms. 'What beautiful babies you are,' she said. Then as she fed you she started singing. *O sono Belli (how beautiful)* and then she said, 'One day your father, Sargeant Papa is going to come and take us to America.' Then she started singing *God Bless America.* 'Maria, who taught you to sing that song?' I said to her. And she said, 'My Sergeant Joe Martino from America.'

"The next day my mother came to get me. She thought you both were so beautiful. 'E Quando somo Belli questi gemeli,' she said to Maria. Before we left I said to Maria, 'Buona fortuna (good luck). I hope your Sergeant Joe comes back to take you to America. I wish you well.' That was the last time I ever saw her. I always assumed that she did make it to America with her Sergeant Joe. If it wasn't for meeting your cousin Rita in Rome and coming here to meet your grandfather, Carlo, this story wouldn't have had such a happy ending. This is destiny. I'm so glad to meet you both and to be able to tell you about your mother. I'm glad also to have met your grandfather; he's a great man."

Joe and Giorgio hugged him and shook his hand. "Thank you Rino for telling us this story of our mother," Joe said.

Everyone was very touched. Then Papa Carlo picked up his glass and said, "Salute" and gave a little toast. "I give a toast to this wonderful family I have and I wish you all good luck and good health for the rest of your lives. This is the happiest day of my life, to have all of my family around me."

After a while the party wound down. Some people went upstairs to rest before getting ready to go out to dinner. Some people went outside and walked around, while theie children took a nap. Still others just sat around talking.

Everyone gathered at the front door just a little before seven. Carlo knew that this would probably be his last time together with everyone. He kissed and hugged each of them and said, "You've all given me such joy in my life. I hope you'll always remember this day when I'm not here anymore."

"Don't say that, Rino said. "We'll be together many more times before that day comes."

Then everyone piled into the limos that Carlo had hired for the occasion.

A lot of Joe's friends from his football days were at the hotel. The coach, the players, the owner of the team, Mr. Reed. He introduced his brother to them. Mr. Reed really liked meeting Giorgio. He loved his singing. "I'm very pleased to meet you," he said. "Joe's like a second son to me, even though he doesn't play football anymore. I'm just sorry that Tom wasn't here to meet you, too."

Joe's friend Jim had come all the way from Las Vegas for the occasion. He'd wanted to surprise him. He'd very much wanted to meet Giorgio, too. "Giorgio," Joe said, "I want you to meet my good friend, Jim. We've been friends since we were children."

Giorgio enjoyed meeting someone from Joe's past.

After dinner, Joe and Giorgio got up to make a speech. They took Grandpa Carlo by each arm and walked him to the front table and to the microphone. "I'd like to introduce you to my grandfather, Carlo," Joe said. "I've known this man all my life, but I only recently found out he's my real grandfather."

He turned to Carlo and gave him a big hug. Then Giorgio took the mic and said, "Ladies and Gentlemen, life is funny sometimes. Many years ago when I was a young man in Venice singing in gondolas for money, this man asked me to sing *Come Back to Sorrento* because he was born in Sorrento. The song brought tears to his eyes. Then he bought me a cappuccino and we talked. I told him that I wanted to study singing so before he left he gave me a check for ten thousand dollars to help me with my studies. I made a promise to him that I'd do just that. His generosity is what made me who I am today."

He turned to his grandfather and gave him a big hug. "Thank you so much for your generosity. I'll always love you. You have a special place in my heart."

With the help of his two grandsons Grandpa Carlo came to the microphone and with a trembling voice, said, "Ladies and Gentlemen, this is the best day of my life. I've found my two lost grandsons. It's really a miracle that everything happened this way. If I should die tomorrow I'll die a happy man. I'll tell my son in heaven, dear Joseph, about his two beautiful sons that he never knew. Thank you all for being here tonight to celebrate this."

Then he turned to give both grandsons a hug and everyone stood and applauded.

***

The next morning everyone got up late and went down for breakfast. They noticed that Papa Carlo wasn't there.

"I'll go check on him," Lisa said.

Seconds later, they heard a loud scream and then crying. Everyone ran upstairs to see what was the matter.

They found Lisa crying on Papa Carlo's bed. "He's dead," she said. "He must have died in his sleep."

An ambulance was called, even though the obvious had indeed happened. And even though they were all saddened, the knowledge that he died happy tempered their grief. They held hands and said a prayer and thanked him for being so good to them. They prayed that God would take him to heaven. He'd wanted to die in his sleep, not in a nursing home. And his wish was granted.

Joe and Giorgio made the funeral arrangements. They'd have viewing hours the next day. Many people come to pay their respects. Papa Carlo was loved by many people. The next day they had a mass service at the church. A girl usually sang the *Ava Maria* but Giorgio asked if he and Joe could sing it in her place. Of course, given the circumstances, their tone took on a new meaning. Their grandfather had died, just after they'd finally met him. It was an occasion that prompted vocals unlike either had ever experienced, and although the assembled were respectfully silent as the song ended, there wasn't a dry eye to be found.

After mass, they all left for the cemetery. Carlo was going to be buried next to Joseph. Giorgio had never seen his father's grave and he was overcome with grief.

After the short sermon, everyone dropped a rose onto the casket.

"Papa Carlo," Joe said, "I love you. Thank you for everything you've done for me. I've always considered you my grandfather in spirit and I'm glad to find out that you were my grandfather in real life. It gives me great joy to have been part of your life. I hoped you might have had more time with us but it was not to be. I promise that I'll always take care of Grandmother Lisa and to be close to my family. We'll always remember you in our hearts."

"Grandpa," Giorgio said, "you've always been with me, ever since you gave me the money to sing. All these years I've wondered if you were part of my life, and now I find out that you were. I know who I am now and where I come from and it gives me great joy. When I was in concert I always thought about you and thanked you for all that you'd done to help me. At the end of every concert, I always sang your favorite song, the one you loved so much. Know that every time I sing it now, I'll be thinking of you. And I'll be sure to tell all my children and grandchildren about how kind and generous you were. Goodbye, Grandpa, we will all miss you."

Sam and his family walked to the grave. "Mio caro amico e fratello Carlo" (My good friend and brother). We had wonderful years together. I'll never forget you. You'll always be in my heart. And I've named a special dish after you. I'll miss you, old friend, and thank you once again for giving me a job. I'll see you again someday in paradiso."

Sam Junior threw down a flower. "Godfather, I love you. I'm going to miss you. Thank you for taking me into the business and thank you for trusting me. I'll always remember what you told me. Treat people well and they'll treat you well in return. We'll have a party in your honor every Christmas and we'll always salute you the way you used to do."

Lisa was the last one to throw a rose. "Carlo, you'll always be in my heart. Thank you for the past fifty-five years. I couldn't have asked for anything more from a man. I remember when we met on the boat coming to America. You'd say, 'Quando sei Bella.' In the beginning I didn't understand what you said and I had to ask my father. You said how beautiful I was. Then when we got to America and got off the boat, you said, 'Amore mio (my love), I will see you soon.' And I say that now to you, Carlo, Amore mio, I will see you soon. I just wish you had more time to be with your new grandsons and great-grandchildren. But now you can see Joe and tell him all about them."

Little Giorgie went up to the grave and said, "Papa Carlo, I love you even though I've only known you for a short time. I hope someday when I'm grown up I can go back to Italy to where you were born in Sorrento. I'd like to see the house where you were born. My father told me how beautiful it was there and he's sung many of the beautiful songs that were written there. I'd like to do that in your memory."

The service concluded and they all went back to their cars for the trip to Carlo's home.

"I'm glad that you're going to be part of our family," Giorgio said to Rino, "first by marriage through Lisa and then by marrying Rita."

"Rino," Lisa said to her brother, "I'm glad you're marrying Rita. She's a wonderful woman and she'll make you a great wife. I hope to see more of you once you're married."

"We'll be in touch," Gene said to Giorgio.

And to Joe, "We hope to see you again soon."

They shook hands and hugged one another. Then they gathered their children and luggage and left.

Before he left, Rino told Joe and Giorgio, "Next year Rita and I are going to be married in Italy and of course we'd like both of you to be there."

They both said they would.

"We want to see where our mother is buried," Giorgio said, "and to see where she lived. Again, thank you for telling us the story about her. We'll never forget this."

Rita hugged her grandmother. "We'll keep in touch and I hope you'll be able to come to our wedding next year in Italy."

"I hope so too," Lisa said. "God willing, I'll be there." She kissed Rita goodbye. Rino and Rita were going to stay with Gene and Lisa for a few days before catching the plane for Italy.

Gene and Lisa were waiting for them in New York, and they had a nice dinner together. They discussed Rita and Rino's wedding. "Rino," Gene said, "I want you to be best man. I can't think of anyone else I'd have."

"You know we have another family in Russia," Rino said to Lisa. "A half-brother and sister. Should we invite them to the wedding? I talked about it with Father Antonio before we left. When he heard my story he told me I should get in touch with our father and let the past stay in the past."

"Rino, I think Father Antonio was right," Lisa said. "We should forget the past and invite them. I'd love to meet this second family. After all they're a part of our blood and are family, even though we've never met."

Rino went to see the Rabbi a few days later. He took Rita with him and introduced her. "Rabbi, this is Rita, my fiancée. We're going to get married in Italy next year."

When the Rabbi heard that he put his hands on his head and exclaimed, "You want me to come to Italy to marry you?"

"No, no, the padre will marry us," Rino said. "I want you to come to the wedding and then I want you to come and spend time with me and Gene and Lisa. But I want to thank you again for helping me with Lisa's marriage and with our mother. By the way, Father Antonio said hello. He always remembers the day you came to Rome to marry Lisa and Gene. He's been telling all his colleagues the story. They all thought it was a wonderful thing for a rabbi and priest to perform a wedding."

The Rabbi smiled and said, "That's something that I'll always remember. I know now that I made the right choice. I've told others the story and they tell me the same thing. You know, I have to tell you Rino; your sister is a wonderful woman. She's the best thing that ever happened to Gene. Their children are wonderful too, and I enjoy them coming to the Temple. Thank you for inviting me to your wedding. I'll do everything I can to be there. Rita's a wonderful girl and I wish you all the best. I'd also enjoy seeing Father Antonio again and seeing more of Rome."

The next day when it was time for Rino and Rita to leave, they all kissed goodbye and promised to keep in touch. Rino was very happy to be marrying Rita and it was good getting together again with the family he hadn't seen in so long. Finding Rita was the best thing that had happened to him. His mother was right. She'd told him that someday he'd meet the right girl for him, and he had.

For Joe and Giorgio, finding each other was the most wonderful thing that had ever happened to them. Being twins, they'd always felt like a part of them was missing. To find out that they were twins and who they were solved a great mystery. Now that they'd found each other they promised to be as close as they could.

"I hear you raise money for handicapped children," Giorgio said to Joe. "I'd be happy to go with you to Las Vegas sometime and help you. It's a wonderful cause."

Joe was happy to hear that. But before they left, they went into the living room to say goodbye to their Grandma Lisa. They saw a picture on the wall of a happy couple posing together and asked her who it was.

"That's a picture of your grandfather and me when we were married and went to New York City for our honeymoon. Your grandfather's brother, Angelo, gave us a surprise present of seeing Enrico Caruso at the Metropolitan Opera House. He was from the Naples area where your grandfather was born. After the show, we got to go backstage and see him. Your grandfather shook his hand and asked if he would sing his favorite song, *Come Back to Sorrento*. And he said, 'That song is in my heart. I fished there when I was a boy and it always brings back memories of where I was born.' Your grandfather never forgot that. He loved to tell that story."

There was a plaque on the wall next to it with a story inscribed. "That's a story that your grandfather wrote last year when he wasn't feeling well and thought he might die. He wanted it all written down to let others know what happened in his life."

She read it to them.

"I love this country America because it gave me the opportunity to work and the freedom to make what I could of myself. I was very lucky when I came to America. I met this wonderful family on the boat--my future father-in-law, my mother-in-law, my sisters-in-law and my beautiful blue-eyed wife. We had a great life together. I always listened to my father-in-law, Patrick, who was a good friend and so like my own father. My father died when I was little. I'd make him laugh when I called him Patricio because I couldn't pronounce his name the right way. He had a lot of life experience and what he told me made a lot of sense. 'Carlo,' he said, 'remember when we fought in Europe during the war? We fought like brothers. We fought for freedom and a better quality of life and human dignity.' When we came to America, we worked hard together because we saw the opportunities. We succeeded because we worked hard. We learned that if you treat people well, they'll treat you well. That's what helped us make our company grow. I missed Patrick very much when he died, and I'll always keep him in my heart until I see him again. I was lucky to make plenty of money and I've have never been sick. But now I'm eighty years-old and I have heart trouble. All my life I've been very healthy and I thank God for that. But at the same time, with all the money and the love from my wife and my family, I have a broken heart to have missed all the people in my life. My parents, my brother, Angelo who died when I first got married. Then I lost my only son in the war. It broke my heart. And then losing my best friend, my father-in-law, who was like my own father. But I survived that and I understood that life would get better if I kept going on. I'm very blessed to still be here because I believe each of us have a set time to live our life and when it's time to leave, we do. I've had a lot of close calls and I survived. I'm sure there's a reason. I'm very happy and if something happened to me tomorrow, I'd be sad to leave my beautiful wife and family behind. But I'll always remember Sorrento, the place where I was born, because I have so many good memories. The love of my mother because my father died when I was young. I still remember when my mother told me to go milk the goat. That milk helped keep us healthy. I loved going fishing with my friends. We'd lie on our boat and sing songs and play our mandolins. I'll always remember that.

"Giorgio and Joe are very interested in this story. They look at the picture and say, 'Grandpa, we promise we'll always take care of Grandma for you. And now, before we leave, we'll sing the song in your heart, *Come back to Sorrento*. Grandpa, we'll always remember you in our hearts."

It was time for Giorgio and Rosa to leave. With tears in their eyes, everyone hugged each other goodbye. They each had money and fame, wonderful wives and children, but knowing their true identities were worth more than anything money could buy. They were born for a reason. It was their destiny to meet again.

Most adoptees want to find out who they are and where they came from. Only a few lucky ones like Joe and Giorgio get the chance to find happiness, which is what everyone is looking for.

Each of us has our own path to follow in life. Sometimes things happen that we don't expect and lead us somewhere else. That's what makes life more challenging.

Country Waltz

Lucky in Love

Words and Music by
John Scalpa

When we danced thru' the night, and I held you so tight, I saw the love for
me in your eyes...... In my heart burned a flame when you told me your name. Our love was
such a thrill-ing sur-prise...... Nev - er, nev-er be-fore
have I been luck-y in love...... Nev - er, nev-er be-fore has my
life been touched from a-bove...... Dar - ling, dar - ling, since we
met on the danc - ing floor...... I be-lieve in you, and our love so
true will go on for - ev - er - more...... I be-
lieve in you, and our love so true will go

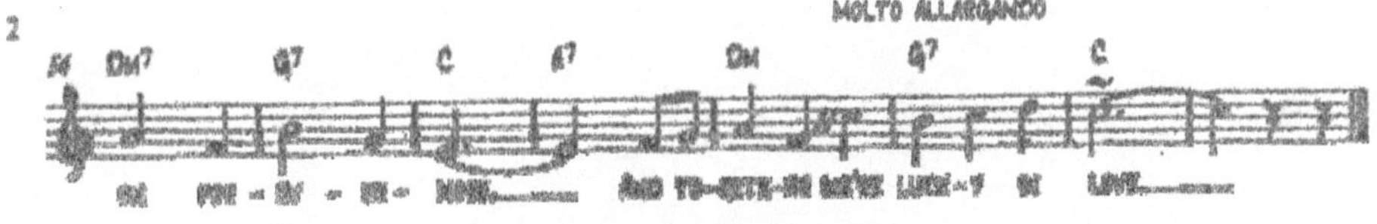

This now concludes the story of the famous twins.

MY DARLING
MODERATELY SLOW
VERSE 1:
WORDS AND MUSIC BY JOHN SCALPA
WHEN I SAW YOU IN MY DREAMS___ YOU WERE SWEET AND KIND___ AND YOUR
SMILE___ NEV-ER LEFT MY MIND___ WHEN I LOOK IN YOUR EYES___ I RE - AL -
IZE___ I SEE YOUR LOVE FOR ME___ IN YOUR EYES___ NO
MAT - TER WHERE I GO, NO MAT - TER WHAT I DO. I'M AL - WAYS THINK - ING OF YOU. WHEN
WE WALK THRU' THE NIGHT___ WE SHARE THE MOON - LIGHT___
VERSE 2:
SA - MO IN - SIE - ME___ STA SE -
RA. IO TI PAR - LO D'A - MO - RE. SO - NO LE ME___ PA - RO - LE SO - LA - MEN - TE PER
TE___ TI DA - RO U - NA RO - SA___ E SA - RAI LA MIA SPO - SA___ I SEE YOUR
SUBITO p mf
LOVE FOR ME___ IN YOUR EYES___ NO MAT - TER WHERE I GO, NO
MAT - TER WHAT I DO. I'M AL - WAYS THINK - ING OF YOU. WHEN WE WALK THRU' THE NIGHT___
___ WE SHARE THE MOON - LIGHT___ AND I SING MY SONG FOR YOU___ OH MY
CRESC
DAR - LING___ I'M GLAD I MAR - RIED YOU___ AND YOU SAID:
MOLTO ALLARGANDO
A TEMPO
"YES, I DO!"___ I WILL SHARE MY LIFE___ WITH YOU!___
SEMPRE CRESC
ff
COPYRIGHT © 1992 JOHN SCALPA

L'AMORE DI PRIMAVERA
COPYRIGHT © 2006 JOHN SCALPA

Words by John Scalpa
I Will Love You Forever
Music by John Scalpa and Mark S. Johnson
Tenderly
Colla voce
A tempo
Poco rall.
In my life, I ne - ver fell in - love with an - y - one but you.
And I know in my heart you love me - too.
Un poco piu mosso
Re - mem - ber the time when I took you to the prom. We danced through the night. And we had a good time.
I know I made you cry. I tried to un - der - stand. I know I was wrong. And I sing for you my song.
A tempo
Your love gives me new life. Your love gives me new strength. And now I know I can play the game a - gain.
Colla voce
Un poco meno mosso
And I feel in my heart my love be - longs to you for the rest of my life. For the rest of my life. For the rest of my life.
Poco a poco rall. e dim. a fine
Copyright © 1982 John Scalpa

www.ingramcontent.com/pod-product-compliance
Lightning Source LLC
Chambersburg PA
CBHW030824310726
48980CB00006B/631/J
9780984650200